"This is a really bad idea. We're business partners."

"What's a bad idea, Lucy? Having a conversation?" Dom asked.

"You liking me. You wanting to kiss me."

"It doesn't change anything."

"Yeah, it does."

Dom was silent for a beat. "I'm not putting any pressure on you, Lucy. Just being honest. I don't expect anything from you."

"How I am supposed to pretend it's business as usual when every time I look at you I'm going to be thinking about this?" she asked. She could hear the panic in her own voice.

"I shouldn't have said anything."

She stared at him, frustration welling inside her. "I don't want this," she whispered. She blinked rapidly, feeling overwhelmed on every level.

"Hey," Dom said. He stepped closer and rested a hand on her shoulder. "It's okay. The last thing I want to do is make things tougher for you. Forget I said anything. We'll just pretend the last five minutes never happened."

Dear Reader,

How I loved writing this book! I think family really does make the world go around, and having the opportunity to explore Dom's and Lucy's families—as well as their lives—really was a pleasure from start to finish.

A Natural Father is set in beautiful, cosmopolitan Melbourne, Australia, my home, and centered on an Italian family working in the fresh produce markets in the heart of the city. While I am not Italian, I grew up with many Italian friends. Frankly, it's impossible to live in Melbourne and not be exposed to the Italian community—they have had such a profound effect on the city. And of course, there is the Italian food! Lygon Street in the Carlton area is famous for its many Italian restaurants and delicatessens. If you are ever in town I highly recommend a bowl of pasta and a glass of Chianti at one of them. Bliss!

This is my first Harlequin Superromance book, and I hope you enjoy reading it. I love to hear from readers, so please don't hesitate to drop me a line via my Web site, www.sarahmayberry.com.

Happy reading!

Sarah Mayberry

A NATURAL FATHER
Sarah Mayberry

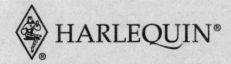

HARLEQUIN®

TORONTO • NEW YORK • LONDON
AMSTERDAM • PARIS • SYDNEY • HAMBURG
STOCKHOLM • ATHENS • TOKYO • MILAN • MADRID
PRAGUE • WARSAW • BUDAPEST • AUCKLAND

Recycling programs
for this product may
not exist in your area.

ISBN-13: 978-0-373-71551-0
ISBN-10:   0-373-71551-X

A NATURAL FATHER

Copyright © 2009 by Small Cow Productions PTY Ltd.

This edition published by arrangement with Harlequin Books S.A.

® and TM are trademarks of the publisher. Trademarks indicated with
® are registered in the United States Patent and Trademark Office, the
Canadian Trade Marks Office and in other countries.

www.eHarlequin.com

Printed in U.S.A.

ABOUT THE AUTHOR

Sarah Mayberry was born in Melbourne, Australia, but is currently based in Auckland, New Zealand, because her partner is also a writer who keeps getting jobs in places that are not home. She loves to travel, cook, read and shop for shoes—oh, and let's not forget sleep. Very important! Writing for a living is her dream job, and one she hopes continues for a long time to come.

Books by Sarah Mayberry

HARLEQUIN BLAZE
380—BURNING UP
404—BELOW THE BELT
425—AMOROUS LIAISONS

Don't miss any of our special offers. Write to us at the following address for information on our newest releases.

Harlequin Reader Service
U.S.: 3010 Walden Ave., P.O. Box 1325, Buffalo, NY 14269
Canadian: P.O. Box 609, Fort Erie, Ont. L2A 5X3

Thanks to the team at *Neighbours* for inspiring this story, particularly you, Mr. Hannam, with your talk of delicious, barefoot Italian men making gnocchi.

As always, this book would not exist if Chris was not by my side, mopping my fevered brow and rubbing my shoulders and making me laugh. And then there is Wanda, who always makes my writing better, always knows best and always makes me laugh even when I think I want to cry. You rock.

CHAPTER ONE

"I DON'T FEEL SO GOOD." Lucy Basso pressed a hand to her stomach. "Maybe I should do this another time."

Her sister Rosetta rolled her eyes and passed the menu over.

"Stop being such a wuss," Rosie said, scanning the menu. "I'm going to have the pesto and goat's cheese focaccia. What about you?"

"How about a nervous breakdown?" Lucy said.

Around them, the staff and patrons of their favorite inner-city Melbourne café went about their business, laughing, talking, drinking and eating as though none of them had a care in the world.

Lucy stared at them with envy.

I bet none of you are unexpectedly pregnant. I bet none of you are so stupidly, childishly scared of telling your Catholic Italian mother that you decided to do it in a public place so she couldn't yell too loudly. I bet none of you are contemplating standing up right now and hightailing it out of here and moving to another country so you never have to look into her face and see how disappointed she is in you.

Her sister placed the menu flat on the table and gave Lucy one of her Lawyer Looks. Over the years, Rosie had perfected several, and Lucy kept a running tally of them.

This was Lawyer Look Number Three—the my-client-is-an-idiot-but-I-will-endure-because-I'm-being-paid one.

"There's no point worrying about something you can't change. And it's not like you've robbed a bank or become a Buddhist, God forbid. You made a baby with the man you love. So what if you're not married to him? So what if he's just left you for another woman? None of that is your fault. Well, not technically."

Lucy narrowed her eyes, for a moment forgetting her nerves. "What's that supposed to mean? Which bit is *technically* not my fault? Us not being married or his leaving me? And please do not tell me that you think us being married would have made a difference to this situation, because that's so not true. I'd just be sitting here with a stupid ring on my finger and he'd still be having tantric sex with Belinda the Nimble."

Rosie smiled. "There, see? All you needed was to get a little temper going, and you're fine."

She looked so pleased with herself, Lucy had to laugh.

"You are the worst. Please tell me you have a trick like that up your sleeve for when Ma starts crossing herself and beating her chest."

"She hasn't beaten her chest for years. Not since we told her it was making her boobs sag prematurely," Rosie said. "And what's with the nimble thing, by the way? You always call Belinda that. Personally, I prefer 'that slut,' but I'm hard like that."

Lucy reached for the sugar bowl and dug the teaspoon deep into the tiny, shiny crystals.

"It's one of the things Marcus said when he told me he was leaving. That he'd met someone, and she was beautiful and captivating and *nimble*."

Even though two months had passed since that horrible, soul-destroying conversation, Lucy still felt the sting of humiliation and hurt. She'd been so secure in Marcus's love. So certain that no matter what else was going wrong in her life—and the list seemed to be growing longer by the day—he'd always be there for her.

Ha.

"Nimble. What the hell does that mean? That she can put her ankles behind her ears? Like that's going to see them through the hard times," Rosie said.

Lucy shrugged miserably, then caught herself. She was wallowing again. The moment she knew she was pregnant, she'd made a deal with herself that self-pity was out the window. The days of self-indulgent cannoli pig-outs were over. She had another person to consider now. A person who was going to be totally dependent on her for everything for so many years it was almost impossible to comprehend.

"Hello, my darlings, so sorry I'm late."

Lucy and Rosie started in their seats. When it came to sneaking up on people unawares, their mother was a world champion. It was a talent she'd mastered when they were children, and it never failed to unsettle them both.

"Why you had to choose this place when the parking is so bad and my cornetti are ten times better, I don't know," Sophia Basso said as she scanned the busy café, clearly unimpressed. "We could have had a nice quiet time at home with no interruptions."

"Ma, you've got to stop sneaking up on us like that. You're like the Ninja Mom," Lucy said.

"I can't help that I step lightly, Lucia," Sophia said.

Small and slim, she was dressed, as always, with elegance in a silk shirt in bright aquamarine with a bow at the neck, a neat black skirt and black court shoes. Over it all she wore the black Italian wool coat her daughters had bought her for her birthday last year.

"I know it's hard to park here, but Brunetti's make the best hot chocolate in town," Rosie said.

Sophia sniffed her disagreement as she folded her coat carefully over the back of her chair. Then she held her arms wide and Rosie stood and stepped dutifully into her embrace, followed by Lucy a few seconds later.

"My girls. So beautiful," Sophia Basso said, her fond gaze cataloging their tall, slim bodies, dark shiny hair and deep-brown eyes with parental pride.

She sank into her chair and Lucy and Rosie followed suit.

Sometimes, Lucy reflected, meeting with her mother was like having an audience with the queen. Or maybe the pope was a better comparison, since there was usually so much guilt associated with the occasion, mixed in with the love and amusement and frustration.

"You've put on weight, Lucia," Sophia said as she spread a napkin over her lap. "It's good to see. You're always much too skinny."

Lucy tensed. She was twelve weeks pregnant and barely showing. If she lay on her back and squinted, she could just discern the concave bump that would soon grow into a big pregnancy belly. How could her mother possibly notice such a subtle change?

Lucy exchanged glances with her sister.

Just say it. Spit it out, get it over and done with.

Ever since she found out she was pregnant five weeks ago, she'd been coming up with excuses for why she couldn't tell her mother. First, she'd decided to wait to make sure the pregnancy was viable before saying anything. Why upset her mother for no reason, after all? But the weeks had passed and she'd realized she was going to start to show soon. The last thing she wanted was for her mother to find out from someone else. She could just imagine Mrs. Cilauro from the markets or old Mr. Magnifico, one of her customers, asking her mother when Lucia was due.

The thought was enough to make her feel light-headed. For sure the chest-beating would make a reappearance. And she would never be able to forget causing her mother so much pain. Not that being single and pregnant wasn't going to score highly on that front. Her mother had struggled to raise her and Rosie single-handedly after their father died in a work-site accident when they were both just toddlers. Sophia's most fervent wish, often vocalized, was that her two daughters would never have to go through the uncertainty and fear of single motherhood.

Guess what, Ma? Surprise!

"I saw Peter DeSarro the other day. He asked me to say hello to you both," Sophia said, sliding her reading glasses onto the end of her nose. "He asked particularly after you, Rosetta. You broke his heart when you married Andrew, you know."

"Oh yeah, I was a real man killer," Rosie said dryly. "All those guys panting on my doorstep all the time."

Sophia glanced at her elder daughter over the top of her glasses.

"You were too busy with your studies to notice, but you could have had any boy in the neighborhood."

Rosie laughed outright at that.

"Ma, I was the size of a small country in high school. The only boys interested in me were the ones who figured I was good for a free feed at lunchtime."

"Rosetta! That is not true!" Sophia said.

Lucy squeezed her eyes tightly shut. Any second now, the conversation was going to degenerate into a typical Rosie-Sophia debate about history as they both saw it, and Lucy would lose her courage. She took a deep breath.

"Mom, I'm pregnant," she blurted, her voice sounding overloud in her own ears.

Was it just her, or did the world stop spinning for a second?

Her mother's eyes widened, then the color drained out of her face.

"Lucia!" she said. Her hand found Lucy's on the tabletop and clutched it.

"It's Marcus's. We think maybe a condom broke. I'm due in late October. Give or take," Lucy said in a rush.

Her mother's face got even paler. Lucy winced. She hadn't meant to share the part about the condom breaking. She'd never discussed contraception with her mother in her life, and she wasn't about to start now.

"You're three months already?" her mother asked, her voice barely a whisper.

Lucy nodded. She could see the stricken look in her mother's eyes, knew exactly what she was thinking.

"I didn't want to tell you until I was sure," she said. It was flimsy, and all three of them knew it. "I didn't want you to worry about me," she said more honestly.

Her mother exhaled loudly and sat back in her chair. Her hand slid from Lucy's.

"Now Marcus will have to step up and take care of his responsibilities," Sophia said. "You are angry with him, Lucia, I know, but for the sake of the baby you will take him back. You will buy a nice house, and he will get a real job to look after you and the baby."

Lucy blinked. Fatten her mother up, give her a sex change and stuff her mouth with cotton wool, and she'd be a dead spit for Marlon Brando in *The Godfather* right now, the way she was organizing Lucy's life like she was one of the capos in her army.

"Ma, he's with someone else now. He loves her," Lucy said flatly.

Sophia shook her head. "It doesn't matter anymore. He has responsibilities."

"Since when did that ever make a difference with Marcus?" Rosie said under her breath.

Lucy's chin came up as the familiar urge to defend Marcus gripped her. She frowned.

He's not yours to defend anymore, remember?

"This child needs a father," Sophia said, her fist thumping the table.

Lucy knew that her mother's words were fueled by all the years of scraping by, but they weren't what she needed to hear. She couldn't undo what had happened. She was stuck. She was going to have to do the best she could with what she had. And she was going to have to do it alone.

Rosie's hand found her knee under the table and gave it a squeeze.

"It's not like I planned any of this," Lucy said. "It was an accident. And I can't make Marcus love me again. I have to get on with things. I've got the business, and Rosie and I have been talking—"

"The business! I hadn't even thought about that! How on earth will you cope with it all on your own?" Her mother threw her hands in the air dramatically. "All those fruit deliveries, lifting all those boxes. And it's just you, Lucia, no one else. This is a disaster."

"Ma, you're not helping. You think Lucy hasn't gone over and over all of this stuff?" Rosie said.

"She hasn't gone over it with me," Sophia said, and Lucy could hear the hurt in her voice.

"I know this is the last thing you want for me," Lucy said. "I know you're disappointed. But it's happening. I'm going to have a baby. You're going to be a grandmother. Can't we concentrate on the good bits and worry about the bad bits when they happen?"

Suddenly she really needed to hear her mother say something reassuring. Something about how everything would be all right, how if she had managed, so would Lucy.

Tears filled Sophia Basso's eyes and she shook her head slowly.

"You have no idea," she said. "Everything becomes a battle. Just getting to the grocery store, or keeping the house clean. Every time one of you was sick, I used to pace the floor at night, worrying how I was going to pay for the medicine and who was going to look after you when I had to go into work the next day. All the times the utilities were cut off, and the times I couldn't find the money for school excursions… I would never wish that life on either of you."

"It won't be the same, because Lucy has us," Rosie said staunchly. "What Lucy was about to tell you is that she's moving into the granny flat at the back of our house. When the baby comes, Andrew and I can help out. Between all of us, we'll get by."

Lucy saw that her mother's hands were trembling. She hated upsetting her. Disappointing her. Deep down inside, in the part of her that was still a child, Lucy had hoped that her mother would react differently. That she'd be more pleased than concerned, that she'd wrap Lucy in her arms and tell her that no matter what happened she would be there for her.

The nervous nausea that had dogged her before her mother's arrival returned with a vengeance.

She was already scared of what the future might hold. Of having a baby growing inside her—a crazy enough concept all on its own—and then taking that tiny baby home and having to cope with whatever might happen next without Marcus standing beside her. She'd told herself over and over that hundreds of thousands of women across Australia—probably millions of women around the world—coped with having babies on their own. She would cope, too. She would. But she knew it would be the biggest challenge she'd ever faced in her life. And it would be a challenge that would never stop, ever. At seventy, she would still be worrying about her child and wanting the best for him or her. She only had to look at her mother's grief-stricken face to know that was true.

She stood, clutching her handbag.

"I can't do this," she said. "I'm sorry, Ma. But I can't do this right now."

It was too much, taking on her mother's trepidation and doubts as well as her own.

Her mother gaped and Rosie half rose from her chair as Lucy strode for the entrance, fighting her way through the line of people waiting for service at the front counter.

Outside, Lucy stuffed her hands into the pockets of her coat and sucked in big lungfuls of air. She stared up at the pale blue winter sky, willing herself to calm down.

It's going to be okay. I'm twenty-eight years old. Last year, I started my own business. I can do this. I'm a strong person.

She found her car keys in her bag and started to walk, chin up, jaw set.

After all, it wasn't as though she had a choice.

A month later

DOMINIC BIANCO RAN his hands through his hair and stifled a yawn. If anyone asked, he was going to blame the jetlag for his tiredness, but the truth was that he'd gotten out of the habit of early starts while he'd been visiting with family back in the old country. Six months of touring Italy, hopping from one relative's house to the next had made him lazy and soft. Just what he'd needed at the time, but now he was back and there was work to do. As always.

Around him, the Victoria Market buzzed with activity. Situated in the central business district, the markets were the heart of the fresh produce trade in Melbourne, supplying suburban retailers, restaurants and cafés across the city. Bianco Brothers had occupied the same corner for nearly thirty years, ever since new immigrants Tony and Vinnie Bianco started selling fruits and vegetables as eager young men. Today, the family stall sprawled down half the aisle and turned over millions of dollars annually.

Dom checked his watch. Five o'clock. One hour until customers started arriving.

He wondered if he would see her today. Then he shook his head. What was he, sixteen again?

"Grow up, idiot," he told himself as he turned toward the pallet of boxed tomatoes waiting to be unloaded.

She might not even come. For all he knew, she might not even be buying her produce from his father anymore.

He flexed his knees and kept his back straight as he hoisted the first box of tomatoes and lugged them over to the display table. His uncle Vinnie was fussing with the bananas, ensuring the oldest stock was at the front so they could offload it before the fruit became too ripe.

"Be careful with your back, Dom. You know what happened with your father," he said as Dom dumped the first box and went back for another.

Dom smiled to himself. For as long as he could remember, his uncle had said the same thing every time he saw anyone carrying a box. Dom figured the hernia his father had had while in his twenties must have really messed with his uncle's head.

By the time Dom had unloaded all the tomatoes, he'd worked up a sweat beneath the layers of sweatshirts and T-shirts he'd piled on that morning. He peeled off a couple of layers, enjoying the feeling of using his muscles again.

It was good to be back. He'd felt a little uneasy as the plane took off from Rome two days ago, but it was nice to be home. Even returning to the old house hadn't been that big a deal.

Danielle's stuff was gone. The only sign that she'd ever lived there was the pile of mail addressed to them both that his sister had left on the kitchen counter.

Mr. and Mrs. Bianco. He wondered if Dani was planning on reverting to her maiden name now that their divorce was final. It wasn't something they'd ever discussed. He frowned as he thought about it. It would be strange to learn she was calling herself Dani Bianco. As though the only part of him that she still wanted was his name.

"Dom, how many boxes iceburg lettuce we got?" his father called from the other end of the stand.

Dom shook his head when he saw that his father had his clipboard out and pencil at the ready. For thirty years Tony

Bianco had kept track of his stock and sales in the same way—on paper in his illegible handwriting. Any notation he made would be indecipherable to anyone else.

Dom did a quick tally of the boxes stacked beneath the trestle tables.

"We got two-dozen boxes, Pa," he called. Enough to see them through the day.

Before he'd left for Italy, he'd spoken to his father about bringing the business into the twenty-first century. There were a bunch of user-friendly, highly efficient software systems available for running businesses like theirs. Knowing what stock they had on hand, what it was costing them, how much they were selling and who their best customers were at the touch of a button would be of huge benefit to Bianco Brothers. Currently, all that information was stored in his father's head and consequently Tony's business decisions were often based more on gut-feel and instinct than hard figures.

Predictably, his father had been resistant to the idea of change.

"I do it this way for thirty years," he'd said, then he'd gestured toward the long rows of produce and the customers lining up to make their purchases. "We do okay."

His father was being modest. They did more than okay. They did really, really well. But, in Dom's opinion, they could do better. He'd backed off last time because he'd been too messed up over Dani to concentrate on the business, but now that he was back it was time to start pushing harder. He was going to be running this business someday, since none of his cousins were even remotely interested. He didn't want to have to deal with boxes full of his father's scrawlings when he tried to work out where they stood.

He dusted his hands down the front of his jeans and glanced over the stand, checking to see that all was as it should be. Everything looked good, and he turned back to the stack of pallets piled behind their displays. Might as well get rid of those before the rush.

By the time he'd tracked down one of the market's forklift drivers and arranged for him to shift the pallets to the holding area, half an hour had passed. The bitter cold was starting to burn off as the sun made its presence felt, and Dom shed another layer as he made his way back to the stand.

He'd just finished pulling his sweatshirt over his head when he saw her.

She was wearing a long, cherry-red coat, the furry collar pulled up high around her face as she talked to his father. Her long, straight dark hair hung down her back, glossy in the overhead lights. She turned her head slightly and he watched her smile, noting the quick flash of her teeth, the way her eyes widened as she laughed at something his father said.

As always when he saw her, his gut tightened and his shoulders squared.

Lucy Basso.

Man, but she was gorgeous. Her sleek hair. The exotic sweep of her cheekbones. Her ready smile. The elegant strength of her body.

Gorgeous—and now he didn't have to feel guilty about noticing.

He stepped closer, automatically smoothing a hand over his hair to make sure he didn't have any goofy spikes sticking up from dragging off his sweatshirt. Just to be safe, he checked his fly as well. Never could tell when a clothing malfunction was loitering in the wings, waiting to bring a guy down.

All the while, he drank her in with his eyes. She looked even better than he remembered.

Lucy and her sister had grown up in Preston, just one suburb across from his own family's stomping ground in Brunswick. They'd gone to different schools but the same church, and he'd been aware of her from the moment he'd first started noticing girls. There was something about the way she held herself—tall and proud, as though she knew exactly what she was worth.

He hadn't been the only guy in the neighborhood who'd noticed. He'd never been put off by competition, but somehow the timing had never been right to make his move. Life kept intervening—other girlfriends for him, then, when he was free, she'd be with some other boy. Then they'd stopped running into each other altogether as they grew up and went out into the world. He'd only reconnected with her in the past year when she'd approached his father about the new door-to-door fresh produce delivery service she was starting up. After that, he'd seen her every day for six months before he bailed on his life for Italy. And he'd felt guilty every time he looked at her and felt the pull of desire. It wasn't like he'd needed the added hassle as he and Dani battled through the ugly death throes of their marriage, and often he'd resented the attraction he'd felt.

Bad timing—again.

But things were different now. He was a single man. Divorced. Not exactly a shining badge of honor, not something he'd ever planned, but it was what it was.

And Lucy Basso was standing in front of him, looking amazing, daring him to reach out for something he'd always wanted.

She'd been one of the reasons for coming home. Not the main reason, not by a long shot. But he'd always wondered where she was concerned. What if…? And now there was nothing stopping him from finding out.

He was about to take the last step forward when a voice piped up in his head.

What are you doing, man? What happens if things get serious and she discovers you're an empty promise?

He pushed the thought away. He refused to live half a life, no matter what had happened with Dani. Especially when Lucy was standing within reach.

"Lucy Basso. Good to see you," he said.

She was already smiling as she turned to face him, her olive skin golden even under the harsh fluorescent lights.

"Dom! Hey, long time no see. I heard you'd taken off for Italy," she said.

She had an amazing voice. Low and husky.

"Decided it was time to take a look around the old country, see what all the fuss was about," he said. He tucked a hand into the front pocket of his jeans and rested his hip against the side of the stall.

"And?" She cocked an eyebrow at him, a small smile playing around her mouth.

"The Vatican is an okay little place. And they did some nice work at the Coliseum. But, to be honest, it would have been much more impressive if they'd finished building it."

She laughed and pulled a face at him. "Bet you didn't make that joke when you were in Rome."

"As a matter of fact," he said, "I didn't."

She laughed again.

He shot a glance toward his father, aware that Tony was watching their exchange with a big smile on his face.

Go away, he urged his father silently. *There's no way I'm asking her out with you standing there. I'll never hear the end of it.*

"I bet you're glad to have him back, Mr. Bianco," Lucy said.

"I save work especially for him," Tony said, rubbing his apron-covered belly with his hands, his smile broadening. "To make up for long holiday."

His father was looking at Lucy with admiring eyes and Dom realized he wasn't going anywhere soon. He might be pushing sixty, but Tony knew a beautiful woman when he saw one and he wasn't above a little harmless flirtation in his old age.

"Six months in Italy. I can only imagine," Lucy said, closing her eyes for a beat. "Heaven. The way I'm going, I'll get over there when I'm ready to retire," she said.

"Make the time. It's worth it," Dom said. "Even if you only go for a few weeks."

She shrugged, her hair spilling over her shoulder. "Nice idea, but it's not going to happen," she said ruefully.

Then she reached for her purse to pay for her order, and her coat fell open.

The words Dom had been about to say died in his throat as he registered the gentle bump that had been hidden by the long lines of her coat.

She was pregnant.

Lucy Basso was pregnant. Which meant she was married. Not free. Not available. And definitely not about to go out with him.

Bad timing again. The worst timing in the world, in fact.

Fifteen years of lust, blown away in a few seconds.

Damn.

CHAPTER TWO

SOMEHOW DOM MANAGED to make coherent conversation for the next few minutes, but his gaze kept dropping to the bump swelling Lucy's sweater. After a while, she placed a hand there and blushed.

"Starting to show now, I guess," she said.

"Uh, yeah. When are you due?" he asked.

"Just before Christmas."

"Wow. I guess your husband must be over the moon," he said, fishing unashamedly.

Who had she married? How come his mother hadn't mentioned it in one of her letters to him? He'd gotten updates on every other birth, death or marriage in the neighborhood. Why would she miss Lucy Basso's?

Lucy tugged her coat closed and slid a button home to keep it that way.

She shrugged casually, as if to say that her husband's happiness was a given.

"You know, I'd better get going with all of this." She gestured toward the trolley she'd filled with her supplies for the day.

Dom frowned as he noted several large boxes and bags of produce in her order.

"I'll give you a hand," he said, stepping forward.

"It's okay. I've got a hydraulic tailgate in the back of the van," she explained.

"Right." He rocked back on his heels.

She was nothing to him, a neighborhood acquaintance and now a customer, but he hated the idea of her lugging groceries around all day when she was four months pregnant.

She laughed, obviously interpreting the look on his face.

"Italian men," she said, shaking her head. "Honestly, I'm fine. I wouldn't do anything to put my baby in danger."

She curved her hand possessively over her bump, and he felt that tight feeling in his gut again.

Forget it, buddy. Forget her. It's over.

"Okay. If you're sure," he said.

"I'm sure. I'll see you tomorrow. You, too, Mr. Bianco."

She smiled once more before pushing her trolley up the aisle.

He wasn't aware that he was staring after her until his father came and stood next to him.

"Beautiful girl."

Dom forced a casual shrug. Beautiful, married and pregnant. Not exactly a winning combination.

"Yeah, she's nice," he said.

He turned back toward the stand. Ridiculous to feel as though he'd just lost something valuable. For all he knew, she was a ball-breaking shrew with bad breath and a worse temper. There was nothing for him to mourn, no loss had occurred. They barely even knew each other.

He was so absorbed in trying to look busy that he almost missed his father's next words.

"Such a shame. Her mother very worried, I hear."

"Worried? Why?" Dom asked. Then his mind jumped to the obvious. "Is there something wrong with the baby?"

He knew what it was like to hope each month for good news, only to learn that once again all the wonders of modern medicine could not make up for the failures of nature. For four years he and Dani had tried in vain to have a baby. He could only imagine how wrenching it would be to have all the joy of finding out you were pregnant, only to learn there was something wrong with your child.

"Something wrong with the baby? How would I know?" his father asked, giving him a look.

Dom returned it in full measure.

"You're the one who said her mother's worried. What's she worried about if it's not the baby?"

Tony rolled his eyes, then held up his left hand, pointing to his own well-worn wedding ring.

"No husband. Lousy no-good left Lucy for other woman," he said. He looked like he wanted to spit, the notion offended him so much. "Poor Lucy, she left with business and bambino all on her own."

Dom stared at his father.

"She's not married?" he asked, just in case his ears were deceiving him, feeding him what he wanted to hear.

"Didn't I just say that?" his father asked. Muttering to himself in Italian, he strode off to serve the customer hovering nearby.

Dom stared blankly into space for a few long seconds.

Not married.

Single, in fact.

A smile curved his lips. He even turned on his heel, ready to race after her and ask her out.

He stopped before he'd taken a step.

She was pregnant.

Four months pregnant with another man's child.

Not exactly your typical dating situation.

"Hey, Dom, those arms of yours painted on?" his uncle Vinnie called from the other end of the stall.

Dom blinked. A queue of customers had formed in front of him, waiting to be served.

Right. He was at work. There was stuff to do. He could think about Lucy Basso later.

It was a great theory, but he found it impossible to stop himself from thinking about her as the morning progressed. The flash of a red coat glimpsed briefly through the crowd. The sight of a woman pushing a baby stroller. A young couple walking hand in hand, both glowing with obvious contentment over her big, swollen belly. Everything seemed to remind him of her. She'd rocketed from being a vague incentive to come home to the most important thing on his agenda in the space of a few minutes.

Why was that? Because of the profound disappointment he'd felt when he'd thought she was married, lost to him for good?

Man, she's pregnant, he reminded himself for the twentieth time that day.

But did that really matter? Really?

THAT NIGHT, Lucy sat with her laptop at her dining table and stared at the number at the bottom of her monthly spreadsheet. It wasn't abysmal. It was almost respectable, considering her business, Market Fresh, had been in operation just over twelve months. But would it be enough to impress the man at the bank tomorrow?

Market Fresh had seemed like such a great idea when she came up with it two years ago. She'd been working as hostess in a busy suburban restaurant and listening to the chef's constant complaints. He didn't have time to get into the city markets every day to pick produce for himself, and he was perpetually disappointed in what he could source locally. Because she lived close to the city, Lucy had offered to stop by the markets on the way into work each day and fill his shopping list. The restaurant paid her for her time, and she selected the best produce at the best prices, going straight to the wholesaler rather than allowing a retailer to act as the middleman.

The chef had been so impressed with what she'd brought back and how much money she'd saved him, he'd bragged about it to his chef friends. Before long, Lucy had two, then three, then four shopping lists to fill each day. After a while, she realized that she'd accidentally discovered a niche in the market, and Market Fresh was born.

She did her homework for a whole year before jumping in. She took some small-business courses, and she went through the sums over and over with her sister. Finally, she leased the van and pitched herself to her former employer and his friends. After a few ups and downs, the business was now holding its own.

Except she'd reached a difficult stage in her company's growth. She needed more clients, but she couldn't afford to put on an extra driver to service them until she had more money coming in. Also, she needed to up her game to ensure she retained her existing clients. The answer to all her problems was obvious but expensive: the Internet. Ever since she'd found out she was pregnant, Lucy had been exploring the idea of taking Market Fresh online. With a Web site, she could deliver a real-time list of available produce to her clients each day and receive and collate their orders automatically. She already knew from discussions she'd had with several of her key clients that they were attracted to the convenience of the idea. She was confident that new clients would be equally drawn.

She just had to find the money to get online. Hence her appointment with the bank tomorrow.

Lucy rubbed her belly. She hated the thought of taking on more debt. She already made lease payments on the van, and while she was keeping her head above water, it would take the loss of only a few clients or a hike in fuel costs to put her in the red again. She didn't want to risk that, not with the baby on the way.

But she also wanted to ensure her child's future. Build something that would keep them both safe and warm for many years, without having to rely on the generosity of Rosie and Andrew, or handouts from her mother.

She closed her eyes at the very thought. Since the meeting a month ago when she'd told her mother she was pregnant, she'd been on the receiving end of all the fussing a pregnant woman could endure. Home-cooked meals appeared magically in her fridge, and every time her mother visited she brought something for the baby—stacks of disposable diapers, a baby bath, receiving blankets, tiny baby clothes. The study nook where she planned to put the baby's cradle was already jammed to overflowing with her mother's gifts.

It was incredibly generous, and it also took a huge burden off Lucy's shoulders in terms of her baby budget. But every time her mother handed over an offering, Lucy remembered the nights her mother had stayed up late ironing business shirts for fifty cents apiece. And the weekends she'd spent sewing wedding and bridesmaid dresses, and confirmation dresses for the girls in the neighborhood. And all the times Lucy had watched her mother carefully count her change into the rainy-day jar. Her mother was retired now, living off a small pension and her savings, and Lucy knew that every gift to her came at her mother's expense.

Her mother had sacrificed so much to give her and Rosie a good home, and now she was sacrificing again to support Lucy's unplanned pregnancy.

Lucy shoved her chair back so sharply it screeched across the timber floor.

She had to convince the people at the bank that she was a good risk. Somehow she had to push the business into the next phase, and she had to look after herself and her baby without leaning on her mother. It wasn't right. It wasn't the kind of daughter Lucy wanted to be. She remembered how proud she'd felt when she and Rosie had presented their mother with the lush, expensive Italian wool coat. Sophia's eyes had lit up then filled with tears when she'd understood that the beautiful garment was hers, a token of her daughters' esteem and affection.

That was the kind of daughter Lucy wanted to be—the kind of daughter who gave instead of took, the kind of daughter who could give her mother the retirement she deserved after all her hard years of work.

Lucy ran a hand through her hair and let her breath hiss out between her teeth, wishing she could release her tension as easily. She had her business papers in order and her best suit was hanging at the ready—even though she had to use a couple of safety pins and leave the zipper down to get the skirt on. As long as she didn't take her jacket off, no one would ever know.

"They'll listen," Lucy said out loud, trying to convince herself. "They'll see my vision. They have to."

"First sign of madness, you know," Rosie said from behind her, and Lucy started.

"For Pete's sake!" she said, one hand pressed to her chest. "Have you been taking lessons from Ma or something?"

"I knocked," Rosie said, gesturing toward the door that

connected the flat to the kitchen of the main house. "You were too busy talking to yourself to hear me."

Lucy punched her sister on the arm. "That's for scaring the living daylights out of me."

Rosie rubbed her arm. "If you weren't knocked up, you'd be in so much trouble right now," she said. "But even a lawyer has to draw the line at taking on a pregnant woman."

"Very noble of you."

"I'm good like that. You coming in to watch *Desperate Housewives* with us?" she asked.

Lucy shot a look toward her laptop. She had her accounts in order, but her nerves demanded she go over them one last time, just to be sure.

"I think I've got too much work to do," she said.

Rosie's face immediately creased with concern. "Everything okay? You're all good for the bank?"

"Sure. No problems," Lucy said, careful to keep her voice casual.

"I can still cancel my afternoon appointment and come with you," Rosie said.

While a part of Lucy wanted her support more than anything, she knew she had to do this alone. The whole point of getting the loan and growing the business was to become more independent and self-sufficient. Lucy didn't want to be a charity case for the rest of her life. She owed her baby a better start than that.

"It's all good. Really. I've already ironed my shirt and everything," she said.

Rosie looked like she wanted to argue some more, so Lucy said the first thing that popped into her head.

"Hey, guess who's back in town? Dominic Bianco. Saw him at the market this morning."

As she'd hoped, her sister stopped frowning and got a

salacious, speculative look in her eye. Rosie had always had a thing for Dom Bianco.

"How long was he away? And is he as hot as ever?" Rosie asked.

"Six months. And he looks the same as always," Lucy said.

"Ow. Must have been some divorce that he needed six months time-out to recover," Rosie said with a wince. "Nice to know he hasn't lost his looks, though. Tell me, does he still wear those tight little jeans?"

"At this point I feel honor-bound to remind you that you're a married woman."

"I can still admire from a distance. And Dominic Bianco is worth admiring. Those cheekbones. And those black eyes of his. And that body." Rosie fanned herself theatrically.

"Careful or I'm going to have to hose you down."

"How can you look at that man and not have sweaty, carnal thoughts?"

"Um, because I'm four months pregnant," Lucy said, "and about to become a walking whale?"

"Irrelevant."

"Maybe he's not my type."

"You have twenty-twenty vision and a pulse, and you're pregnant so it proves you're heterosexual. He's your type. Next," Rosie said, wiggling her fingers in a gimme-more gesture.

Lucy frowned. She'd never seriously given the matter much thought before. In fact, she'd never really paid much attention to Dominic, truth be told. He'd been married until recently, and she'd been living with Marcus, and Rosie had always had a thing for him—he'd been out of bounds for a bunch of reasons, really. And Lucy wasn't the kind of person who got off on lusting after the forbidden.

"I don't know. Maybe I never let myself notice," she said finally.

"Ha!" Rosie said triumphantly. "I knew it!"

"You want to share what you know? 'Cause I'm still in the dark here."

"You have the hots for him. Only someone who really has the hots for someone would completely block out the other person's attractiveness like that. And The Bianco definitely qualifies as attractive. The man is a god. Sex on legs. H-O-T."

"Okay, I got it." Lucy shook her head at both her sister's convoluted logic and her use of her teen code name for Dom. "Is this the kind of argument you try on in court, by the way? Do judges buy this crap?"

"It's the only explanation," Rosie said, crossing her arms smugly over her chest.

"Really? How about this—you've been hot for Dom for so many years that you're trying to live vicariously through me?"

Rosie cocked her head. "Hmmm. That's not bad."

They both laughed.

"You're a dirty birdy," Lucy said, reaching out and tugging on her sister's shoulder-length hair.

"Thank you. I do try." Rosie turned toward the door. "Sure you're not up for ice cream and *Housewives?*"

Lucy bit her lip, tempted now that she'd let go of some of her anxiety. It wasn't as though she hadn't already gone over and over her application. "What flavor have you got?"

"New York cheesecake *and* macadamia toffee," Rosie said.

Lucy slung an arm around her sister's neck. "Have I told you lately that I love you?" she said, planting a kiss on her sister's cheek.

"You, my dear, are an ice-cream hussy," Rosie said. Then she slung her arm around Lucy's fast-disappearing waist and kissed her back. "Love you, too."

LATER THAT NIGHT, Rosie finished smoothing moisturizer into her face as she sat in bed. She dropped her hands into her lap, her thoughts on her sister. Lucy was so strong and bright and determined, but Rosie couldn't help worrying about her. It was part of the job description of elder sister, but it also came down to simple empathy. Her sister was in a tough situation and Rosie would feel for any woman faced with the same challenges. The difference was, Lucy *was* her sister, and Rosie had a lifetime of feeling responsible for her to add to her natural sympathy. It made her want to move mountains for her, even though she knew her sister was determined to stand on her own two feet.

If only Marcus wasn't such a loser. It wasn't the first time Rosie had had the thought, and it wouldn't be the last. From the moment she'd met him she'd spotted him for what he was—a moocher, content to pursue his "art" while someone else footed the bill for all the everyday things like food, water, shelter. That someone else had been Lucy for so many years that Rosie had almost gone crazy biting her tongue. And now Marcus had shown his true colors and bailed on her sister when she needed him the most.

What an asshole. Lucy deserved so much better.

"What time are the Johnsons coming in tomorrow?" Andrew asked as he exited the ensuite bathroom.

He had stripped down to his boxers, and as usual the sight of his solid, muscular body filled Rosie with a warm sense of comfort and proprietorial pride. He worked hard to stay fit, and she made a point of admiring the results as often as possible because she knew that, like her, he'd been an overweight teen and the ghosts of past shame still lurked in the corners of his mind.

"Looking fine, Mr. James. Looking fine," she said, giving him her best leer.

Andrew struck a few muscleman poses, each more ridiculous than the last. She was laughing her head off by the time he slid into bed beside her.

"Come here," he said, sliding an arm around her waist.

She went willingly, curling close to his big, warm body, her head resting on his shoulder. She wondered for perhaps the millionth time how she'd gotten so lucky. She'd had the hots for Andrew James since she walked into her first common-law lecture at Melbourne University. He'd been sitting in the third row, his long legs stretched out in front of him. He'd glanced up from his notebook, and her brown eyes had met his blue, and the deal had been sealed then and there. He hadn't even needed to smile, but when he did, she'd literally gone weak at the knees.

Rosie smiled as she remembered. She hadn't believed in love at first sight until that moment. Life sure showed her.

"What are you smiling about?" Andrew asked.

"Just thinking about the first time I saw you," she said.

"That old thing," he said. "What is it with women, always mythologizing the past?"

She dug an elbow into his ribs. "Don't ruin my sentimentality with your man-logic."

Her thoughts inevitably clicked to the subject she'd been worrying at before Andrew came through from the bathroom.

"I wish Lucy could have met someone like you instead of Marcus the moocher," she said.

"She'll be fine. Stop worrying."

"I can't help it. It's in my genes."

"It's not like she's in this alone. She's got Sophia and she's got us. We'll all pitch in."

"It's not the same."

"I know. But it's close, and it's more than a lot of people have. Lucy's a lot tougher than you give her credit for, you know."

"I know."

"Anyway, it'll be good practice for us, being Uncle Andrew and Aunty Rosie. By the time our own kids come along, I'll have mastered the whole diaper thing, no problems."

She tensed.

"Wow. I'll have to tell Lucy you're volunteering for pooper-scooper duty," she said.

She felt his chest rise as though he'd taken a breath to say something, but he didn't speak. For a moment there was a whole world of not-talked-about stuff hanging in the air between them.

"Oh, I forgot. The Johnsons. They rebooked for eleven," she said.

"Right. Yeah, I'd forgotten," he said.

He stretched to the side and clicked off the bedside lamp.

"Good night," he said, kissing the top of her head.

She kissed his chest one last time and slid back to her side of the bed. As much as she'd love to fall asleep on him, she knew she'd just wake up in half an hour with a numb arm.

The sheets were cool on her side and she stared up at the ceiling, reliving that telltale little hitch in their conversation.

You have to pay the piper sometime.

There was a conversation coming, looming on the horizon. She knew that. And it filled her with fear. Because she knew how much Andrew wanted children—and she had no desire at all to be a mother.

CHAPTER THREE

ROSIE'S WORDS RETURNED to haunt Lucy as she approached the Bianco Brothers stall at the market the next morning. Dom was at the front of the stand and she was about to call out a greeting when he stooped to lift a box of potatoes. He was wearing a pair of well-worn Levi's, and the soft denim molded his butt and thighs as he lifted the heavy load. His biceps bulged, visible against the tight cotton of a long-sleeved T-shirt, and Lucy found herself swallowing unexpectedly.

Then Dom turned and saw her, and his dark eyes lit up and his straight, white teeth flashed as he smiled. His black hair was curly and unruly around his face, and he was tanned from his months in Italy.

Okay. Maybe Rosie was on to something when she said he was a god, Lucy admitted to herself as she stared at him. *Maybe he is attractive.*

"Lucy. Be with you in a minute," he said, dropping the potatoes onto another customer's trolley.

Then he grabbed the hem of his long-sleeved T-shirt and tugged it over his head. Lucy's eyes widened as she scored an eyeful of tanned, hard belly as whatever he was wearing underneath clung to the top he was removing.

Okay. Attractive is the wrong word. Sexy. Very, very sexy.

Lucy dragged her eyes away, frowning.

She was pregnant. Having a baby. With child. She had no business ogling hot guys at the market. She cursed her sister mentally. This was all Rosie's doing, planting stupid suggestions in her head. If she hadn't said all that stuff about Dom last night, there was no way Lucy would be standing here right now feeling like a pervert.

"How can we help you today?" Dom said, closing the distance between them.

Lucy smoothed her hands down the sides of her skirt and shook her head slightly to clear it.

"All the usual staples. Plus I need eggplants and a whole lot of fresh herbs," she said, consulting her list.

"May I?" Dom asked. He held out a hand for the list.

"Sure."

She'd given her list to Mr. Bianco a hundred times. So why did it feel different giving it to Dom?

Damn you, Rosie, and your stupid teen crush.

"Sorry, did you say something?" Dom asked.

"No! At least, I don't think I did," Lucy said.

"The eggplants are down here. You want to come check them out?" he asked after a small silence.

"Sure." She waited until his back was turned before she hit herself on the forehead with her open palm. Then, just in case her stupid brain hadn't gotten the message, she slid a hand over the baby bump beneath her suit coat.

The smooth, taut curve of her belly grounded her in an instant. She was pregnant and scheduled for an important meeting with the bank. Her days of getting goofy over guys were over.

One hand on her tummy, she followed Dom.

"Nice and shiny," Dom said as he showed her the eggplants. "Just the way we like them."

"Definitely," she said.

She kept her gaze focused on the dark purple vegetables in front of her.

"I'll take three boxes," she said.

"Not a problem."

She stood back as Dom hefted a box from beneath the trestle table, lifting it easily onto her trolley. When all three boxes were stacked neatly, he turned to face her.

"What next?" There was a smile in his eyes and it quickly spread to his mouth. For the first time she noticed that he had a single dimple in his left cheek.

Rosie hadn't mentioned that last night.

"Um, the herbs," she said.

They were about to move to the other end of the stall when Mr. Bianco found them, a clipboard in hand and a frown on his face.

"Dom, you remember how much onions we order last week? Oh, hello, Lucy. You looking lovely today."

For some reason, Dom's father's compliment made her blush. Which was stupid. Every morning he said something along the same lines to her. Why should today feel any different to any other time?

Because you were eyeing up his son like a side of beef five minutes ago? Because all of a sudden a part of you would like to really be looking lovely today?

She squashed the little voice with a mental boot heel. She really was going to have words with her sister for causing all this crazy, too-aware-of-Dom stuff.

"Hi, Mr. Bianco," she said. "How are you today?"

"No complaints," he said, patting his belly complacently. "But I interrupting. I wait."

"It's fine. No worries," she said, gesturing with her hand that they should go ahead and have their conversation.

Dom shot her an appreciative look. "Two seconds," he promised as he turned to talk with his father.

She moved away a few steps to inspect a pile of zucchini while they talked, but she was aware of lots of hand gesticulating and the frustrated tone of their conversation as father and son discussed something intently.

"Okay, sorry about that," Dom said a few minutes later as he rejoined her.

He was frowning and the smile had gone from his eyes.

"If there's a problem, I can wait for one of the other servers to be free," she said.

Dom shook his head. "No problem. Just stubborn pig-headedness."

"Right."

He sighed, and his frown eased a little.

"You see that clipboard he's holding? That's the complete record of our stock on hand for the week," he said.

Lucy's gaze took in the many feet of frontage the Bianco Brothers occupied, all of it filled to overflowing with fresh produce.

"You're kidding me."

She carried a tiny fraction of the inventory the Biancos did, and she kept it all neatly organized via a simple computer program. She couldn't even imagine how Mr. Bianco kept track of his stock with paper and pen.

"It gets worse. He's the only one who can read his own handwriting. So whenever Vinnie or I or one of the others needs to check on something, we have to find him and get him to interpret for us."

"Wow," Lucy said.

"Yeah," Dom said, a world of frustration in his voice.

"Driving you crazy?" she guessed.

"Just a little. There's so much stuff we could be doing.

Even having an up-to-date list of what's available on a Web site would be a huge bonus. We get fifty phone calls a day from customers asking what we've got on hand. But Pa thinks that because his way has worked for thirty years, there's no reason to change."

He ran a hand through his hair, his gaze distant as he looked down the aisle. Then his eyes snapped back into focus and he gave her a rueful smile.

"Sorry. This isn't getting your order filled, is it?" he said, pulling her list from his pocket again.

"It's okay. I can barely have a conversation with my mother these days. I can't even imagine working with her," Lucy confessed.

Dom's gaze instantly flicked to her stomach. She felt heat rise into her face. Yesterday when she'd seen him, she'd deliberately been vague when he'd asked about her husband. But she could tell by the awkward silence that had fallen that he knew the truth. There were precious few secrets in the close-knit Italian community they'd grown up in, and she should have known he'd soon find out she was single. Why she'd even bothered to cover yesterday she had no idea. At the time, it had seemed…messy to try to explain about Marcus and the fact that she was all alone.

At least be honest with yourself if you can't be honest with anyone else, Lucia Basso.

The truth was that she'd been embarrassed. She stopped short of labeling the emotion she'd experienced shame. She wasn't ashamed of her baby. She refused to be. But there was no getting around the fact that she was a good Catholic girl who was having a baby on her own because her boyfriend had abandoned her for another woman.

She opened her mouth to try to explain her omission, then swallowed her words without speaking them. Dom wouldn't care. Her being pregnant or not or married or not meant nothing in his world. They had a business relationship, nothing more.

But still she felt uncomfortable. And the feeling seemed to be mutual. Dom shoved a hand into the back pocket of his jeans and shifted his feet.

"She'll come around. Once she sees that little baby, she'll be putty in your hands," he said.

It was too complicated a situation to explain over a trestle table of zucchinis. Lucy smiled and waved a hand.

"It's fine. We're fine. It's all good," she said.

Dom hesitated a beat before nodding. "Okay, let's get you those herbs."

They were both careful to keep things surface-level for the rest of the transaction, and Lucy left the stall feeling oddly depressed. Which was as stupid as blushing over Mr. Bianco's compliment. There was nothing in her relationship with Dominic Bianco that she had any reason to feel depressed about.

Still, she found herself going over their conversation again as she broke up her stock into separate orders in the back of the van prior to her first delivery of the day.

It was the fact that he'd confided about his father that had made her drop her guard, she decided. Dom had always been friendly, but in a professional way. Today was the first time that either of them had offered each other anything beyond polite small talk.

"Ow." Lucy looked to where she'd caught her knee against the corner of one of her crates.

Great. She'd been so distracted thinking about Dominic that she'd put a run in her panty hose. Now she'd have to find the time to buy a new pair and wriggle into them before her bank appointment that afternoon.

A surge of nerves raced through her as she thought about the bank and the loan and what it meant for her future.

Get your head together, girl, because you will not get a second chance to get this right.

It was a scary thought—more than scary enough to sweep any other thoughts away. She didn't have the luxury of being distracted right now.

Grimly determined, she finished breaking up her orders.

LATER THAT AFTERNOON, Dom stood in the refrigerated storeroom Bianco Brothers rented and broke the tape seal on the small box in front of him. Inside was a state-of-the-art handheld data unit, ideal for inputting stock information and orders for a wholesale company like his father's.

Dom had picked up the unit yesterday after work, and today he was determined to start phase one of his plan to modernize the business. His father was going to be resistant to change, he knew that. But Dom would show him how much easier and more efficient life could be. In essence, that was what phase one was all about—massaging his father into letting progress do its thing.

It wasn't like he was asking his father to take on the burden of learning the new software himself. Dom would do all that. At worst, Tony would have to learn how to pilot one of these handheld units, and the literature promised that they were as simple to use as a pocket calculator.

After studying the instructions for a few minutes, Dom powered up the unit and experimented with a couple of functions. Satisfied that he had the basics sorted, he turned to the stacks of crates towering around him. He'd catalog the stock in the storage space, then download the data into the new software program on his computer, then he'd show his father what they could do with the information. His father was stubborn, maybe even a little scared and intimidated by new technology, but Dom was confident that the old man would switch on to computerizing once he understood the benefits.

His thoughts drifted to Lucy as he began to punch in data. She'd looked good today, if a little pale. The bulge of her pregnancy was still in the burgeoning stage, cute and round rather than big and heavy. She'd always been beautiful, but being pregnant had added an extra dimension to her appeal.

He shook his head as he caught his own thoughts. He was not hitting on a pregnant woman. He'd already decided against it. She was vulnerable, for starters. Abandoned by her boyfriend, running a business on her own. She had too much at stake and inserting himself into the mix was only going to make things worse. Plus—pure selfishness here— he didn't want to have any doubt about why Lucy was attracted to him. If that miracle ever happened. Not that he figured her for the type of woman who would seek out a man to provide security for herself and her unborn child, but he didn't want there to be any confusion around the issue.

Once again they were the victims of bad timing. But maybe when she'd had the child, when her world was more settled... Maybe then he'd make his move, try his luck.

"Dom. We're starting to close up. You ready in here?"

Dom turned to find his father standing in the doorway, his body a dark silhouette against the pale winter sunlight. There was a small pause as his father's eyes adjusted to the difference in light, and Dom didn't need to see his father's face to know that he'd spotted the handheld unit.

"What you doing?" Tony asked. His voice was flat, absolutely expressionless.

Bad sign.

"I picked this up yesterday on the way home from work," Dom said, facing his father. "I wanted to show you what it can do."

"I told you, we not interested. Vinnie and me have discussed."

"But, Pa, we can do so much more with this software in place. Project sales, pick up on trends. Cut down on spoilage."

Dom hated that he sounded like a beseeching child trying to cajole a parent into taking him to an amusement park. This was a smart business decision and he should not have to cajole his father into anything. He was part of Bianco Brothers, too. It was time his father and uncle started respecting his opinion more.

"Take it back. I hope they give you money back," Tony said dismissively.

"Why don't you come over and take a look at what it can do? I've just entered this whole wall of stock in about five minutes," Dom said. "It's every bit as fast as writing it down on your clipboard, and everyone can have access to the data."

"Don't talk like I am little child," Tony said. His voice was sharp. "I not idiot. Your uncle not idiot. We know how to run business. You bide time, be good boy, and one day you will run. Until then, you do things our way."

Dom flinched from the tone and intent of his father's words.

"Speaking of talking to people like children. In case you hadn't noticed, I'm not a boy anymore," he said. "Also, just so you know, Luigi Verde and his son have installed a computer system. And the Kerrimuirs have had one for two years. We're going to be left behind if we don't step up now and start offering our clients more services."

He hadn't meant for things to get this heated so quickly, but he also hadn't expected his father to be so adamant on the issue. At the least, he'd expected his father to be curious, to explore the idea a little before rejecting it.

"It not matter. Our clients are loyal. They not forget us."

Dom couldn't help himself: he laughed.

"Pa, welcome to the twenty-first century. There's no such thing as loyalty anymore. As soon as our customers know they can get a better deal or more value for money from one of our competitors, they're gone. Don't believe for a second that they come to you and Uncle Vinnie for any other reason except that it lines their pockets."

His father waved a dismissive hand in the air and made a spitting noise.

"What you know? Your generation not understand. You not understand sticking to something, making work no matter what. You think if something hard, must be wrong. You walk away from commitments like mean nothing."

Dom went very still.

"You're talking about me and Dani, aren't you?"

If his father wanted to throw accusations around, Dom was going to be damn sure they both knew what they were talking about.

Tony shifted his bulk, then tucked his thumbs into the waistband of his apron and just stared back at Dom. His stillness was his answer: yes, he thought his son had given up on his marriage rather than do the hard yards to fix it.

Hot anger stiffened Dom's neck and squared his shoulders. He'd known that his father was unhappy about the divorce, but not this unhappy.

"I guess I should thank you for the honesty. At least we both know where we stand."

"You think your mother and I not have hard times? You think I never look at other women and wonder if they wouldn't be easier to love?"

Dom held his hand up. "Wait a minute. You think I *cheated* on Dani? Is that what you're saying?" he asked. His voice had slipped up an octave.

His parents had known he and Dani were trying for children, that there had been problems, but Dom had never discussed the finer points of the issue with them. He'd never quite known how to explain to his father that thanks to the case of mumps he'd had when he was twenty years old, he was sterile and would never be able to father children of his own. He'd figured he'd get around to it, eventually.

And now his father was suggesting that the reason his marriage had fallen apart was because he'd strayed. So. Not only was Dom a man who couldn't go the distance and honor his commitments, he was a cheat, too.

"Why else marriage break up? Dani was nice girl. She would never cheat," his father said.

Dom rocked back on his heels. "This is unbelievable. How long have you felt this way, Pa? How long have you thought your son was a no-good sleaze?"

It was his father's turn to rock back on his heels. "That not what I said. You never talk, you never say anything. You come to me and your mother and say marriage over. What we supposed to think?"

"Shit, I don't know. Maybe the best of me? Maybe that there was a bloody good reason for my divorce and that I'd tell you once I could handle talking about it?"

"Talk now. Tell me now," Tony demanded, thumping his chest.

"Why would I bother?" Dom said. "You have your own ideas about me, and you obviously like them a lot more than the truth."

He grabbed his jacket and strode toward the doorway. He

couldn't remember ever being more furious with his father—and they'd had some rip-roaring fights over the years.

His father held his ground until the last possible moment, then stepped to one side.

Dom thrust the handheld unit at him as he passed.

"Do what you like with it. You won't hear another word from me on the subject," he said.

Then he marched back toward the stand. There was work to do, after all. He'd hate for his father to think his no-good son was adding shirking to his list of crimes.

"I CAN'T BELIEVE they said no."

Lucy forced a small smile. "Well, they did. Apparently I'm a bad risk. No assets, no security."

"But you're making a profit. And you'll make a bigger one once you get the site up and running and you attract more business," Rosie said.

"Said all that. They didn't care."

"Crap," Rosie said. Then she sat straighter. "We'll try another bank. There's got to be someone out there with a bit of vision."

"Rosie, I have my van lease with them, do all my banking through them. If they don't want to do business with me, no one else is going to step up to the plate."

"You don't know that. We have to try." Rosie pulled her cell phone from her bag. "What's the name of that new bank, the one advertising all the time?"

"I've already called the other three major banks, and two of the building societies," Lucy said.

"And?"

"Like I said. No one wants to take a risk on me. And that's before they've gotten an eyeful of this." She indicated her belly.

Rosie stared at her, clearly at a loss as the facts sank in. "Crap," she said again.

"Oh yeah," Lucy said.

A waiter appeared at their table and Rosie waved him away.

"No, wait. I need chocolate," Lucy said.

"Good idea," Rosie said.

They both ordered hot chocolates and cake before returning to the crisis at hand.

"There has to be some way around this," Rosie said.

Lucy pushed her hair behind her ear. She was tired, exhausted really, but she was hoping the chocolate would give her a much needed kick. Crawling into bed and sleeping for a day was not an option open to her right now.

"I've been doing some sums. If I save my ass off between now and when the baby is due, I can put aside enough to cover my bills for three months. Ma mentioned the other day that Cousin Mario is looking for work. I thought I could offer him the driver's job for three months. He can take my wage, I'll live off my savings. It might work."

Rosie was staring at her. "What if you need more than three months? What if Mario won't do it for what you pay yourself? Which, let's face it, is a joke."

Lucy felt the heat of threatening tears, and she clenched her jaw. "I guess I'll cross that bridge when I come to it."

"No. It's a make-do, Band-Aid plan, and it's not going to cut it. You need that twenty thousand."

"Really? Do you think?" Lucy said. She so didn't need her sister pointing out the obvious to her, not when she was trying to be stoic.

"We'll lend it to you," Rosie suddenly announced, slapping her hands onto the table so hard she made the sugar dispenser jump.

"What?"

"Andrew and I have got some money put aside for renovations at the office. We can put them off and lend it to you instead," Rosie said.

Lucy stared at her sister. "God, I love you, you idiot, but there's no way I'm taking money from you and Andrew. Forget about it. I'll talk to Cousin Mario tonight, get something else sorted. It'll be fine."

"Listen to me," Rosie said, leaning across the table until she was right in Lucy's face. "That money is just sitting there. We've been talking about hiring an architect for years and it hasn't happened. We'll draw it up like a loan, if that makes you feel any better. You can pay us interest, make regular payments. We'll be just like the bank, only nicer."

Lucy shook her head. "No. You've already taken me into your home. You won't let me pay more than a token rent. I can't keep taking your charity forever, Rosie. What kind of a mother am I going to be if I can't stand on my own two feet?"

"Exactly. And the fastest way for you to get there is to get that Internet site happening and grow your business. I know it hurts your pride, but taking a loan from your family is the best thing for you and the baby. And that's the truth." Rosie sat back in her chair, her case made.

Lucy stared at her, her mind whirling.

It was so tempting. Rosie and Andrew had the money. Lucy could stick to her original game plan. She'd already spoken to a Web site design company in anticipation of today's bank appointment. She could go full steam ahead with her schedule and be online within a month.

"Say yes. Be smart. For the baby," Rosie said.

"It's so much money," Lucy said. "And you guys have got plans for it."

"They'll wait."

"What about Andrew? It's his money, too."

"He loves you almost as much as I do, and he'll understand."

Lucy closed her eyes. So many big decisions lately. If only she had a crystal ball. She opened her eyes again.

"Yes. Okay. I can't believe I'm saying that, but thank you. Thank you so much. Where would I be without you?"

"Good girl!"

"I won't let you down," Lucy said. "I promise I'll pay back every cent."

"I know you will. I know where you live, remember?"

They were both blinking rapidly. Lucy shook her head.

"I feel like I just got off a roller-coaster. Talk about up and down."

"Welcome to parenthood, I guess," Rosie said. "From what I hear, this is just the beginning."

They both smiled, and Lucy reached across to grab her sister's hand, overwhelmed with gratitude and relief.

"Hey there. Long time no see," a familiar male voice said.

Lucy looked up to see Dominic Bianco standing next to the table. She felt her sister's fingers convulse around hers in reaction and had to fight the urge to giggle. Truly, Rosie's crush on The Bianco was a hoot.

"Dom. You're not just finishing work for the day, are you?" Lucy asked, noting he was still wearing his Bianco Brothers shirt.

"Something like that. Hey, Rosetta, how are things?"

Rosie was smiling at Dom with slightly glazed eyes. "G-good. Things are good. I'm married now, you know," she said.

Dom's eyebrows rose a bit at her sister's odd segue.

"Congratulations. When was the wedding?" he asked politely.

"Eight years ago," Lucy said.

"Right," Dom said. He looked confused, as well he might.

"Lucy tells me you've come back from six months in Italy," Rosie said.

Now it was Lucy's turn to be embarrassed. She didn't want Dom to think she spent her spare time talking about him.

"Yeah. Had a few months in Rome, Florence and Venice, checked out the countryside."

"Andrew and I were going to go for our honeymoon, but we wound up in Thailand instead," Rosie said. "I guess you got a bit of sun while you were there, huh? You're really tanned."

Rosie's eyes were on Dom's forearms as she spoke, and she looked as though she was about to lunge across the table and sink her teeth into him. Lucy drew back her knee in case she had to kick her sister.

"It was summer over there. What can I say?" he said.

He turned his attention to Lucy. "Your client happy with the herbs for his wedding dinner?"

"As happy as he can let himself be. He's French. He makes it a point to never smile too much."

Dom laughed, and Lucy felt a surge of satisfaction that she'd amused him.

"We've got a few French chefs as clients. They like to keep us on our toes, that's for sure."

"Pretty amazing, Lucy winding up as one of your customers after all these years," Rosie said. "It's a small world."

"Even smaller when you're Italian," Dom said. "Lucy is one of our favorite clients. My father and I fight over who gets to serve her."

Even though she knew he was only joking, Lucy shifted in her chair.

"That's rubbish. You almost always serve me," she said, aware of her sister's speculative glance bouncing back and forth between them.

"That's because I cheat," Dom said with an unrepentant grin.

The waiter arrived with their hot chocolates and cake, and Dom checked his watch.

"I'll leave you to it—looks as though you've got your work cut out for you," he said, indicating the generous slices of cake.

"See you tomorrow," Lucy said.

Dom smiled and gave a small, casual wave before moving to the other side of the café, out of sight behind the central counter.

"Oh. My. God. Pass me the chocolate. I need emergency therapy," Rosie said, slumping in her chair and fanning herself. "He's better-looking than ever. What a hunk. I mean, wow."

"Oh, look, there's Andrew," Lucy fibbed.

Rosie immediately sat up straight. Then she realized her sister was yanking her chain.

"Good one. Very funny."

"Just a timely reminder."

"Hey, I love Andrew with everything I've got, don't you worry. I'm not going anywhere, with anyone. But I can still admire The Bianco. It's a sentimental thing."

"It's sad. And, can I say, just a little embarrassing. You almost got drool on your good shirt."

"Pshaw," Rosie said, flicking her fingers in the air. "I was in total control the whole time."

Lucy rolled her eyes and spoke to the ceiling. "Delusional. The woman's delusional."

"Anyway, he never even noticed me. He was too busy looking at you like he wanted to lick you all over."

Lucy stared at her sister.

"He was not!"

"Uh-huh. He was, and he was flirting with you, too."

"Get out of here. I look like I've got a beach ball stuck up my top. He was not flirting with me."

"Lucy is one of our most favorite clients ever. My father and I wrestle to the death over who gets to serve her. What do you call that?"

"Being polite. Or being funny. Maybe both. But not flirting."

Rosie gave her a get-real look. "Seriously? You seriously didn't think he was flirting with you?"

"Of course not. Duh," Lucy said, pointing to her belly.

"Man. We are going to have to do something about your dating skills, because if you're not picking up signals that strong, you are never going to find another man," Rosie said.

Lucy knew her sister was only joking, but her words still caught her on the raw.

"Hey, what's wrong?" Rosie asked as Lucy reached for her hot chocolate and concentrated on stirring it.

"Nothing. Nothing's wrong."

"Bad at flirting and bad at lying. What am I going to do with you?"

Lucy stopped stirring her drink and met her sister's eyes.

"I don't want another man. I want Marcus. I want the father of my baby," she said in a small voice.

Her sister stared at her, her face full of sympathy.

"Go on, say it. Tell me I'm pathetic for wanting some-one who doesn't want me," Lucy said.

"I don't think that's pathetic. Marcus is the pathetic one. I just feel sad that I can't give you what you want."

Lucy sighed heavily and picked up a fork.

"I guess all this chocolate is still very necessary, after all," she said.

"Chocolate is always necessary, whether it be for cele-bration or commiseration," Rosie said.

Her sister waited until Lucy was swallowing a chunk of sinfully rich frosting before speaking again.

"And he was flirting with you. The Bianco was fully, blatantly, balls-out flirting with you."

CHAPTER FOUR

"Did you even consider discussing this with me first?" Andrew asked.

Rosie put down her knife and fork and gave her husband her full attention.

"I should have waited to talk to you, I know—"

"You think?"

Rosie blinked. Andrew didn't often lose his temper but when he did it was usually well-earned. Like tonight. As soon as she'd given it some thought, she'd known she should have spoken to him before offering the money to Lucy. But she couldn't undo what had already been done.

"I'm sorry. I got carried away. All I was thinking about was Lucy and how I could help. I hate that she's in such a difficult position."

"I hate it, too. But we've already given her a home. We can't afford to give her our savings, too."

"I hear what you're saying, but that money's just sitting in the bank, collecting interest. Why not use it to help Lucy? She'll pay us interest like the bank. It's a win-win situation."

Andrew pushed his chair back from the table and stood.

"What about our plans to renovate the practice? What about getting a junior partner? All that just goes by the wayside, does it?"

"No, of course not. But it's not like we were actually ready to do any of that. We haven't even decided on an architect yet."

"Because you keep putting it off."

Rosie stood, hating being at a disadvantage. "I haven't put anything off. Neither of us has pushed for the renovation. We've been too busy building the practice."

Andrew looked at her, his face tense.

"Rosie, every time I suggest we start talking to architects you come up with a reason for why we can't. First it was the Larson trial, then it was the Bigalows' divorce. The time after that you strained your Achilles' at the gym and you didn't want me doing all the legwork on my own." He stared at her, his jaw set. "If you're not ready to have children, tell me and stop stringing me along."

Rosie took a step backward. She hadn't been expecting such a direct confrontation, not after the way they'd both been sidestepping the issue for so long. It had become a game of sorts, the way they skirted around the all-consuming subject of when to start a family.

"I'm not not ready," Rosie said quickly, even though her stomach tensed with anxiety. "I'm not stringing you along. The time simply hasn't been right before."

Andrew sighed heavily. His blue eyes were intent as he looked into her face. "So when will the time be right if we give all our savings to Lucy? Five years? Ten years? You're thirty-one. How old do you plan on being when our kids are in college? You're the one who insisted we needed to add a junior partner to the firm before we even considered starting a family. And we both agreed we couldn't do that until we'd renovated the practice to create an extra office."

Again the tightness in her belly.

"Lucy probably only needs the money for a year or

two," she said. "As soon as she's paid us back, we'll renovate and start trying."

"Rosie. Be serious. It will take longer than two years for Lucy to pay out a loan. She'll be working part-time, she'll have expenses for the baby. It could take her years to get on top of things. We've dealt with enough bankruptcies to know that most small businesses don't survive the first few years."

"Lucy is not going to go bankrupt!"

"I didn't say she was. But she's also not going to suddenly become Martha Stewart, either."

He watched her, waiting for her to acknowledge that he was speaking the truth.

Finally she nodded. "Okay. You're right. It probably won't be two years."

He returned to the dining table and sat. His meal was only half-eaten, but he pushed it away.

"So we need to make a decision. Do we invest in our dream or your sister's?" he asked quietly.

She sat, too. Suddenly she felt very heavy.

"We could remortgage," she suggested.

"We're already leveraged because of buying the office. And once you have a baby and we put a partner on, our income will be reduced. That was the whole point of socking away extra money to pay for the renovations rather than taking on more debt. You know I would have been happy if we were pregnant years ago. But I know financial security is important to you, so we did things your way. Now you're telling me you want to put things off again while we lend our renovation fund to your sister?"

Rosie picked up her fork and pushed it into the pile of cold peas on her plate.

"Do we put off having a family or not, Rosie?" he asked.

She raised her gaze to him. She knew exactly how much he wanted children. It was one of the first things they'd discussed when they got together all those years ago. He wanted at least three children, wanted to build a family that would make up for the lack in his own shitty childhood. Even though the thought had scared her even back then, she'd invested in his dream, built castles in the air with him. And for the past eight years she'd been burying her head in the sand, pretending this day would never come.

"I shouldn't have offered the money to Lucy," she said quietly. "I'm sorry."

Andrew waited patiently for her to answer properly.

"We're not putting off starting a family," she confirmed. "I'll tell Lucy that we can't lend her the money after all."

Andrew's shoulders relaxed. She saw for the first time that there was a sheen of tears in his eyes. This meant so much to him.

"I'll come with you. We'll explain together," he said.

Rosie shook her head.

"No. It was my mistake. I'll do it."

She stood. She hated to think of how disappointed Lucy would be. Her sister had been so excited this afternoon.

If only she hadn't acted so impetuously. If only she'd stopped to think, waited to talk to Andrew tonight. But she hadn't, and now she had to go break her sister's heart to avoid breaking her husband's. And then, somehow, she had to overcome this terror that struck her every time she thought about becoming a mother.

LUCY DRAGGED HERSELF to the market the next morning. Never had she wanted to stay in bed so badly, not even the morning after Marcus left.

She felt defeated, and it scared her that she couldn't see a way out. She had no choice but to keep on working for as long as she could and hope that her cousin was prepared to drive for her at minimum wage and that she had a problem-free pregnancy before giving birth to the world's most perfect baby.

She didn't blame her sister for reneging on the loan. Rosie's offer had been generous and impulsive, and Lucy totally understood why she and Andrew had decided they had to retract it once cooler heads had prevailed.

She just wished she had an Option C to fall back on now that Option B had gone up in flames.

"Lucy. Managed to brave the cold, I see," Dom said as she stopped her trolley in front of the Bianco Brothers stall.

"Yeah," she said. Today even Dom's smile and charm couldn't nudge her out of her funk. All she wanted to do was to go home, curl into a ball and sleep until the world had righted itself. She fished in her bag for her shopping list, growing increasingly frustrated when she couldn't put her hand on it.

"Sorry. Give me a minute," she said. She pulled handfuls of paper from her bag, angrily riffling through them for the one she needed. She was such a train wreck—couldn't even get one little thing right today.

She could feel Dom watching her as she went back and forth through the papers. The list had to be in here somewhere. And if it wasn't, it meant a trip home to collect it from her flat. She felt dangerously close to bursting into tears and she blinked rapidly.

"Here."

She looked up to find a takeout coffee cup under her nose. She automatically shook her head.

"I can't drink coffee."

"It's hot chocolate. And you look like you need it more than I do."

As he spoke, the smell of warm chocolate hit her nose and her mouth watered.

"Come on, take it," he said, waving the cup invitingly.

"Thanks." She took the cup with a small smile. The first mouthful was hot and full of sugar. Just what she needed.

"Better?" Dom asked.

"Thanks."

He smiled, the dimple in his cheek popping. She glanced down at her papers and realized her shopping list was right on top of the pile.

"Typical," she muttered as she handed it over.

Dom scanned it quickly. "No problems here. Why don't you kick back and I'll get this sorted?"

He was already moving off. She knew she should object, at least pretend to inspect the produce on offer. But she trusted him. And today—just today—she needed a break. Tomorrow she would take on all comers again.

She rested her elbows on the push bar of her trolley, watching Dom sort through produce for her as she sipped his hot chocolate.

He was a nice man. Sexy, too. Although she still wasn't sure that she was grateful to her sister for pointing that fact out. She wondered what had gone wrong with his marriage. Then she realized what she was doing and dragged her attention away from his broad shoulders and flat belly.

"Okay. I think that's everything. I threw in some extra leeks for you. We overordered, and I'm sure you can find a customer to give them to," Dom said when he'd finished loading her trolley.

Lucy looked at him steadily for a moment before speaking.

"Thank you," she said. She hoped he understood that

she meant for everything—the produce, the hot chocolate, giving her a helping hand when she was bottoming out on self-pity.

He shrugged. "It's nothing. You look after yourself."

She opened her mouth to say more, but he was already greeting another customer. She'd taken up far too much of his time. Her stomach warm, she headed to her van and a full day of deliveries.

DOM FOUND THE PAPERWORK sitting among the boxes of broccoli in front of the stall. Four pages, stapled together with a brochure for a Web site design company. They looked important, and he put them aside in case a customer came looking for them. It was only when they were packing up the stall for the day that he noticed the papers again.

The sheets obviously couldn't have been too vital, since no one had claimed them. He was on the verge of throwing them out when something about the loopy handwriting on the front page jogged his memory. He flicked through, and Lucy Basso's signature jumped out at him from the last page. He remembered her agitation this morning, the way she'd fumbled in her bag. She had to have lost this when she was looking for her shopping list.

Dom stared at her signature for a long beat. He could wait till tomorrow and hand them back to her.

Or he could take them to her.

He folded the papers in two, sliding them into his back pocket. Lucy Basso was not in the market for romance. He knew that, absolutely. And yet he was still going to take advantage of the opportunity these papers represented.

Later that night, he balanced a takeout pastry box in one hand while knocking on Lucy's front door with the other.

Music filtered out into the night, Coldplay's "Everything's Not Lost." He glanced over his shoulder at the backyard of the house her flat was piggybacked onto. He'd had to decipher his father's handwriting on the much-thumbed index cards that constituted the Bianco Brothers' customer database to find her address. He eyed the flattened moving boxes stacked against the house and wondered how long she'd been living here.

Footsteps sounded on the other side of the door, and he blinked as it opened and light suddenly flooded him.

"Dom! Hi," Lucy said. She sounded utterly thrown, and her hands moved to tighten the sash on her pale-blue dressing gown.

She was ready for bed. He gave himself a mental slap on the head. Of course she was ready for bed—she was pregnant, and like himself she had to be up at the crack of dawn.

"Hi. Sorry to barge in like this. You left some papers at the stall today and I thought they might be important," he said.

"Oh. Wow. Thanks."

She smiled uncertainly and pushed a strand of thick dark hair off her face. For the first time he noticed her eyes were puffy and a little red.

She'd been crying.

That quickly his self-consciousness went out the window. The thought of Lucy crying on her own made him want to hurt something.

He lifted the pastry box.

"And I brought dessert, in case you hadn't had any yet."

She frowned as though she didn't quite understand what he was saying.

"Dessert?" she repeated.

"You know, the stuff everyone tells us is bad for us but that we keep eating anyway."

She laughed. "Right. Sorry. I wasn't expecting… Come in," she said.

She stood aside and he stepped past her into the flat. He took in her small combined living and dining room, noting her rustic dining table and her earthy brown couch with beige and grass-green cushions. A number of black-and-white photographs graced the walls—the desert at sunset, an empty beach, an extreme close-up of a glistening spiderweb.

"You really didn't have to do this," Lucy said as she moved past him to the kitchenette that filled one corner of the small flat.

"It was no big deal. It's on my way home," he said.

Technically, it was kind of true. If he was taking the really, really scenic route.

Lucy placed two plates on the counter.

"Would you like coffee or something else with… I don't even know what you brought," she said. She sounded bemused again but he refused to feel bad about ambushing her.

"Tiramisu. Like a good Italian boy," he said.

"I love tiramisu."

"It's in the blood. We've been trained from birth to love it."

He handed over the pastry box and she peeled away the paper.

"Good lord, this thing is monstrous. There's no way we can eat all of this," she said.

He made a show of peering into the box.

"Speak for yourself."

She smiled and gave him a challenging look as she divided the huge portion into two uneven servings, sliding the much larger piece onto a plate and pushing it toward him.

"I dare you."

"You should know I never back out on a dare," he warned her.

She handed him a fork, a smile playing about her lips. He followed her to the dining table where she sat at the end and he took the chair to her left. She'd barely sat before she was standing again.

"Coffee! I forgot your coffee. These bloody pregnancy hormones have turned my brain into Swiss cheese," she said.

He grabbed her arm before she could move back to the kitchen.

"Relax. I don't need coffee," he said.

Her arm felt slim but strong beneath his hand. He forced himself to let her go, and she sank into the chair.

For a moment there was nothing but the sound of forks clinking against plates as they each took a mouthful.

"Before I forget," Dom said.

He leaned forward to pull her papers from his back pocket, then slid them across the table.

Lucy's face clouded as she looked at them.

"Thanks."

"Why do I feel like I just handed you an execution order?"

Her gaze flicked to his face, then away again.

"It's nothing. Less than nothing. I'm sorry you wasted your time on them."

She pushed the papers away as though she never wanted to see them again.

He took a mouthful of his dessert and studied her. She looked tired. Maybe even a little beaten. The same vibe he'd sensed from her this morning.

"You want to talk about it?" he asked quietly.

She looked surprised. Then she shook her head. "You

don't want to hear all my problems," she said after a long moment.

"Come on, you have to talk to me. You made me come all this way for papers that mean nothing, you're eating my tiramisu. What's in this for me?" he said.

She huffed out a laugh at his outrageous twisting of the truth. "When you put it that way…" She gave him a searching look then shrugged. "Just yawn or fall face-first into your food when you've heard enough."

"Don't worry. I have plenty of cunning strategies to escape boring conversations. I have three aunts and four uncles."

Briefly she outlined her plans for Market Fresh—her goal to go online to grow the business, her plans to lease a second delivery van. She sat a little straighter as she talked and color came into her cheeks. She loved what she was doing, what she was building. And he was quietly impressed with her strategy. Apart from the all-too-apparent hiccup curving the front of her dressing gown, she sounded perfectly situated to take the next step.

"Absolutely," she agreed with him. "Except for one tiny little thing—the bank doesn't agree with me. They won't lend me the money I need to get my Web site built. Without the site, I can't generate more business, and without more business I can't afford to put on a second van."

Lucy looked down and seemed surprised that she'd polished off her dessert.

"So, basically, I'm screwed," she said.

"Lucia Basso. If your mother could hear you now," he said, mostly because he hated the despairing look that had crept into her eyes.

"It's okay. She already thinks I'm screwed. It won't be news to her."

She met his gaze across the table, and they both burst into laughter. She laughed so hard she had to lean back in her chair and hold her stomach. By the time she'd gained a modicum of control, tears were rolling down her face.

"God, I needed that," she said. Then her eyes went wide and she straightened in her chair as though someone had goosed her. "Oh!"

Both hands clutched her belly and she stared at Dom.

"What? Is something wrong?" he asked, already half out of his chair.

"The baby just moved!"

"Right." He felt like an idiot for being on the verge of calling the paramedics.

"It's the first time," she explained excitedly. "All the pregnancy books say I should start feeling something about now, and I've been waiting and waiting but there's been nothing—"

Her eyes went wide again and she smiled.

"There he goes again!" she said. "This is incredible! Dom, you have to feel this."

Before he knew what she was doing she'd pushed aside her dressing gown to reveal the thin T-shirt she was wearing underneath, grabbed his hand and pressed his palm to her belly. He could feel the warmth of her skin through the fabric, the rise and fall of her body as she breathed.

"Can you feel it?" she asked, her voice hushed as though the baby might overhear her and stop performing.

He shook his head, acutely self-conscious. He didn't know what to do with his fingers, whether to relax them into her body or keep his hand stiff. He could smell her perfume and feel the swell of her breast pressing against his forearm.

"Relax your hand more," she instructed, frowning in

concentration. He let his hand soften and she slid it over her belly, pressing it against herself with both hands.

Still he could feel nothing. She bit her lip.

"Maybe he's tired," she said.

Beneath his palm, he felt a faint surge, the smallest of disturbances beneath her skin.

He laughed and she grinned at him.

"Tell me you felt that?"

"I felt it."

They smiled at each other like idiots, his hand curved against her belly. He knew the exact moment the wonder of the moment wore off and she became self-aware again. He pulled his hand free at the same time that she released her grip on him. They both sat back in their chairs, an awkwardness between them that hadn't been there a few minutes ago.

"I should go," he said. "You've got an early start tomorrow."

"Yours is earlier," she said.

They both stood.

"About the business…something will come up," he said.

She shrugged. "Or it won't. I'll muddle through, I'm sure."

Her hand found her stomach, holding it protectively. He followed her to the door.

"Thanks for the tiramisu," she said with a small smile. "And for bringing my Web site stuff back."

"Like I said, it was on the way home. And I would have eaten all the tiramisu on my own if I'd had the chance. You saved me from myself."

He patted his stomach and she laughed, as he'd known she would. He hovered on the doorstep, unwilling to leave her just yet.

"What does it feel like?" he asked suddenly. "When the baby moves inside you?"

Her expression grew distant, and she cocked her head to one side. He had to resist the urge to reach out and touch her cheek to see if her skin really was as soft and smooth as it appeared.

"The books say it's like butterflies fluttering," she said after a moment. "Some women say it's like gas."

"Butterflies or gas. Right."

She smiled. "The closest thing I can come up with is that it's like when a goldfish brushes up against your hand. Only on the inside, if that makes sense."

She was so beautiful, standing there with her uncertain eyes and her smiling mouth and her rounded stomach. He wanted to kiss her. He took a step backward.

"Good night, Lucy Basso," he said.

"Good night, Dom."

He told himself he was being smart and fair as he walked down the darkened driveway to the street. She was pregnant. He had no business chasing her.

And yet he felt like he was letting yet another opportunity slip through his fingers.

He flexed his hand as he remembered the flutter of movement he'd felt beneath his palm. A smile curved his mouth as he started his car. She'd been so delighted, so amazed. He was stupidly happy that he'd been there to share the moment with her.

He sobered as he registered where his thoughts were going. This wasn't his baby. Lucy wasn't his wife or partner. He wouldn't be sharing any more moments of discovery with her—or with any other woman, for that matter.

There was a message from his father on his answering machine when he arrived home, asking him to call back. His father sounded sleepy when he answered the phone.

"You are late. Where have you been?"

Dom raised his eyebrows at his father's nosiness. "Out. What's up?"

"Out where? Out with girl?"

The joys of working with his family—they felt they owned his life.

"Pa."

He heard his father sigh.

"I need you to make run to Lilydale tomorrow to collect more zucchini from Giametti's. We short and I promise dozen boxes to Vue De Monde," his father explained.

Dom rubbed his eyes and stifled a yawn. What his father was suggesting would mean he had to get up an extra two hours early in order to have the stock on hand for their customers.

"You know, if you'd let me manage the stock on the computer, we wouldn't have these kinds of problems," he said lightly.

To his surprise, his father blew up, sending a string of expletives and curses down the phone.

"I sick of hearing about computers. You said you not talk about them again. I expect you to honor this even if you honor nothing else!"

Dom let his breath out between his teeth. He loved his father, but he wasn't a little boy anymore, and he certainly didn't have to take crap from him—especially when it was out-of-line, unearned crap.

"Am I part of Bianco Brothers or not?" he asked.

"You are my son. This is stupid question."

"Answer the question, Pa."

"You are part of business. You there every day. You can't work out for yourself?"

"So I'm an employee. Like Steve and Michael and Anna?"

"You are my son."

Dom didn't say a word, waiting for his father to stop hedging. The silence stretched tensely for long seconds before his father spoke again.

"What you want from me? You my right-arm man," his father said, messing up his Anglo phrasing the way he often did. "I not manage without you. There. Happy now?"

"If that's true, if I'm your second in command, I want a say. I want a vote. And I want a bit of respect while you're at it," Dom said.

"Respect! You talk respect when you speak to your own father like he is idiot who doesn't know anything about anything. You have place in my business, good job. You should be grateful, counting your lucky stars, instead of whining and complaining."

Dom held the phone away from his ear and swore long and loud. Why did he bother? Hadn't he banged his head against this brick wall just the other day? His father didn't want to change. He was old. And the truth was, Bianco Brothers was so successful that his father wouldn't notice the business they would lose over the coming years as their competitors got leaner and meaner and more efficient. By the time his father was ready to retire—or he dropped dead on the job, which was just as likely—Dom would be left with the task of picking up the pieces and trying to claw back market share.

If he chose to take it.

"Good night, Pa," he said. Then he ended the call.

"My business," his father had said. Not "our business."

Dom leaned against the kitchen counter. He had some decisions to make. If his father wasn't going to allow him to grow, to have a say… Well, maybe Dom needed to forge his own way.

LUCY FELT RIDICULOUSLY shy as she arrived at the market the following morning. Last night she'd pressed Dom's hand against her belly, practically strong-arming him into sharing her baby's first movements.

What had she been thinking? As if he cared what was going on in her belly. He was her wholesale supplier, for Pete's sake. The guy who used to sit two pews forward of her own family in church when they were kids. He didn't want to know what her baby felt like when it kicked. Every time she remembered how she'd pressed his hand against herself her toes curled in her shoes.

It wasn't until after he'd gone that she'd looked in the mirror and seen how puffy and red her eyes were. There was no way he wouldn't have guessed she'd been crying. She could only imagine what he thought of her: poor, lonely Lucy, desperate for company.

She was relieved when she approached the stall and saw Dom was busy with another customer and his father was free. Mr. Bianco could help her with her order, and she wouldn't have to talk to Dom today. One small thing going her way for a change.

"Lucy. You look beautiful," Mr. Bianco greeted her, his chubby arms spread wide.

Dom glanced up from where he was standing nearby. His dark gaze was unreadable as he noted her.

"I'll look after Lucy, Pa," he said.

"You are busy," Mr. Bianco said dismissively.

"I'll just be a minute," Dom said, addressing Lucy and not his father.

There was a definite tension between the two men, and Lucy shrugged uncomfortably.

"Sure. Whatever suits you guys," she said.

Mr. Bianco opened his mouth to protest, but Dom nailed

him with a look that had Mr. Bianco muttering under his breath as he moved off to serve someone else.

Lucy fiddled with the strap on her bag, nervous all over again now that she was going to have to face Dom after all. Maybe she should apologize for last night, for thrusting her baby bump at him. Just get the awkwardness out of the way and move on.

"Okay. Sorry about that," Dom said.

She looked up, words of apology on the tip of her tongue.

"Listen, have you got time for a coffee? Sorry, a hot chocolate? Twenty minutes?" Dom asked.

She opened her mouth but no sound came out. Why did this man keep taking her by surprise?

"Sure," she finally managed to croak.

Dom called out to his father that he was taking a break. Lucy left her trolley next to the stall and followed him to a café in the group of permanent shops that ran along Victoria Street beside the market. The woman behind the counter greeted him with a smile.

"We'll have two hot chocolates, Polly," he called as they sat.

Lucy clasped her hands nervously in front of her as Dom gave her his full attention. She had no idea what he was going to say to her, and she found his intense gaze unnerving. Suddenly all she could think about was how hot and heavy his hand had felt against her body last night.

Talk about inappropriate.

"I've been giving some thought to what we talked about last night," he said. "About your business and your plans for the future."

Lucy nodded. Right. He was going to offer her some advice, probably suggest she talk to one of the second-tier banks like everyone else had. She schooled herself to be patient. He was being kind, after all. And she'd shown herself to be in need of kindness last night.

"How would you feel about taking on a business partner?" Dom asked.

She blinked. "Excuse me?" she asked stupidly.

He smiled. "Bit out of the blue, huh? I think you've got some great ideas for your business, and I think you've tapped into a strong niche market. Market Fresh has a lot of potential. There's no reason why you couldn't be operating across the city, even expanding into other states."

He smoothed some papers out on the table between them.

"What I'm proposing is a fifty-fifty business partnership. I'll put up the capital to expand the business and build the Web site. You'll bring the existing business and your expertise to the table." He paused to look at her, his eyebrows raised in question.

She was too busy grappling for a mental foothold to say anything. Dom wanted to buy into her business? Become her partner? Give her the money she needed to make her business a success?

"But you already have a business," she said, blurting out the first thought that popped into her mind.

"No. My father has a business. I just work for him," he said. There was a tightness around his mouth that hadn't been there yesterday. A determination.

"You don't know anything about my business. You haven't seen the books. You have no idea what my turnover is," she said, frowning.

"Of course I'd want my accountant to take a look at things before we signed anything. I guess what I'm asking at this stage is if this sounds like something you might consider?" Dom asked.

Their hot chocolates arrived, and Lucy bought some time by fiddling with her cup and saucer.

Did she want a business partner? Being her own boss had been part of the appeal of starting Market Fresh, but taking on a partner wouldn't necessarily mean she wouldn't still have her independence. It would mean compromises though, having to listen to other ideas and incorporate them into her plans.

She eyed Dom assessingly. She hardly knew him really. Didn't know if he was hot tempered or easygoing, impulsive or rational. All she knew was what she'd observed of him over the year she'd been a customer at Bianco Brothers. He was good with customers. He was smart. He knew his product. He knew the industry.

"I've never thought about taking on a partner. Mostly because it's never come up before." She studied his face. She didn't quite know how to ask her next question, so she decided to just go for it.

"Why me? Why Market Fresh?"

He took a sip of his hot chocolate before answering.

"I'm thirty-one and I've been working for my father all my adult life. I've always thought I'd take over when he retired. But I'm beginning to realize that that might be a long way off. And that maybe I don't want to be Tony Bianco's boy anymore. I have ideas, things I want to try, and he's not open to them."

"Okay. I get that part. But you could do anything."

"Sure. I could start my own business. Go through all the pain of establishing myself, learn a new industry. Or I could find someone like you who has done all that hard stuff already."

He eyed her over the rim of his cup.

"And you need help," he added. "Which, speaking from

a purely selfish point of view, means I've got a certain amount of leverage."

Lucy dipped her head in acknowledgment of his brutal honesty. "Well. I asked," she said ruefully.

"Yep."

He sat back in his chair, his hands toying with his cup, spinning it on the saucer. His eyes never left hers as he waited for her to think things over some more.

What did she have to lose, after all? Her business, was the answer. And she was very afraid that she would do just that if she *didn't* take him up on his offer. She needed capital to grow. That was the bottom line.

"Okay. I'm interested," she said.

He smiled slowly. Suddenly she wished that her sister had never made her take a second look at him. Two weeks ago, he was a man, a human being like any other. Today, thanks to Rosie's teen obsession, Lucy felt a distinct frisson race up her spine as she registered how very, very good-looking he was.

Again, so not appropriate. Especially given her situation and the offer he'd just put on the table.

"Great. Why don't we meet on Sunday? That will give me time to get a preliminary offer drawn up. Rosetta will probably want to take a look at it, right?"

"Oh yeah. She'll probably want to pat you down and ransack your house and run an FBI check on you," Lucy said.

He smiled again. "I've got nothing to hide."

He leaned across the table and held out his hand. She hesitated a second before taking it. His hand was warm and firm.

"To new beginnings," he said.

She nodded, unable to speak for some reason while he held her with his dark gaze.

"We'd better get you on the road," he said.

She followed him to the stall, feeling more than a little dazed. After what had happened with her sister's offer of a loan, she knew it would be stupid to get too excited. So many things could go wrong. Dom could change his mind after he'd looked at the books. His lawyer or accountant might have objections. Anything could go wrong.

And yet a slow excitement was bubbling through her blood. If this came off, her problems were solved. She'd have the capital she needed to grow. She'd have a fighting chance to secure her and her baby's future.

She closed her eyes for a minute.

Please, please, please let this happen.

She wasn't quite sure who she talking to, but she hoped like hell they were listening. It was about time she scored a break.

CHAPTER FIVE

"YOU'RE NOT WEARING that," Rosie said as Lucy loaded paperwork into her tote bag.

After two weeks of negotiations and discussions, she and Dom had signed a partnership contract the previous day. Lucy still couldn't quite believe that her money problems were over. Well, not over, but at least in a holding pattern for a while. She had a chance now to do what she needed to grow her business. Which was what today's lunch meeting with Dom was all about—planning for the future.

"Lovely. Thank you for the confidence boost," Lucy said.

"I didn't mean you look bad. You just look…ordinary," Rosie said.

Lucy looked down at the plain black pants, black turtleneck and black boots she was wearing. The pants were new, the first of her true pregnancy wardrobe. The turtleneck was old and would probably never look the same again after being stretched over her belly.

"I *am* ordinary," she said dismissively.

"Why don't you wear that red stretchy shirt? That always looks great with black."

"It makes my boobs look huge."

"Exactly," Rosie said with a grin.

Lucy rolled her eyes. "You are seriously turning into a pimp. You need help." She was only half joking—her sister's continual comments about Dom were starting to wear her down.

"He asked you to lunch," Rosie said.

"It's a work meeting, not a date."

"He likes you, Lucy. He flirts with you every time we see him. Yesterday, when we signed the contract, he even ordered you food from the bar without asking because he knows you get hungry all the time. How many more signs do you want that this man has the hots for you?"

"None. I just signed a partnership contract with him. I don't want him to have the hots for me." Lucy shook her head. "Why are we even having this conversation? He does not have the hots for me. He's a nice guy. He's considerate. He's like that with all his customers. He's like that with you."

"He doesn't look at me the way he looks at you," Rosie said.

"And how does he look at me?" Lucy asked, hands on hips.

"Like he wants to take a bite out of you," Rosie said. "Like a starving man looks at a feast."

Lucy hooted with laughter.

"You are so deluded. Starving man, my ass. He's newly divorced, he's just spent six months traveling through Italy. He's probably got women lined up around the block to throw themselves at him. There's no way he's interested in a five months pregnant woman. No. Way."

"You're nineteen weeks," Rosie said a little sulkily. "Not quite five months."

"Which means I'm only cow-like instead of elephant-like. You need to stop trying to live out your teen obsession through me."

"It wasn't an obsession," Rosie said.

Lucy gave her a look.

"Okay, it was slightly obsessive. But that's not why I want you to wear the red shirt. He's a nice guy. I think he'd make a great father."

Lucy stilled, the smile fading from her lips.

"I'm not looking for a father for my baby," she said.

"Marcus isn't going to help you carry the load, Lucy," Rosie said.

Lucy eyed her sister steadily. She needed Rosie to understand that she couldn't buy into the romantic fantasy she was spinning. She didn't have the luxury to indulge those kinds of dreams anymore.

"I know you're trying to help, but please can we stop it with the whole Dom-likes-me thing? He's my business partner. All I want from him is hard graft and a cash injection. I don't want him to like me. And I don't want to like him. We're business partners, and I need one of those much more than I need a man in my life. Even if that was an option that was on the table. Which it isn't."

For a moment Rosie looked as though she was going to object, then she sighed and shrugged a shoulder.

"Fine. Bury your head in the sand."

Lucy palmed her car keys. "Thank you. You know how much I like it there."

Dom had given her directions to his house in Carlton and she found it easily. A double-fronted terrace house, it was a pale cream color, the trim painted heritage green and red. Someone had placed terra-cotta planter boxes along the front edge of the front porch, but they were full of dirt and nothing else. She wondered if Dom's ex-wife had been the gardener and felt sad for him. No one got married expecting it to end in divorce.

Warm air rushed out at her when he opened the door to her knock.

"Lucy. Come on in. I'm just finishing up the gnocchi dough," he said.

She managed a greeting of some description, but she had no idea what she'd actually said. She was too busy reeling from the impact of Dominic Bianco in bare feet, well-worn jeans and a tight, dark gray T-shirt. His hair was ruffled and casual, his eyes warm.

He was so earthily, rawly sexy it took her breath away.

She barely noticed the polished hardwood floor beneath her feet or the ornate plasterwork on the cornices and ceiling as she followed him down the hall.

She gave herself a mental slap. She had no business being so aware of Dom as a man. It was ridiculous and counter-productive and she needed to get a serious grip. Right now. Dom was her business partner. End of story.

"I'm making my mama's secret gnocchi," Dom said over his shoulder. "If you notice any of the ingredients, you have to take the information to your grave with you."

They entered a wide, spacious living area with a vaulted ceiling. Immediately in front of them was a sleek, dark stained table. To the left was a modern white kitchen with dark marble countertops. Beyond she could see comfortable-looking brown leather couches and French windows that opened onto a deck.

"I promise not to look," Lucy said.

She noted the two place settings at the table. Everything looked perfect, from the red roses in a sleek vase to the snowy white linen napkins folded neatly across each side plate. She frowned.

Dom moved behind the island counter and reached for a handful of flour. She watched as he dusted the counter prior to rolling out the dough.

She smiled uncertainly when he glanced up at her.

"You want to take your coat off? I should have asked before I got flour on my hands again. Just throw it on the couch."

She took advantage of his suggestion to try to pull herself together, but nothing could stop the way her brain was suddenly whirring away.

He'd gone to a lot of trouble for a simple business meeting. The flowers, the beautifully set table. Unless she was hugely mistaken, he'd even ironed the napkins. And he was making pasta by hand for her.

Was it just her, or was Dom pulling out all the stops for what was supposed to be a simple working lunch, their first as business partners?

She studied him carefully as she crossed to the kitchen. His hair was slightly damp, as though he'd just had a shower. But that could mean anything. Maybe he'd slept in, maybe he'd been to the gym. Maybe he'd even had someone stay the night and they'd whiled away a weekend morning in bed together before he'd had to get ready for this meeting.

She frowned as she registered her distinct unease at the thought of Dom with another woman.

"You want to open the wine?" he asked as he began to roll out thin ropes of dough with his fingertips. He indicated a bottle of red wine.

"Um, sure. Where can I find the bottle opener?"

"Top drawer, on the left," he said.

She found the opener easily and began twisting it into the cork.

"Haven't seen one of these for a while," she said.

Dom frowned. "I thought pregnant women were allowed to have the occasional glass of wine these days. My sisters drank through their pregnancies."

Lucy laughed. "I meant the cork. It's the real deal, not plastic. And definitely not a screw cap."

"Oh, right. I brought some bottles of Chianti back from Italy. They won't have anything to do with screw caps over there."

She collected the glasses from the table and poured the wine, then placed his within reach on the counter.

"Thanks." The smile he gave her was warm. Then his gaze dropped below her face.

He did not just do an eye-drop on me, she told herself sternly, even though it had looked distinctly like he was checking out her breasts. *He's probably worried that my turtleneck won't withstand the pressure of being stretched over my bump and that the whole thing will suddenly rip in two like the Hindenburg.*

Even though she was limiting herself to just one small glass of wine, she took a healthy sip and welcomed the distracting warmth as it slid down her throat. When she dared look at Dom again he was cutting the dough into one-inch sections.

See? He's not interested in your boobs. You've been spending too much time with your delusional sister.

"Do you cook often?" she asked.

She did a mental eye roll at the question. She might as well have asked about the weather. She'd had several meetings with him since he'd proposed their partnership and yet each time she seemed to feel less comfortable, not more so. Now she was trotting out the kind of polite, stiff chitchat she usually saved for new acquaintances.

"When I can. I try to make some meals on the weekend for during the week. It's easy to get lazy when I'm home late from the market," he said.

He began marking the gnocchi with a fork, expertly rolling each piece off the tines and onto a floured plate.

"You've done this before," Lucy noted. "Don't tell anyone, but I buy mine from the supermarket."

He tsk-tsked and shook his head.

"Lucia, Lucia. Don't you know that food is the way to a man's heart?" he said in a flawless impersonation of any number of elderly Italian women she knew.

"Damn. That was where I went wrong," she said, snapping her fingers in mock chagrin.

Dom winced.

"Sorry," he said. His gaze dropped to her belly. "I didn't think."

She shrugged. "It's okay. It wasn't my store-bought gnocchi that scared Marcus away. He fell for his yoga instructor."

"Yoga instructor. That's a new one. I thought it was usually the secretary."

"Marcus is a photographer, so he had to improvise. But he's making out just fine. Apparently what she lacks in the dictation department she makes up for in flexibility," Lucy said. Then she flushed as she realized how jealous and bitchy she sounded.

The corners of Dom's eyes crinkled as he grinned at her.

"Saucer of milk, table two," he said.

She pulled a face. "Sorry. I didn't mean to say that."

"Yeah, you did. It's okay. You're supposed to be pissed off. The only people who are cool with being betrayed are people I don't want to know."

He took the gnocchi over to the stove and slid them into a pan of boiling water. His arms flexed as he brushed the last pieces from the plate. He hadn't shaved today, she noted, and his jaw was dark with stubble, enhancing his rumpled, casual appeal.

Bare feet and stubble ought to be banned, she thought. *I'd have to turn the hose on Rosie if she was here.*

Dom turned his head and caught her staring. A slow smile spread across his mouth. She tore her gaze away and frowned down into her drink. Her heart was suddenly pounding, and she didn't know what to do with her hands.

"So, um, what did your father say about us becoming partners?" she asked abruptly, desperate for distraction.

"I haven't told him. It's none of his business what I do with my investments," Dom said.

"Wow. You guys must have had one hell of an argument."

His mouth quirked wryly. "You could say that."

He didn't offer any more information, and she wasn't about to push. They were business colleagues, not friends. On the personal front, they owed each other nothing.

"So, Lucy, the big question—do you like it hot?" he asked.

She blinked. "Um, sorry?"

He laughed. "Maybe I should rephrase that. Can you eat chilies without getting heartburn?"

"Oh. So far, so good. But I'm definitely more on the coward's side of the chili divide than the courageous."

"Okay, why don't you come over here and try the sauce, let me know if I've gone too crazy with anything." He gestured for her to join him at the stove.

She came to a halt a few feet away, and he dipped a wooden spoon into a saucepan.

"Come a little closer so I don't spill."

She stepped forward, feeling acutely self-conscious. She was standing so close now that if she inhaled deeply her baby bump would jostle him. He lifted the spoon to her mouth.

"Blow on it a little, it's hot," he said.

She pursed her lips and blew gently. She could feel him watching her and heat stole into her cheeks. She told herself it was because she was standing near the stove and she was wearing a turtleneck, but she knew it had more to do with how broad his shoulders were up close and how good he smelled and how acutely aware she was of all of the above.

Desperate to get the moment over and done with, she leaned forward to taste the sauce. Tough luck if she burned her mouth. It would be worth it to gain some distance and some perspective.

The flavors of rich tomato, fresh basil, subtle garlic and the perfect amount of chili chased each other across her palate.

"Oh, that's good!" she said, closing her eyes to savour the flavors.

When she opened her eyes again Dom was staring at her, his eyes very dark and very intent. Her breath got caught somewhere between her lungs and her throat and her gaze dropped to his mouth. He had great lips, the bottom one much fuller and softer-looking than the top. She wondered what it would feel like to kiss him.

Dear God.

She took a step backward.

"You know, I might go powder my nose before we eat," she said in a high voice she barely recognized as her own.

"Second door on your right," he said easily.

She nodded her thanks and scooped up her handbag on the way. She heaved a sigh of relief when she was safely behind the closed bathroom door. Then she dived into her bag and found her cell phone. Rosie answered on the second ring.

"Aren't you supposed to be in a meeting with The Bianco?" her sister asked, not bothering with a greeting.

"I need advice. He's cooking for me," Lucy whispered into the phone.

"What? Why are you whispering? Of course he's cooking for you—he invited you to lunch," Rosie said.

"I'm whispering because I'm in the bathroom, and I'm in here because he's set the table with flowers and linen napkins and he's made gnocchi from scratch and there's wine and he just fed me sauce and looked at me as though maybe he really does want to take a bite out of me," Lucy explained in a rush.

"Oh boy. I need to sit down."

"Me, too," Lucy said. She put down the lid on the toilet and sat.

"I'm freaking out here, Rosie. I have no idea if I'm reading things into the situation that aren't there or I don't know what," she whispered, glancing toward the door.

"Calm down. Let's assess the situation logically. You said there were flowers. What kind?"

"Roses."

"And linen napkins. And he's making pasta for you?"

"Yep. And there's wine. And I think I saw some kind of cake sitting on the counter for later."

"He *baked* for you? Maybe I need to lie down," Rosie said. "I can't believe The Bianco is making a move on you."

Lucy sucked in an outraged breath. "What do you mean you can't believe it? You're the one who told me he wanted me. You're the one who told me to wear the red shirt and that this was a date, not a business lunch."

"Yeah, but this is *really happening!*" Rosie said excitedly.

Lucy closed her eyes. She felt dizzy, scared, even a little sweaty. She couldn't handle this. She didn't want Dom to look at her with bedroom eyes. She didn't want to be aware of him as a woman. She was pregnant. A tiny little person was growing inside her body. Soon, she'd be looking after that little person night and day.

"I think I should leave," she told her sister. "I'll tell him I don't feel well and come home."

"Are you kidding me? Stay. Stay and see what happens."

Lucy clutched the phone.

"Rosie. Be serious. This is not a game. This is my life. Isn't it complicated enough already? I just signed a contract to share my business with Dom. If anything happened between us—" She broke off, shaking her head. She couldn't even allow herself to go there. It was so absurd, so crazy. She still couldn't believe that she'd seen what she'd thought she'd seen in his eyes.

"But he likes you," Rosie said, as though that resolved everything.

"I don't like him," Lucy fired back.

"Liar. If you didn't like him, you wouldn't be hiding out in the bathroom calling me because he looked at you."

"Rosie. Be serious. I just gave half my business to this man."

Rosie sighed. "Fine, be sensible then. Tell him you're not interested. Get it out of the way now, off the agenda. That way you both know where you stand."

Lucy realized that every muscle in her body was tense and made a conscious effort to relax.

"Okay, good. That's what I'll do, nip it in the bud," she said, nodding her agreement. "Thanks, Rosie. I needed to hear that."

"Did you?"

"Stop trying to be Dr. Freud. You don't have the beard for it."

She ended the phone call after promising to call Rosie the

moment the meeting was over. Then she flushed the toilet and washed her hands and eyed herself sternly in the mirror.

The very next time Dom smiled at her in that special way or looked at her as though she were chocolate-coated, she'd call him on it. They'd lay their cards on the table, establish some ground rules and move on. Problem solved.

Dom was dressing a salad when she returned to the living room.

"We're about two minutes away. Would you mind taking our wineglasses over to the table?" he asked.

"Sure."

She placed the wine on the coasters he'd provided and hovered awkwardly beside one of the chairs.

"Does it matter where I sit?" she asked.

"Help yourself."

He brought the salad to the table, then served the pasta. Aromatic flavors wafted up from her meal as he placed it in front of her.

"This looks wonderful," she said.

"I take no credit. My ma perfected this recipe over twenty years. All I did was follow instructions," he said.

He smiled and she searched his face for any of the heated intent she'd registered earlier. But for the life of her she could find nothing apart from friendly warmth and welcome.

"You want Parmesan?" he asked, offering her a small bowl of freshly grated cheese.

She sprinkled Parmesan on her gnocchi and took her first mouthful. It really was fantastic—the tomatoes tangy, the chili providing the exact right amount of background burn. The gnocchi was light and fluffy, with the hint of something elusive in the mix.

"This is great," she said, gesturing toward her plate with her fork.

"Yeah? Glad you like it. I made so much, you can take some home with you, save you cooking dinner."

There was a solicitous note in his voice. She darted a look at him, ready to deliver her clear-the-air speech at the first sign of anything remotely unbusinesslike. But again he simply looked friendly and interested. The perfect business partner, in fact: cooperative, personable, intelligent.

She was on tenterhooks throughout the entire meal, waiting for a repeat of the moment by the stove. It never happened. After they cleared the table, he brought out his paperwork and notepad and got down to business in earnest. Not once over the subsequent hours did he so much as hint that he saw her as anything other than his business partner.

No hot looks. No lingering glances. No intimate smiles. Nothing except sensible, incisive business discussion.

After two hours of intense strategizing, Lucy retreated to the bathroom again.

She was confused. She'd been so sure…. The butterflies in her stomach, the pounding of her heart, the steamy intent in his eyes—was it really possible that she was so out of practice with all things male-female that she'd misread his signals? Could she have simply imagined that moment of connection? Was that really possible?

She checked her reflection in the bathroom mirror and groaned as she realized she'd spilled sauce on herself, her baby bump having obligingly caught it. She stared at the red splodge, bright against the dark of her turtleneck, like a beacon drawing attention to her belly.

"You're an idiot," she told her reflection.

The tension she'd been carrying with her all afternoon dissipated as she sponged her top clean, shaking her head all the while.

Call it hormones, call it nerves, call it whatever—she'd

clearly misinterpreted Dom's behavior. Of course she had. She was pregnant. Hardly an object of desire. She had to have been temporarily deranged to even entertain the idea in the first place.

Feeling calm and centered for the first time all afternoon, she returned to their meeting.

Thank God she hadn't delivered her little speech.

CHAPTER SIX

DOM COULDN'T STOP thinking about Lucy. While he cleaned up after their lunch, he thought about how she didn't take herself too seriously, how she liked to laugh. How smart she was in a school-of-hard-knocks kind of way.

During his run afterward, he thought about how gutsy and brave she was.

He liked her. He liked her a lot. The admiration and curiosity and attraction he'd felt for her previously had been based on what little he knew of her via their brief daily encounters at his father's stall. Now, however, he'd seen Lucy at home, watched her interact with her sister, had numerous meetings with her, and he was beginning to understand just how special she was.

As he paused at a traffic light, he registered that he'd spent the past hour thinking about Lucy Basso. And not in a business kind of way.

Sweat ran down his back and the smile faded from his lips as he remembered the moment by the stove. He'd almost kissed her. She'd been standing so close and he'd been staring into her face and the need to taste her lips, to touch her to see if she was as smooth and warm and soft as he imagined had almost overwhelmed him.

He was a bastard. The light changed and he took off across the intersection.

The moment he'd decided to offer her a partnership, he'd known it meant the end of his chances with her. Lucy did not need her new business partner lusting after her. She needed help, support, money. Anything beyond that was simply not on the agenda. And he was a selfish prick for even letting himself go there. He lengthened his stride, angry with himself. He needed to get a grip on his attraction to her.

Ten minutes later, he slowed his pace, switched off his iPod and opened the gate to his parents' house. His mother looked up from the kitchen table when he entered via the back door.

"Dominic! At last you come. I was beginning to forget what my boy looks like," she said, pushing herself to her feet with an effort.

Like his father, his mother had turned into a round little barrel as she aged, her love of pasta and rich meats catching up with her. Her long gray hair was pinned on the back of her head, and she wore a voluminous apron over her dress. Her hands were dusted with flour, and she held them out from her sides as he kissed her.

"You all sweaty," his mother said, eyeing him with concern. "You should get out of those damp clothes. Have a shower. Put on something of your father's."

"I'm fine. I just dropped in for a quick hello," he said.

His mother's lips immediately thinned.

"I never see you anymore. First you go away for six months, then you come home and still you are stranger."

Guilt stabbed him. He *had* been avoiding home—or, more accurately, he'd been avoiding his father. At the market, work acted as a buffer between them, but at home there was no place to hide the fact that he and his father were barely on speaking terms.

"I've been busy. Work and some other things."

His mother sat back at the table and resumed rolling out the mixture for her biscotti.

"Your father is in the front room. You should go say hello to him," she said.

He hesitated a fraction of a second before nodding.

"Sure."

He could feel her watching him as he walked up the hallway.

His father was in his favorite chair, the seat reclined as far as it could go, the Italian-language newspaper, *Il Globo,* spread across his belly. Dom watched him sleep for a moment, noting how old his father looked without his larger-than-life personality to distract from the new wrinkles in his face and the sag of his jaw. Age spots had appeared on his hands in the past few years and the gray in his hair was turning white. He was fifty-nine and still he woke every day at 5:00 a.m. to tend the stall at the market, despite the fact that they could easily afford to hire staff to cover the early shift.

Stubborn bastard.

"Pa," he said quietly.

Tony started, the newspaper rustling. He frowned, jerking the chair into the upright position.

"Was reading newspaper," he said.

Dom gestured back toward the kitchen.

"I dropped in to see Mama for a bit," he said.

Tony nodded. "Good, good. She worries when she not see you."

Conversation dried up between them. Dom felt the silence acutely. He and his father had had their moments over the years, but he'd never felt as distant as he had recently.

He cleared his throat. "There's something I've been meaning to tell you. Lucy Basso was looking for an investor in Market Fresh, so I've bought in. We're partners."

"What is this? Partners? How can you be partners with another business when you have Bianco Brothers?"

"It's not a full-time gig. At the moment, at least. When things pick up, I might have to rethink. But in the meantime nothing has to change."

His father's face reddened. "You work for me! You always work for me."

"I'm not resigning, Pa. I'm just exploring other opportunities."

His father glared at him for a long moment.

"This is because of computers."

"I want to make my own business successes," Dom said, sidestepping the issue.

"After everything I give you, everything I do for you. You tell me this, no discussion, nothing."

Dom refused to feel guilty. He had a life to live, too.

"I'm not a kid, I don't need to ask your permission." He felt like he'd been saying that a lot lately. "I just thought you'd like to know what was going on."

He headed for the kitchen. His mother looked up from spooning biscotti mixture onto a tray when he entered.

"Listen, I have to go. But maybe I could come around for dinner during the week?"

His mother frowned, then her gaze slid over his shoulder.

"Bianco Brothers is for you. For all my children. And you throw back in my face," Tony said from the doorway.

Dom saw his father's hands were shaking and his eyes were shiny with tears. Dom rubbed the bridge of his nose and reached for patience.

"What am I supposed to do, Pa? I have a business degree, I have ideas, but you won't listen to any of them. So either I sit around and suck it up and stew in my own juices, or I do something for myself. I chose Option B. You still have Vinnie and the rest of the staff. There's nothing I do that they can't."

"What is going on? What is happening here?" his mother asked.

"Dominic is leaving business," Tony said, his chin stuck out half a mile.

Dom raised his eyebrows. "That's not what I said."

"What do you call when you buy another business?"

"I'm a partner. Lucy will still run it. I'm just helping out. I promise this won't be a problem, okay?" he said. "Look, we can talk about this more tomorrow at work."

When you've had a chance to cool down and think instead of react.

He turned to his mother.

"Save some biscotti for me," he said. She nodded absently and kissed him good-bye.

Out in the street, Dom took a deep breath, then let it out again. He'd done it. It hadn't been pleasant, but it was over.

The look on his father's face flashed across his mind. He'd looked betrayed. Hurt. Baffled.

Dom started to run, lengthening his stride with each step. Soon he was breathing heavily, sweat running down his chest and spine.

He refused to look back, and he couldn't stand still forever. His father was going to have to come to terms with his decision. And if he didn't…well, they would cross that bridge when they came to it.

LATER THAT EVENING, Rosie stood in the kitchen making spaghetti with meatballs with her husband. As usual, he was cutting the onions because they made her howl like a baby and she was mashing the canned tomatoes in the saucepan.

"Do you think it would be wrong for me to invite

Dominic Bianco to the Women's Institute fund-raiser next week without telling Lucy first?" she asked during a lull in their conversation.

"Why would you do that?" Andrew asked.

"Because if I tell Lucy, she'll tell me not to invite him."

"Okaaaay," Andrew said, frowning. "Why do I feel like I'm missing a vital part of this conversation?"

"I think Dom likes Lucy."

His eyebrows rose toward his hairline.

"She's pregnant," he said.

"So?"

He clanked a frypan onto the stove.

"You're serious? You need me to explain?"

"It's happened before in the history of the world." Rosie was aware she sounded defensive. Was she the only one who saw the potential here? "Lucy is still gorgeous and fantastic. Would it be any different if she was a single mom and she met a guy?"

Andrew looked confused for a minute as he thought it over.

"Yes. And I don't know why, it just is. Pregnant women are for protecting and admiring, not lusting after," he said unequivocally.

She grunted.

"Hey, I can't help the way the male mind works. This stuff is hardwired in, along with the ability to kill spiders and take out the garbage."

She rolled her eyes but couldn't help smiling.

"I'm still going to invite him," she said.

"I'd be disappointed if you didn't."

She threw the tea towel at him.

"I almost forgot. I picked up that new George Clooney movie for you on the way home," Andrew said as he measured olive oil into the frypan and added the onions.

"Have I told you lately that you're the man of my dreams?" she said.

"Yeah? Prove it," he said. He pulled her close for a kiss, and only the hiss of the olive oil forced them to call a halt.

"Phew. Someone's looking for some action tonight," she said, fanning herself with a hand.

"You know it, babe."

She smiled at him, anticipating the night ahead. A couple of hours with George on the TV and her husband beside her on the couch—the perfect man sandwich. Then bed, with sleep not on the immediate agenda. Sounded pretty damn fine to her.

"You know, I've been thinking," he said as she began to form the meatballs. "This whole thing with Lucy—the baby, the renovation fund."

She tensed, forewarned by the odd stiffness to his speech. Almost as though he'd rehearsed what he wanted to say.

"I'm thinking we should start the office renovation now," he said.

She let out a silent sigh of relief.

"Okay. Good. That sounds good," she said.

"And that maybe we should start trying for a baby at the same time."

She suddenly had trouble swallowing.

This is it, the moment of truth. Speak now or forever hold your peace.

"I thought we were going to wait until we had a junior partner on board," she said slowly.

"Sure. But the odds are good we won't get pregnant straight away. Even if we do, there's a whole nine months to find someone and train them. I was talking to Lincoln Sturt during the week, and he thinks the renovation would only take a month or two to finish. He even suggested his draftsman for the design work."

Rosie stared at him. Lincoln Sturt was one of their clients, a builder. That Andrew had consulted him without talking with her first was unsettling.

"You never mentioned this before," she said.

Andrew shrugged, but he darted her a quick, assessing look. The rehearsed speech, his obvious tension, the homework he'd put in—this was important to him. But she'd always known that. And crunch time had to come sometime, right? This was what she'd signed up for when she married him.

He wanted to be a father. He wanted to have children with her.

She licked her lips. Took a deep breath.

"Okay. All right. Let's do it," she said.

For a long moment there was only the sound of the onions cooking. Andrew stared at her. Then a smile lifted the corners of his mouth.

"Really?" he asked. He looked slightly dazed and she realized he'd anticipated more resistance from her.

"Sure. Let's go for it," she said.

Andrew gave a whoop of joy then swept her into his arms. She found herself laughing along with him, her head whirling as he spun them both around.

"No more sleep-ins. No more weekends away. No more dinners for two," Andrew said.

"Nope. Not for at least twenty years. And even then we'll have to pry them out of the house with a crowbar."

Andrew laughed and kissed her soundly. Then, to her surprise, he dropped her back on her feet and headed for the door.

"Hey! Where are you going?"

He merely waved a forefinger in the air to tell her she'd have to wait. He was back in seconds with something shiny in his hand.

It took her a moment to realize it was the blister pack for her contraceptive pills.

"I've been wanting to do this for ages," he said, pulling a pair of scissors from a drawer.

Rosie lifted a hand in protest, but the scissors were already slicing through the shiny foil. The pack fell into the rubbish, slice by slice.

Andrew threw her a triumphant smile.

"There. Done," he said.

"Yep," she said dryly.

He looked so happy. Alive in a way that she hadn't seen him in a long time.

"I love you," she told him. "You know that, don't you?"

He kissed her. "I love you, too, babe."

Rosie closed her eyes and held him tight. She could do this. Thousands of women took the plunge into motherhood every day. She was smart, resourceful, kind. She would be a good mom. Of course she would.

A WEEK LATER, Lucy smoothed on lip gloss and stepped back from the mirror to check the effect. She'd decided to wear her hair up for the Women's Institute fund-raiser, a fashion show where all the clothing would be auctioned off at the end of the night, the money going toward the local women's shelter. She'd added another element to her pregnancy wardrobe for the event, a sleeveless black stretch dress that promised to give as she grew. Paired with a bolero cardigan with intricate beading on the front, she figured she looked about as good as she was going to. Her lips were shiny, her hair loosely gathered on her head in big, loopy curls, and if nothing else the dress underlined the fact that she'd gone up a whole cup size since becoming pregnant.

A rap sounded on the connecting door. Before she could call out that it was okay to come through, it opened to reveal her mother and Rosie, both also done up to the nines.

"My goodness, Lucia!" her mother said, stopping in her tracks. "You are so big all of a sudden!"

Sophia's eyes were glued to Lucy's belly.

Lucy looked down at herself. "No, I'm not. The doctor said the baby is normal size, and that I'm normal size."

Her mother tilted her head to one side and did a slow walk around Lucy as she stood in the center of the living area.

"It is this dress—it is too tight. I think maybe you should wear something different," Sophia said. "Something less revealing. What about that long coat you have?"

Lucy felt her hard-won confidence seeping out the soles of her shoes.

"I think you look stunning," Rosie said. "If I had boobs like that, I'd show them off, too."

Lucy glanced down at her chest then. Great. Huge belly, enormous breasts. Probably there was something wrong with her hair and makeup, too.

"I think it's too late to hide that I'm pregnant," Lucy told her mother.

"What about a brooch? Do you have a thing for me to pin this shut with?" her mother asked, holding the two sides of Lucy's bolero top shut over her cleavage.

Rosie laughed.

"It's too late to preserve Lucy's virtue now, Ma. She's been got at, good and proper."

"You're hilarious," Lucy told her sister.

Rosie blew her a kiss.

"Are we ready, ladies?" Andrew asked from the doorway. He was wearing a dark navy pinstripe suit and a white shirt with no tie. With his midbrown hair freshly cut, he was looking very sharp.

"Hey, you look great," Lucy told him.

Andrew shrugged a shoulder.

"Thanks."

He shot Rosie a long, warm look. Lucy watched as her sister blushed, then got busy picking a piece of lint off the hem of her dress as though nothing had happened.

That sealed it. Something was going on. Her sister and Andrew had been acting weird all week, but until now Lucy had been half-convinced she was imagining it.

Not the only time she'd imagined something lately, of course, so her track record wasn't exactly spotless. She still squirmed with self-consciousness every time she remembered that panicked phone call to her sister from Dom's bathroom. She had to have been temporarily insane. Not once since that afternoon had he been anything less than professional and friendly with her. Scrupulously so. No lingering looks, no checking out her breasts, nothing.

Andrew jingled his car keys.

"Let's hit the road."

Lucy turned back to check herself in the living-room mirror one last time. She could only see her top half but what she saw looked pretty good, her family's comments aside.

For just a second, she wondered what Dom would think if he saw her like this. He'd only ever seen her bundled up for work in the mornings or dressed for comfort for their meetings. Or—worse still—in her pyjamas, ready for bed. Would he even notice the difference?

Lucy shook off the thought with a frown. It didn't matter what Dom thought of how she looked, for Pete's sake. It was irrelevant.

Her mother chattered all the way to the community center, discussing carpet colors and window furnishings for the office renovation. Lucy smiled to herself as she heard the rising frustration in her sister's voice as Rosie tried to put forward her own opinions. For once, it was nice not to be the center of her mother's attention.

The center had been professionally decorated for the fashion parade with lots of draped black fabric on the walls, small nightclub tables with candles and big, arty tangles of fairy lights. A T-shaped runway bisected the room, and a bar had been set up immediately to the left of the entrance.

Andrew slipped off to grab drinks for them all as Lucy craned her neck to see if she recognized anyone. She started when a warm hand landed on the small of her back and a deep voice sounded near her ear.

"I was wondering when you guys were going to show up."

Lucy's heart did a strange shimmy in her chest as she breathed in Dom's spicy, woody scent. She turned to face him, not registering how close he was standing until her breasts brushed his arm. She took a hasty step backward, alarmed by the rush of heat that raced through her body.

"Dom. I didn't know you were coming," she said.

"Didn't you? Rosie invited me," Dom said.

He threw a curious look her sister's way. Rosie just did her impersonation of the sphinx. Clearly she had done this on purpose.

"You look great," Dom said, drawing Lucy's attention back to him. He did a slow scan of her body, taking in every curl on her head and every curve on her body. "Beautiful."

For some reason she was having trouble finding her voice. She told herself it was because he'd surprised her, but she suspected it had more to do with how good he looked in a finely cut leather coat, crisp charcoal shirt and charcoal trousers with a fine red pinstripe. He looked like he should be up on the runway, not down here with the plebs.

"Um, thanks. You look nice, too."

Immediately she felt like a dork. Dom smiled, the corners of his eyes creasing attractively.

"I even ironed, so it must be a special occasion," he said.

Lucy felt a pronounced dip in the region of her stomach as he held her gaze.

Okay, there's that look again. And this time I am definitely not imagining it.

His gaze dropped below her chin and into her cleavage. She forgot to breathe. She could feel his attention like a touch, skimming across her skin.

That *is definitely an eye-drop. Dear lord. Is it hot in here or is it just me?*

"Good to see you, Dom," Rosie said pointedly from somewhere behind them.

Dom grinned as he transferred his attention to her sister.

"Rosie," he said. "You look lovely, too."

"Sure I do," Rosie said dryly. "You remember our mother, Sophia Basso? Ma, this is Tony Bianco's son, Dominic."

Lucy started for the second time that night. She'd been so busy staring at Dom, being mesmerized by his intense regard, she'd completely forgotten her mother was with them.

"Dominic. Yes, I remember you from church," Sophia said slowly. "I hear you and Lucia are in business together now."

Dom leaned forward to shake her hand.

"Yes, that's right. It's nice to see you again, Mrs. Basso."

Lucy darted a look at her mother. Sure enough, her mother was watching her like a hawk, waiting to swoop in and demand what was going on between her daughter and Tony Bianco's son. Lucy groaned mentally. Now she was in for it.

"I reserved us a table," Dom said.

He led them across the room to a table with a good view of the runway. Andrew joined them with a carafe of wine and a cluster of wineglasses.

"There's juice for you, Lucy, but I only had two hands," Andrew said as he set his load down.

"I'll get it," Dom said.

He headed for the bar. Lucy found herself following his progress compulsively, unable to take her eyes off his broad shoulders and dark head.

"I thought he was your business partner," her mother said sharply.

Lucy dragged her attention back to the table.

"He is."

"I am not an idiot, Lucia."

"I didn't say you were."

"That is not the way a man looks at a woman when they are in business together. Not the kind of business I am used to, anyway."

Lucy straightened the skirt of her dress. "You're as bad as Rosie."

"Hey, I didn't say a word. I told you I wouldn't and I haven't," Rosie said, holding both hands in the air as if to proclaim her innocence.

Lucy glanced toward the bar and saw Dom was already on his way back to them.

"Nothing's going on," she said firmly. "Can we just drop it, please?"

The thought of Dom overhearing the women of her family discussing his purported attraction to her made her want to cut a hole in the floor and jump through.

Sophia sat back in her chair and crossed her arms over her chest, her posture announcing more clearly than any words that this discussion was far from over.

Dom placed the carafe of orange juice on the table and took the empty seat next to Lucy. She looked at him, searching for confirmation of what she'd seen. But, once again, she could find nothing in his face or demeanor that even hinted at the desire she'd read in him moments before. One minute it was there, the next it was gone.

He caught her staring and smiled slightly, cocking an eyebrow.

"Everything okay?"

You tell me.

"Of course," she said.

She looked away, a frown on her face.

"So, Mrs. Basso, Lucy tells me you're retired now," Dom said politely.

For the next twenty minutes, conversation ebbed and flowed around Lucy as she sipped her orange juice, her mind racing. To quote her sister, Dominic Bianco had looked at her as though he wanted to lick her all over. Slowly. She had not imagined it—even though he was sitting next to her now looking as though butter wouldn't melt in his mouth. As shocking and impossible and scary at it seemed, he saw her as a woman and not just a business partner or a life-support system for a baby. And he wanted her the way a man wanted a woman.

The thought alone was enough to make her heart slam against her rib cage. She shifted in her chair, recrossing her legs.

She felt fifteen again, unable to look a boy in the eye. He was her business partner and, she hoped, her friend. She didn't need this added complication to their relationship.

For a moment she felt a rush of frustrated anger toward him. Why did he have to make things harder? Having him on board was supposed to make things easier, not more difficult. Now he'd messed everything up by noticing she was a woman.

You hypocrite, a voice whispered in her ear. *Like you never noticed he was a man.*

Again she shifted, crossing her legs the other way. No matter what she wanted to tell herself, there was no denying the thump of awareness she'd felt when his hand landed on the small of her back, or the heat she'd experienced when his arm brushed against her breasts when she'd turned.

She wasn't immune to Dominic Bianco.

There, she'd admitted it, if only to herself. Despite what she'd told her sister, she was powerfully aware of Dom.

For example, right now, without looking at him, she knew how he was sitting, who he was talking to, whether he was smiling or not. She could feel the warmth coming off him although he was surely too far away for her to really register his body heat.

I don't need this.

The thought stood out among the chaos in her mind. It was too much. She had been swimming against the tide since Marcus left and she'd found out she was pregnant. She didn't need or want this added complication in her life. Nausea swirled in her stomach, and she put her hand to her mouth.

"Are you okay?" It was Dom—of course—leaning solicitously toward her as the lights lowered and the music came up for the start of the fashion show.

"I need the bathroom," she said.

He nodded and stood, helping her to her feet. Rosie and her mother glanced across but Dom leaned toward them, murmuring something. Then he was leading her to the restrooms at the back of the hall.

Her stomach had settled by the time she was alone in a

cubicle. She sat on the closed lid and reflected that she'd spent more time hiding in bathrooms since she'd become Dom's business partner than she had in her entire life previously. Closing her eyes, she took a handful of deep breaths. Slowly her heart rate calmed. She exited the cubicle and ran cold water over her wrists.

Dom was waiting for her when she emerged from the ladies' room.

"Better?" he asked. She could read concern in every line of his body, and she was terrified by how much she wanted to drop her head onto his shoulder and let him comfort her.

"I think I should go home," she said.

Behind them, the first of the models were strutting down the runway. The music was loud and spotlights roamed and flashed. It was all too hectic when she was feeling so confused and confronted.

"Let me tell the others where we're going and I'll take you," he said.

"No! I'll get a taxi. I don't want to ruin it for everyone. I think I just need an early night."

"No one is going to let you get a taxi home on your own, Lucy."

His expression dared her to argue, and she knew he was right—one of the many crosses a pregnant woman had to bear was communal concern about her welfare. Rosie and her mother would be all over her if they thought she was unwell.

"Okay. But I'll come with you to tell them. They'll freak otherwise."

It took her five minutes to assure her mother and Rosie and Andrew that she really was fine, merely tired and a bit overwhelmed by all the noise. She insisted that they stay and enjoy the show—Dom was going to drop her home and come right back again. Finally they let her go.

She heaved a sigh of relief when they stepped out into the cool night air.

"Thank God."

Dom threw her an unreadable look. "My car's over here."

He led her to a sleek black two-door Mercedes and opened the door for her. She looked around with dismay as she sank into soft leather. The car was intimate and luxurious, with burled wood inserts on the dash and deep seats. She felt as though she'd just agreed to step into a closet with him, and the feeling only intensified as he settled into the driver's seat and shut the door.

Out of the corner of her eye she could see his long legs stretching out in front of him and his hand selecting a gear. She swallowed and clenched her hands around the sash of her seatbelt.

Chill out, she told herself. *We're only five minutes from home. This will all be over in a minute or two.*

Then she'd have the time and space she needed to come to terms with the ridiculous nervousness and awareness that had dogged her since she'd looked into Dom's eyes and realized he wanted her.

"You sure you're okay?" Dom asked as he pulled away from the curb.

"Yes," she said.

He didn't say anything more. She only loosened her grip on the seat belt as they turned into her street.

"Thanks for this, I really appreciate it," she babbled as she slid out of the car, barely waiting for it to stop rolling. "I'll, um, see you at the market on Monday, okay?"

Dom didn't say anything, simply turned off the ignition and exited the car.

"I'll see you to the door."

"There's no need," she said.

He looked very tall standing next to her. The streetlight made his hair shine, but his eyes were masked by shadow.

"My mother would skin me alive if she knew I'd left you out on the street. Then your mother would step in to finish me off."

She made an impatient noise.

"Fine," she said. She was being ungracious, but couldn't the man take a hint? She wanted—needed—to be alone.

Her high heels tapped briskly on the driveway as they walked past the main house to the door to her flat. She searched in her handbag for her house keys, fumbling them awkwardly as she pulled them free. They hit the ground with a metallic clink.

"Damn it."

"I'll get them," Dom said.

She was already sinking to her knees.

"It's all right."

"Lucy. For God's sake," Dom said.

He knelt, too, and they groped around in the dark together. She found the ring of keys at the same time he did. She snatched her hand back when she felt the warmth of his fingers beneath hers.

There was a long, tense pause. Then Dom stood and held out his hand. Wordlessly she took it and let him help her to her feet.

"What's going on, Lucy?" he asked quietly.

She pulled her hand from his grasp, but she could still feel his warmth on her skin.

Before she could think, the words were out her mouth.

"Do you want to kiss me?"

Her armpits and the back of her neck prickled with embarrassed heat, and she rushed into speech again, trying to explain her impulsive words.

"I mean, the other day at your place, when you asked me to taste the sauce. I got the feeling… It seemed to me that something…" She shook her head, unable to articulate her thoughts now that she'd blurted her stupidest suspicions.

She wished for a minor earthquake or some plummeting space station debris or even an escaped animal from the zoo—anything, to distract him and give her the opportunity to bolt inside her flat and barricade herself behind the door and never come out again.

"Yes," he said after what felt like a long time.

She blinked.

"Yes?"

"Yes," he said. "I wanted to kiss you the other day at lunch. And yes, I want to kiss you right now."

For a moment the world was very, very quiet. She wanted to pinch herself to make sure she wasn't dreaming. She wanted to pinch *him* to make sure he was fully *compus mentis*. Did he have any idea what he'd just said? How big a can of worms he'd just opened?

"Why?" she asked.

He laughed, the sound deep and low.

"For all the usual reasons. You want me to draw a picture?"

"This can't be happening."

"Why not?"

Because I'm carrying another man's baby. Because I am so far from being available it's not funny. Because this is nuts, absolutely insane and I can't believe we're even having this conversation.

"Because," she said.

She wasn't about to lay all her defects and liabilities out

in front of him. Surely it was obvious why his admission was so shocking to her?

"Look, I know this is a difficult time for you," he said. "That's why I wasn't going to say anything. But since you brought it up… I've always been attracted to you."

"Really?" Her voice came out as a squeak of incredulity.

"Since we were kids. I used to watch you walk to church in that little blue skirt you used to wear…. Let's just say I have fond memories. When I got back from Italy and learned you were single, I thought about asking you out. But I figured it wasn't great timing."

He didn't need to gesture toward her stomach for her to understand what he meant.

"That blue skirt wasn't that little," she said vaguely, too overwhelmed by his words to make sense.

"My imagination was plenty big enough to compensate, believe me."

She didn't know what to think, how to feel. She hadn't expected him to say yes. In her heart of hearts, she'd still believed she'd imagined his interest. And yet he was standing in front of her, telling her she hadn't.

"I don't know what to say."

"Maybe we should go inside," he said.

"No."

For some reason, going inside with him felt too scary right now.

"Okay. What do you want to do, then?" he asked.

"We're business partners," she said. "This is a really bad idea."

"Having a conversation?"

"You liking me. You wanting to kiss me."

"It doesn't change anything."

"Yeah, it does."

He was silent for a beat. "I'm not putting any pressure on you, Lucy. Just being honest. I don't expect anything from you."

"How am I supposed to pretend it's business as usual when every time I look at you I'm going to be thinking about this?" she asked. She could hear the panic in her own voice.

"I shouldn't have said anything."

She stared at him, frustration welling inside her.

"I don't want this," she whispered. She blinked rapidly, feeling overwhelmed on every level.

"Hey," Dom said. He stepped closer and rested a hand on her shoulder.

"It's okay, Lucy," he said. "The last thing I want to do is make things tougher for you. Forget I said anything. We'll pretend the last five minutes never happened."

A single tear slipped down her cheek. He swore quietly. "Don't cry."

His hand moved from her shoulder to cup her face. His thumb swept across her cheekbone, catching her tear. He felt so warm and strong. She could smell his aftershave intensely. She turned her head slightly, instinctively seeking more of the woody spiciness. Her lips grazed his palm. She froze and so did he.

For a long moment there was nothing but the heavy beat-beat of her blood in her ears.

"Lucy," he said, his voice very deep. It was part warning, part declaration of intent.

She saw him lower his head. Knew she should step back or at least turn her head away, especially since she'd just told him she didn't want this. But she didn't do either of those two things. Instead, she lifted her face and closed her eyes and waited.

If she was honest with herself, she'd been waiting for

this ever since he'd smiled at her that morning at the market after Rosie had awakened her to how attractive he was and she'd caught that flash of his hard belly. All these weeks she'd been waiting and wondering….

His lips were warm and firm yet gentle. He kissed her lightly, teasing first one corner of her mouth, then the other. His hand slid to the back of her neck, palming her nape and drawing her closer. His tongue traced the fullness of her lower lip and she shuddered. She opened to him and his tongue slid inside her mouth. He tasted of wine and coffee. Deep inside her, desire roared to life. Her hands curled around his arms. He felt so good, so real and strong.

It had been so long since anyone had kissed her, wanted her, needed her, and she'd wanted and needed in return. Not since Marcus left, nearly six months ago—

She stiffened and jerked her head back. What was she *doing?*

"Lucy," he said as she took a step away from him.

"I can't believe—"

A sudden, searing pain stabbed through her abdomen. She clutched her belly, her mouth open in a silent cry. Between her thighs, she felt a flooding warmth.

"No," she whispered. "Please, no."

She pressed her hand between her legs, dreading the worst. When she lifted her hand, something dark and wet shone in the dim light.

"You're bleeding!" Dom said.

Pain gripped her again and she hunched forward, wrapping her arms around herself.

"Oh God," she groaned.

Lost in a world of pain, she could hear Dom on the phone, speaking urgently.

"I need an ambulance for 56 Parkside Street, Northcote. She's twenty weeks pregnant and she's bleeding."

"My baby," she said, her eyes closed tight. "My baby."

Strong arms closed around her, bracing her.

"Hang in there, Lucy. They're on their way."

She leaned forward, pressing her face into the cool cotton of his shirt. She was too afraid to move, too afraid to breathe lest anything she did made things worse.

My baby.

"It's going to be all right," he said.

She knew he couldn't possibly know that for sure, but she was endlessly grateful for the confidence and determination in his voice. In the distance, she head the wail of a siren.

"Ambulance," she said unnecessarily.

Thank God. Thank God.

"They said they weren't far away."

Another cramp hit her and she gasped into Dom's chest. His arms tightened around her.

She wasn't supposed to be cramping or bleeding. Her baby was tiny, nowhere near close to being able to survive in the outside world.

This was wrong. All wrong.

CHAPTER SEVEN

DOM TURNED HIS PHONE over and over in his hands as he sat in the waiting area of the emergency department, his thoughts on Lucy and what might be happening up the corridor in the curtained cubicle they'd whisked her into the moment they'd arrived. As far as he knew, she'd had a problem-free pregnancy. She was fit, young, healthy. Surely that had to count for something?

"Damn."

He stood and shoved his phone into his pocket. One minute she'd been warm and willing in his arms, then she'd pushed him away. Seconds after that she'd doubled up with pain. It was all inextricably bound together in his memory—the kiss, her rejection, her pain.

And now they were in hospital, and he could do nothing to help her.

"Mr. Bianco? Dominic Bianco?"

He spun toward the doorway. It was a middle-aged nurse with short steel-gray hair.

"Ms. Basso is asking for you," she said.

His long stride ate up the corridor as he followed her to Lucy's cubicle.

"Dom," Lucy said when she saw him, reaching out a hand.

He took it and tried not to show how shocked he was at its icy coldness. She was terrified, he told himself. It was nothing more sinister than that.

They'd put her in a hospital gown, and it was folded back to expose her belly. Two black belts spanned her bump, and an electronic display beside the bed recorded the rapid beats of her baby's heart.

"How are you doing?" he asked.

"They've given me something to stop the cramping," she said. "The doctor wants to do an ultrasound to find out what's going on."

"Okay, fair enough."

She squeezed his hand tightly and closed her eyes.

"I'm so scared," she whispered. "Would you mind staying with me?"

He couldn't help himself. For the second time that night he reached out to cup her face. She opened her eyes and stared at him.

"I'm not going anywhere," he said.

"I want this baby," she said. "I know it's been tough and I've been scared, but I want this baby so much."

"I know you do." He cleared his throat. "I called Rosie. She's on her way."

"Oh. Good. Thank you. I didn't even think…" She frowned. "God. Marcus. I should tell him what's going on. He'd want to know."

"Give me the number, I'll take care of it for you."

He punched the number into his phone and walked back to the waiting area to make the call, since cell phones were not allowed in the emergency department. The phone rang out and went to a machine. He left a brief message explaining where Lucy was and what was wrong, then snapped his phone shut.

She was being prepped for a portable ultrasound when he returned. She reached for his hand again as a guy in his late thirties wearing a white coat smoothed gel onto her belly.

"This is Dr. Mason," Lucy explained.

Dom exchanged nods with the other man.

"You've had one of these before, right, Lucy?" Dr. Mason asked.

"Yes. At twelve weeks and then again a few weeks ago," she said.

"Then you know how this works."

"Yes."

Dom held his breath as Dr. Mason pressed the wand firmly against her belly and began moving it back and forth. Beside the bed, a portable monitor threw up grainy black-and-white images from inside Lucy's womb: a rounded shape, then something that looked like a leg, then a whirling, pumping round thing.

"Do you know the sex of your baby, Lucy?" Dr. Mason asked, his gaze fixed on the monitor.

"No. Is that important?" she asked earnestly.

The doctor smiled. "Not at all. I just don't want to give anything away if you decided to wait."

Lucy huffed out a little relieved laugh.

"Sorry. I thought you meant…" Her eyes widened as the import of what he'd said hit home. "My baby's going to be all right?"

"From what I can see, everything looks normal with the fetus. And it's pretty clear what's causing the bleeding."

The doctor moved the wand lower on Lucy's belly. They all stared at the blurry images appearing on the monitor.

"What you're looking at is your placenta. It's very low in your womb, close to your cervix. That's what caused your bleed tonight. It's called a marginal placenta previa, and it's not that uncommon a complication of pregnancy."

Lucy's hand tightened around Dom's.

"But doesn't the baby have to come out through the cervix?"

"In a natural birth, yes. If things don't change, you'll be looking at a caesarean delivery."

"Oh. That means I won't be able to do much for about eight weeks after the birth, right?"

Dom knew what she was worried about.

"Forget the business. I'll cover everything," he said.

Her gaze shifted to his face and her frown cleared.

"Right. I'm so used to worrying about everything on my own, I keep forgetting I don't have to anymore," she said.

"Well, get used to it. Whatever happens, we'll work it out."

Lucy bit her lip and nodded, and he squeezed her hand.

If she was his, he would never let her get that hunted look in her eyes again. He would ban it from their lives, no matter what it took.

"You may not necessarily need a caesarean. In many cases of previa, the placenta shifts farther up as the womb enlarges to accommodate the growing baby. If that happens, there's no reason why you can't have a natural birth," the doctor explained.

"When will we know if that's happened?" Lucy asked hopefully.

"We'll get you in for more regular scans from now on. We should have some indication of how we're going in about four weeks. The good news is, with marginal previa like yours, the placenta almost always shifts."

"What about the bleeding? Does that mean tonight was a one-off and it won't happen again?" Lucy asked.

Dr. Mason shook his head.

"We can't guarantee that. Because of the precarious position of the placenta, previa mothers are more prone to bleeds than other women. We'll keep you in overnight to make sure things have settled, and then you can go home. But you'll have to be careful. No heavy lifting. Nothing too vigorous. No sex."

He gave Dom a significant look.

"Oh, we're not… Dom is my business partner," Lucy explained.

Her cheeks were pink with embarrassment.

"Right. Well, important for you to know, just the same," Dr. Mason said.

Dom avoided looking at Lucy, giving her a moment to compose herself. Hell, maybe he was giving himself a moment, too. Not many guys in their thirties were warned off sex before they'd even gotten to second base.

The doctor reached for a tissue to wipe the gel off Lucy's belly.

She bit her lip again. Dom could feel her indecision.

"What?" he asked.

"Did you have another question, Lucy?" Dr. Mason prompted.

"When I had my last scan, they said they couldn't tell whether it was a boy or a girl because of the position the baby was in. I decided it was a sign that it was supposed to be a surprise."

"But now you've changed your mind?" Dr. Mason asked.

"Maybe." Lucy looked up at Dom. "What do you think? If it was your baby, would you want to know?"

The question hit him like a blow to the solar plexus.

If it was his baby…

The world would be a very different place indeed if that were the case.

For a moment he felt a tight, fierce ache in his chest. He would never stand beside his wife and have this discussion. Ever.

But Lucy didn't know that.

"I'd want to know," he said. His voice was low and thick with emotion. He cleared his throat. "I'd definitely want to know."

She nodded. "I think I do, too."

She turned back to the doctor with an expectant look. Dr. Mason smiled.

"You're having a girl," he said simply.

Lucy's eyes filled with tears.

"A little girl!" she said.

"Get ready for the joys of the teen years," the doctor said dryly as a nurse began to pack away the ultrasound machine. "I'll check in with you later, Lucy."

"Thank you," Lucy said, distracted by the news.

Dr. Mason and the nurse left the cubicle and Lucy spread her hands over her stomach. Her eyes were liquid with unshed tears as she looked up at Dom.

"I'm going to have a daughter," she said.

He couldn't speak. He looked into her face, filled with hope and excitement, and the pain was back in his chest.

If you were mine…

If this baby were mine…

He forced a smile.

"Yep. Hope you like pink," he said.

She laughed. "I hate pink! But I'll get used to it."

A nurse stepped through the curtain.

"Excuse me. We need a moment with Ms. Basso," she said. She was holding a washcloth and a bowl of water.

"I'll wait outside," he said.

He sank into a chair in the waiting room and tried to pull himself together. He wasn't the kind of man who relished being helpless, especially when someone he cared about was in pain.

He scrubbed his face with his hands.

She was okay. And the baby was okay. Those were the two most important facts. Anything else was unimportant, including how he felt about her and how much he wanted to right the world for her.

IT WAS AMAZING how exhausting it was reassuring people that you were okay—especially when one of those people happened to be your theatrically inclined mother. Lucy had been transferred to a ward by the time Rosie, Andrew and Sophia arrived, and Lucy spent their entire visit telling them over and over what the doctor had told her. Eventually Andrew suggested they leave her to get some rest. Lucy threw him a grateful smile as he herded her sister and mother from the room. She was exhausted, but there was one thing she needed to do before she could even thinking of sleeping.

She leaned out of the bed, trying to hook her hand bag off the floor.

"I'll get it," Dom said from the doorway.

She sank back on the pillows as he handed over her bag. She hadn't seen him since her family had arrived. He'd faded discreetly into the background when they bustled in and clustered around the bed, and the next time she'd looked up he'd been gone.

"Thanks. I thought you might have gone home by now," she said.

"No."

He didn't say anything else and for some reason she couldn't hold his eye. Now that she knew her baby was safe, fear had receded and the memory of their kiss was like a third presence in the room.

Craziness, all of it. What had she been thinking? What had *he* been thinking?

Flustered, she indicated her bag.

"I wanted to check to see if Marcus had called. It occurred to me he might have tried my cell phone."

"Right."

Dom's face and voice were neutral, but she found herself feeling defensive on Marcus's behalf.

"He's probably out doing something and has left his cell at home," she said.

She checked her phone quickly, but there were no messages.

"He mustn't have got the message yet," she said.

"Can I get you anything?" Dom asked.

"No, thank you. I'm going to try to sleep, I think."

"Good. You look tired," he said.

"I feel tired."

He stepped closer to the bed and leaned toward her. She held her breath as his lips brushed her cheek.

"Sleep well. I'll see you tomorrow."

"You don't need to bother," she said. "Rosie and Andrew will take me home in the morning once I've been cleared for discharge, and then I'll probably rest."

"I'll see you tomorrow," he repeated.

She stared at the empty doorway for a long moment after he'd gone, his words from earlier in the evening echoing in her mind.

I've always been attracted to you.

She had no idea what to think or feel about his declaration. She certainly didn't know what to think or feel about his kiss—apart from the fact that it had been the hottest damn thing she'd experienced in a long time.

Craziness.

She reached for the switch beside her bed and turned off the overhead light. Then she rolled onto her side, one arm cradling her belly.

Lying in the dark, the depth and breadth of what had almost happened tonight hit her. She shuddered as she relived the horrible moment when she'd lifted her hand from between her legs and seen blood. She was so lucky. For the long, tense minutes of the ambulance ride and the first hurried moments in the emergency department she'd been so sure she was losing her baby. But her daughter was still alive inside her. It felt like a miracle.

Not that a previa diagnosis was to be taken lightly. She was going to have to be very careful from now on. But her baby was alive.

She closed her eyes as she smoothed circles on her belly and whispered quietly to her little girl.

"You gave Mommy a scare, didn't you, little one? Let's never do that again, okay?"

She was so tired. She wanted to sleep very badly, but her body remained tense. It wasn't until she heard the distant ring of a phone at the nurses' station and realized she was straining her ears, waiting for the footfall of a nurse coming to tell her she had a call that she understood what she was doing: waiting for Marcus to call.

There were a million explanations for why he hadn't shown up at the hospital or at the very least called to check on her and the baby. He could have gone away for the weekend and forgotten his phone. He might have forgotten to charge it. Or he might be at the movies or someplace else where he couldn't have his phone on.

She closed her eyes again. Her baby needed her to sleep. She could worry about Marcus in the morning.

IN THE END, Marcus didn't call until 11:00 a.m. the following day when she was about to leave the hospital with Rosie and Andrew.

"Lucy, what's going on? Are you okay?" he asked when she took the call.

"I'm fine. I have to be careful, but the baby is well and so am I," she said.

Her sister collected Lucy's things and stepped out into the corridor to give her privacy.

"That's a relief. I wasn't sure if I should call the hospital first, but then I figured if you answered your cell things couldn't be too bad," he said.

"I was very lucky. My placenta is low in my womb, but the doctor told me that there's every chance it will shift as the baby gets bigger."

"Well, good to know it was just a false alarm," Marcus said.

He sounded distracted. She could hear noise in the background, as though he had the television on.

"It was more a warning than a false alarm," she said, frowning. "I'm going to have to be very careful the next few weeks."

"Right."

Her hand tightened on the phone.

"I'll be home this afternoon if you wanted to hear more about what the doctor said," she prompted when he didn't ask any more questions.

"I know the important stuff already. You're going to be okay."

"And the baby," she said.

"Right."

Rosie returned to the doorway. Lucy glanced up and met her sister's watchful, sympathetic eyes. She dropped her gaze to her feet.

"I found out the baby's sex," she said.

Marcus was silent for a moment before exhaling loudly.

"Listen, Luce, all that stuff is great, but I don't know if it's the sort of thing I need to know."

"Sorry?"

"This is your baby, not mine. I don't want to get too attached. I've got my own life now. I don't think it's helpful for either of us to get things too confused."

"You don't even want to know if I'm having a boy or a girl?"

He sighed heavily again. "Sure. Why not, if you want to tell me."

Lucy hunched forward as though she could somehow protect her baby from his disinterest.

"On second thought, I've changed my mind," she said in a rush. Then she ended the call and let the phone drop to the bed.

Rosie sat beside her.

"He doesn't want to know anything about the baby," Lucy reported.

"No."

Her sister didn't sound surprised.

"I know he's been absorbed with Belinda the Nimble, but I figured that something like this…"

"He's a selfish little boy, Lucy. Always has been, always will be."

Lucy stared at her sister.

"I'm so stupid."

"No, you're not."

"I am. I expected him to rush to the hospital. I expected him to care."

"That doesn't make you stupid."

Lucy stared down at her hands. "I want to go home now."

"Okay."

She stared out the window all the way from the city to Northcote.

She felt as though the rug had been jerked from beneath

her feet. Which was irrational, because Marcus had been gone for months. He was in love with another woman; he'd abandoned her utterly. Yet somehow, despite all of that, she'd still expected him to be there for her and the baby if she needed him. She'd still expected him to care. To want to know. To participate. To want to be a father, even if he didn't want to be her partner anymore. The baby she was carrying was half his—surely that was an ironclad guarantee that he was as invested as she was?

Apparently not. Apparently he had no interest in his daughter at all.

She stared blindly at the cars and trees and houses flashing past.

It's just me. Rosie and Andrew and Ma are there, but when it all boils down to it, it's just me and no one else.

For a moment, fear gripped her. Could she really be everything to her baby, both mother and father? Was she up to it? Strong enough? Brave enough?

She took a deep breath. She thought about the tiny person she'd seen on the ultrasound last night. She straightened as resolve hardened inside her.

She could handle this alone. She *would* handle this alone. And from this moment on, she wouldn't allow herself the indulgence, the luxury of ever imagining that she didn't have to. No more secret, hidden beliefs that Marcus would come through for her. No more thinking of Dominic Bianco and letting herself wonder what if.

It was tempting to buy in to the fantasy that Dom represented—a new romance with a hot, desirable man who just happened to have no problems whatsoever with the fact that she was about to give birth to another man's child. A man apparently willing to share the load, wake to feed the baby, change diapers, cook dinner, rub her aching back. In short, a man who would slot ready-made into her life and fill the roles of husband, partner, father and lover all in one.

But she would have to be very foolish and very reckless to believe in that fantasy. And she was neither of those things—she couldn't afford to be.

She was almost glad Marcus had been so blunt, so direct in his rejection of her and her child. She'd needed the wake-up call. The time for dreams and fantasies was over.

IT WAS NEARLY MIDDAY Monday and Dom had just finished his last Market Fresh delivery for the day when his cell rang. He smiled to himself when he saw it was Lucy. He knew she'd be unable to resist checking up on him.

He'd seen her the previous day to collect the van and her customer orders, but he hadn't stayed very long. Her family had circled the wagons to fuss over her. He'd felt like he was intruding.

"Are your feet up?" he asked as he took the call.

"I beg your pardon?"

"Are you lying down?" he repeated.

He wondered if she was frowning or smiling at his interference. Maybe a bit of both.

"I'm sitting on the couch."

"Okay, then I can tell you the deliveries are all done for the day and I'm about to head back to the market."

"Already? You were fast." She sounded surprised. "I thought you were usually done by midday."

"I am. But you're the new guy. You're supposed to be slower."

Definitely she was smiling. He leaned against the side of the van. Even over a cell phone call, her voice had the slight husk in it that always grabbed at the pit of his stomach.

"I want you to know, I really appreciate this, Dom," she said. "I know this wasn't part of our deal and that I was supposed to be the one who was hands-on with the business, at least until we got the Web site up and running and a second van on the road."

"You're right, it wasn't part of our deal. So I guess you owe me."

There was a small silence, then she laughed.

"Okay. Sure. When this is over, I owe you two weeks of hard labor. Fair deal," she said.

The sun came out from behind a cloud, and he lifted his face to the warmth.

"Do I get to choose the labor?" he asked.

For a moment the only thing coming from the other end of the line was silence. When she spoke again her tone was brisk.

"I don't think so. But you can trust me to ante up," she said.

He straightened and opened the door to the van.

"I've been thinking, since you're off the road for the next couple of weeks, this is a perfect time to kick-start the Web site development," he said.

"That was what I was going to suggest, too." She sounded surprised.

"Great minds think alike."

"I guess so. I've been going over my plans, but I wanted to talk to you before I brief the development company."

"Why don't I drop in after work tonight and take a look at them?"

"Okay." There was a short pause. "Do you want to stay for dinner? Ma has made me about fifty casseroles. I can barely get a slice of cheese into the fridge."

He hadn't expected to see her until the end of the week. Tonight was much better.

"Sounds good," he said. "I'll see you later."

He was smiling as he ended the call. Then he remembered the little hiccup in their conversation.

Neither of them had mentioned the kiss. Other things had kind of gotten in the way. But he hadn't forgotten. And neither had she, clearly. He stared out the windshield.

She hadn't liked it when he got personal. And he'd promised her that he wouldn't pressure her.

But she'd kissed him on Saturday night. She'd opened her mouth to him and pressed herself against him and held on to his arms as though she wanted to be as close to him as much as he wanted to be close to her. He hadn't imagined that moment.

He started the van. He was seeing her tonight. That would have to be enough for now.

LUCY WAS A BALL of nerves by the time Dom was due at her place that evening. She could feel her heart beating against her ribs, her palms were sweaty and she kept needing to go to the bathroom.

Grow up, she told herself sternly. *You need to do this, and then it's done and you won't need to worry about it ever again.*

She nearly jumped out of her skin when he knocked on the door.

"Hey. I brought dessert," he said when she let him in. "I figured your mother's catering might not run to three courses."

"It doesn't," she said.

He brought the smell of rain with him, and his dark hair sparkled with droplets.

"I hadn't even noticed it was raining," she said.

"Oh yeah. Cats and dogs and even a couple of cows."

She glanced away as he shrugged his broad shoulders out of a navy peacoat.

"Smells good," he said, sniffing appreciatively.

"Well, I can't take any credit for that. It's all Ma," she said.

She fidgeted with the oven mitts she'd left on the kitchen counter. Then she took a deep breath and met his eyes.

"Dom, we need to talk."

"Okay," he said easily. He propped a hip against the counter and raised his eyebrows expectantly.

"What happened the other night was a mistake," she said stiffly. "I just wanted to establish that so we could both put it behind us and move on."

His expression became wary.

"You mean our kiss?"

"Your kiss," she corrected him.

He smiled a little.

"I know a gentleman never brags, but you kissed me back, Lucy," he said.

When she'd rehearsed this in her mind last night, it hadn't been nearly as difficult. But then Dom hadn't been standing there in a snug knit top, dark cords hugging his thighs, his eyes warm on her.

"Fine. Have it your way. The important thing is that it can't happen again."

"Okay," he said slowly. "That's your call. I promised you I wouldn't pressure you, and I meant it."

She blinked.

Wow. That was easy. She'd been nervous all day thinking about having this conversation, but he'd folded like a cheap deck chair.

She wasn't sure if she was pleased or slightly disappointed.

Which is exactly why this conversation had to happen, her better self reminded her sternly.

"Can I ask one question?" Dom asked as her shoulders began to relax.

"What?" Her shoulders tensed again.

He tilted his head to one side, studying her.

"Was it because you didn't like it?"

She picked up the oven mitt and began to twist it in her hands. "Whether I liked it or not has nothing to do with it."

"I just thought that if you didn't like it, if you're not attracted to me, that was one thing. But if it was something else…?"

"It's irrelevant. This whole flirting thing has to stop."

"Flirting. Is that what you think I'm doing?" he asked. He looked and sounded surprised.

She put down the oven mitt.

"I don't know what you're doing, I only know it needs to stop."

"Because you don't like it," he said.

"No." She realized what she'd inadvertently admitted but plowed on anyway. "Because I'm pregnant, in case you hadn't noticed."

His gaze dipped to her belly.

"I noticed," he finally said.

"It's kind of hard to miss." She crossed her arms over her chest.

"But it doesn't change how I feel about you."

He looked deep into her eyes when he said it and her heart pumped out a couple of double-time beats.

She pointed a finger at him.

"That's exactly the kind of thing I'm talking about. You can't keep saying stuff like that and looking at me like that."

"Lucy, I like you. I already told you that," he said.

She hated how calm he sounded, how in control, while she felt like a can of soda that had taken a spin in the clothes dryer. She stared at him, frustrated that she couldn't articulate her feelings more clearly.

"Don't you understand? I can't do this kind of stuff anymore. I can't look at a man and feel weak in the knees and look at his mouth and want to kiss him. I'm going to have a baby. I can't afford to fool around like that."

"This man you're going weak at the knees over and thinking about kissing—can I assume that's me?" he said.

She ran her hands through her hair, then spread them wide. Her Italian blood coming to the fore, she growled low in her throat, an expression of absolute frustration with her inability to explain.

Dom moved closer and took both her hands in his.

"You like me," he said. "That's what you're trying to tell me. We can both feel this thing that's between us."

She looked into his beautiful eyes. At any other time, she would be ready to throw caution to the wind to be with a man who moved her as easily, as readily as he did. But he was an impossible dream.

"I can't afford to like you, Dom," she said quietly.

He frowned. Then, abruptly, his expression cleared.

"You don't think I'm serious."

She closed her eyes. At last, they were on the same page. "Yes."

"I'm not a kid, Lucy. I'm thirty-one years old. I know what I want."

"You hardly know me."

"I know enough."

"No," she said, shaking her head. "Not for the kind of journey I'm about to go on."

"But isn't that what this is about?" he said, gesturing back and forth between the two of them. "Getting to know and understand each other, exploring the attraction?"

She shook her head slowly. She thought back to the terrifying sense of loneliness she'd experienced when she'd realized that Marcus wanted nothing to do with his daughter.

"I can't afford to explore. I'm about to become a single mother. I don't have time for dead ends and experiments."

"This is because of Marcus. Because he didn't show up."

She wasn't sure how he knew about that—Rosie?—but it didn't matter. He took a step closer and lifted a hand to her face. She closed her eyes for a long moment as his fingers slid into her hair and his thumb caressed her cheekbone.

God, it felt good when he touched her. Made her feel like a teenager again, as though everything was hot and new and untried.

"This is real," he said. "This isn't a game, or me killing time or you indulging in a flirtation. This is real, Lucy."

He lowered his head toward her. Her gaze fixed on his lips. She wanted his kiss so much—too much.

"You don't know that," she whispered, as much to herself as to him. "You can't know how real this is, how long it will last. A week, two weeks, a month."

He shook his head, denying her words.

"You. Don't. Know," she said again.

He hesitated, his mouth so close she could feel the heat of him.

Very deliberately, she turned her head to disengage from his hand and took a step backward.

"I'm incredibly flattered," she said, "but this isn't going to happen."

He didn't say anything for a long moment, then he nodded.

"Okay. I told you the other night that I wouldn't put any pressure on you, and I won't. You know how I feel, the ball's in your court."

She eyed him uneasily. "There is no ball," she said. "No court, for that matter, either."

"I'm not going anywhere, Lucy. And my feelings aren't going to change. What you do with that information is up to you."

She frowned.

"And in the meantime, it's strictly business. Okay?" he added.

He held his hand out to seal the deal. She stared at it for a long moment before taking it.

"Nothing's going to change," she warned him.

"I know."

She looked away from the certainty in his eyes.

The important thing was that she'd done it. Cleared the air, created some boundaries.

There would be no more kissing, no more hot looks. From now on, they were about nothing but business.

CHAPTER EIGHT

Two WEEKS LATER, Lucy sat in the van and watched as Dom
exited the rear of The Lobster Cove restaurant, their last
delivery for the day. His jeans rode low on his hips, and his
face was dark with the beginnings of five-o'clock shadow. His
hair was pushed back from his forehead, and he looked big
and strong and beautiful as he strode toward her. She didn't
realize she was staring until he caught her gaze and held it.

She broke the contact well before he reached the van.

Today had been her first day back at work since the
doctor had given her the all-clear to resume duties. To say
it had been awkward driving around with Dom beside her
all day was an exercise in gross understatement.

Things had been weird between them since her clear-
the-air conversation. Nothing she could put a finger on, but
they were both being too polite, too careful with what they
said and where they put their bodies, as though any false
word or move might upset the status quo.

It was exhausting, and she wished she knew how to fix
things but she didn't. She'd been protecting herself and her
baby, but she'd made things weird between her and Dom.

"Okay, that's us for the day," Dom said as he slid into
the passenger seat. They'd had a very civilized, bloodless
battle this morning about who would drive. She'd won, and
she planned to continue to win until she couldn't squeeze

behind the wheel and reach the brake pedal at the same time. He was already doing so much; she needed to know she was pulling at least some of her weight.

"What did John say when you explained about the tomatoes?" she asked.

"He was fine. More than happy to take the romas over the beefsteaks."

"Good," she said.

She started the van and pulled out into traffic. As it had all day, the silence stretched between them. She racked her brain for something—anything—to say but all she could think about were the long legs in her peripheral vision. She wished like hell she was less aware of him, but she wasn't.

She punched the radio on out of desperation. An old Guns 'n' Roses song was playing and she tapped her hand on the steering wheel in time to the beat, doing her best impersonation of a woman at ease.

She pulled up at the lights and caught Dom eyeing her curiously.

"What?"

"Nothing. Just never pegged you as a Guns 'n' Roses fan," he said.

"Well, maybe you don't know me very well."

"Hmmm."

She gave him a challenging look.

"What kind of music are you into?" she asked.

"A bit of everything. Coldplay, Nina Simone, Fat Freddy's Drop—"

"Fat Freddy's who?"

"They're a New Zealand band. Kind of a new take on reggae. Very cool," he said.

"I'll take your word for it."

He shrugged.

"I'll bring them along tomorrow."

"Okay."

"You should bring something, too," he said. "It'll be like a cultural exchange."

"My heavy metal for your reggae?" she said as she stopped at a light.

"Why not?"

She smiled and glanced at him and caught him looking at her. Their gazes locked for a heartbeat too long before both of them looked away. Successfully killing the only decent conversation they'd had all day.

It has to get better. We're both mature adults. Once this stupid physical awareness fades, it will all be good.

Still, she was exhausted by the time she parked the van in front of Rosie and Andrew's place later that evening.

She let herself in and decided she couldn't face cooking. She wondered if Andrew and Rosie were up for pizza and wandered through to the house to find out. She tracked her sister down in her study and found her frowning over a chunky legal text.

"Hey. Feel like pizza for dinner and listening to me moan about Dom?" she asked, propping her hip against the door frame.

Rosie looked up from her book, her reading glasses balanced on the end of her nose. She looked deeply troubled, maybe on the verge of tears.

"Rosie! What's wrong?"

She could count on the fingers of one hand the number of times she'd seen her sister cry. Lucy was the sook, not Rosie.

"Nothing."

"Bullshit."

Lucy shut the door and hooked the leg of the guest chair

with her foot and pulled it toward herself. Then she sat and crossed her arms over her chest.

Rosie took off her glasses and rubbed her eyes. She sighed and let her hands drop heavily onto her thighs.

"Andrew and I have been trying to get pregnant for the past few weeks, but I got my period this morning and we were both disappointed. No biggie, really. It's just the first month. Stupid to think it might happen so quickly. It'll happen soon, I'm sure."

"Oh my God! That's fantastic," Lucy said. "If you get pregnant soon, our kids can grow up together."

"Yep. It's all good." Rosie smiled with her mouth but not her eyes.

Lucy frowned. Her sister had always been a hopeless liar. "Okay. What's really going on?" she asked.

"Nothing. Like I said, it's just a bit disappointing."

Lucy simply stared her sister down. After a few seconds, Rosie sighed and rubbed her eyes again.

"You know Andrew has always wanted to have kids. He's been talking about it ever since we got together. It's not like this is out of the blue."

"But?"

Rosie's eyes brimmed with tears. "I'm scared."

Lucy shifted her chair closer to her sister's.

"Having a baby *is* scary. But it can't be that hard, right? There are billions of people in the world. I figure if other women do it every day, I can probably pull it off."

Rosie stared at her, her face pale with misery.

"I don't mean I'm scared of *childbirth.* Although I'm not exactly thrilled about it. I'm scared about *everything.*"

"Everything. Could you narrow that down for me?"

Rosie held up a hand and started counting things off on her fingers.

"Okay, first, what if I can't get pregnant? All these years I've been sitting around thinking it's my choice, but it might not be. Maybe my body isn't even capable of getting pregnant. Then there's actually *being* pregnant, having something growing inside you. Is it just me, or is that supremely weird? I know there are all these pictures of glowing women with their big bellies and you make it look so easy, but I've seen *Alien* and that's all I can think about when I think about having a baby growing inside me. Which is not natural, right?

"Then there's childbirth itself. You probably don't need me to explain that one. Watermelon, garden hose—we've all heard the jokes. Then there's afterward. The no sleep and the learning to breast-feed and the being tired all the time. You know how cranky I get without my eight hours. And what if there's something wrong with the baby? What if it needs special help or treatment? What if it gets sick? What if we have a child that will never really grow up and will always need us our entire lives?"

Lucy blinked and opened her mouth to respond, but her sister was just getting started.

"Then there's my body. I know I'm no supermodel, but I like my boobs and I know once I've breast-fed they're going to be hanging down around my knees. It's horribly vain, I know, but I don't want to lose my one good feature. And what if I put on weight during the pregnancy and can't take it off again? I don't ever want to be big again, Lucy. I've had my fat years and I won't go there again.

"And sex. It's supposed to be different afterward, right? Again, watermelon, garden hose. How can it not be different after that kind of wear and tear? What if it's not good anymore? What if I'm so tired from all the breast-feeding and sterilizing bottles and pureeing fruit that I never want to have sex again, anyway? Then Andrew will get resentful and frustrated and we'll turn into one of those horrible married couples who are always sniping at each other. I'll be angry with him because he's always at work, and he'll dread coming home because I've been stuck with the baby all day and the moment he walks in the door I'll start nagging him. Pretty soon we'll forget why we ever liked each other in the first place and the only reason we'll still talk to each other at all is because of the fact that our genes are joined together in another human being."

Lucy waited to make sure her sister was really finished this time. When Rosie just stared at her expectantly, she figured she had the floor.

"You've thought about this *a lot*," she said.

"Yes. All the time." Again Rosie's eyes brimmed with tears.

"Everyone worries about all that stuff, Rosie. I worry about it all the time. Having children is a huge leap of faith," Lucy said. "It's like falling in love. You just have to plunge in and hope for the best."

"But what if the best doesn't happen?"

"Then you deal with it. Like you've dealt with every other challenge that has come your way."

Rosie stared at her hands where they were twisted around each other in her lap. Her lips were pressed together so firmly they'd turned white, and Lucy realized there was something else, something her sister couldn't bring herself to say.

"Rosie," she said. "Talk to me."

Tears finally spilled down Rosie's cheeks as she began to talk, the words coming with more difficulty now.

"I had this client a few years ago. She was successful, midthirties, owned her own business. She was a great person, smart, funny, sharp. She got pregnant unexpectedly. Anyway, she had the baby. And it was a disaster. She couldn't bond with it. She had no maternal feelings or instincts at all, Luce. She just felt…nothing. None of that amazing love women talk about. Nothing. She struggled for two years before she realized that the baby would be better off with someone else. So she gave him up for adoption."

Rosie's face was twisted with fear as she stared at Lucy.

"What if that happens for me? What if I have a baby and it turns out I'm a bad mom?"

Lucy didn't know what to say. She groped for the right words.

"That woman is the exception, not the rule. That's not going to happen for you."

Rosie shook her head, wiping tears from her cheeks with shaking hands.

"You don't understand because you've always wanted kids. Until I met Andrew, I didn't think I'd ever have a husband, let alone a family. It never entered my head. Even when we were kids I never played mamas and bambinos. Remember?"

Lucy dredged up a memory. "You always wanted to play shopkeeper," she said slowly.

Rosie nodded. "That's right." She paused and took a deep breath before looking Lucy in the eye. "I've been thinking about this so much lately. Maybe I'm like my client, Luce. Maybe I'm not meant to be a mom."

Every instinct Lucy had wanted to reject her sister's words because they struck so close to the heart of things she'd always held dear—family, children, the need to nurture and create. To her, they were the stuff life was made of, as essential as breathing. But Rosie had been brave enough to bare her soul and clearly she was deeply concerned about this issue. Lucy owed it to her to consider her words as objectively as she could.

It was possible, of course, that her sister was right, that she was missing the maternal instinct—if such a thing even existed.

"Not every woman in the world has to have children," she said after a short, tense silence. In the back of her mind there was a queue of ifs, buts and maybes lining up, ready to insert themselves into the argument. She'd always imagined her and Rosie's children growing up together, a true extended family. But that was her dream, not Rosie's, and she refused to force her own values on her sister when she was already so distressed over the choices before her.

"Andrew wants children," Rosie said flatly.

"I know. Have you guys spoken about this?"

Rosie shook her head.

"It's kind of important stuff, don't you think?" Lucy said gently. "Something only the two of you can work through, at the end of the day."

Rosie squared her shoulders. "I always knew he wanted children. I married him knowing that."

"But if you don't feel the same way—"

"I'll get over it," Rosie said.

Lucy stared at her sister. Rosie had just cried and wrung her hands and literally trembled with fear and doubt over the huge life change that potentially lay ahead of her. Lifting the rug and sweeping all that emotion neatly out of sight hardly felt like an option.

"Rosie. Talk to Andrew."

"I can't. I've stalled and held him off for too long. I love him. I want him to have the family he's always wanted."

"What about you? What if it's not what you want?"

Rosie bit her lip, then her chin came out in a gesture Lucy knew only too well.

"I'll be okay. It's like you say, everyone worries about this stuff. Once I'm pregnant, it will all fall into place."

Rosie turned back to her book then, picking it up in a clear signal that their conversation was over. Lucy remained where she was, deeply troubled by her sister's confession.

She worried about being a good mom. She worried about the future. But not to the degree her sister obviously did. The set of Rosie's jaw, the squaring of her shoulders—she was like a novice skydiver, bracing herself for her first jump even though she'd much prefer to be safely on solid ground.

"Thanks for listening, Luce. I appreciate it," Rosie said.

There was a firm, no-nonsense note to her sister's voice. The time for heart-to-hearts was definitely over.

Lucy stood. "Please come and talk to me if you need to. I hate the idea of all that stuff just percolating inside you all the time."

"I will. I promise," Rosie said with a quick smile.

Lucy let herself out of the study and returned to her own flat.

Rosie and Andrew's marriage had always seemed rock solid, an absolute certainty in a world full of uncertainty. Now, for the first time, Lucy could imagine a future where that wasn't necessarily true. If they weren't talking to each other about such a big issue…

She considered what would happen if they *did* talk. Andrew wanted children. Rosie, it seemed, did not. At the very least she had some serious doubts. Many a marriage had foundered on smaller differences, Lucy knew.

Feeling every ounce of the extra weight she was carrying, she sat on her couch and tucked her legs beneath herself.

As she'd told her sister, sometimes you simply had to

have faith that things would work out. And that if they didn't, that you could handle the consequences.

She hoped her sister found more comfort in the concept than she did right now.

TWO WEEKS LATER, Dom approached the Bianco Brothers' stand with a box full of sealed invitations under his arm. It was early, but the first pallets had already been moved across from the cold storage. Dom slid the box under the nearest trestle table and got to work. Half an hour later, his father arrived, his breath misting in the cold morning air. Even though they were well into August, spring seemed a long way off. Even longer when his father scowled at him by way of greeting.

It had been like that between them since he'd told his father about his investment in Lucy's business. His father was hurt, jealous, offended and probably a bunch of other things that Dom chose not to explore. He was not his father's property or a household pet. His father had had the chutzpah to start his own business when he was still a very new immigrant to Australia. If he couldn't understand Dom's need to be involved and stimulated and challenged, then they were doomed to be this distant and cool toward each other for a very long time.

"You have not given me the time sheets for last week," Tony said hard on the heels of his scowl.

Dom pulled the forms from his back pocket. His father never used to review this kind of paperwork, but he'd started asking for it four weeks ago—ever since Dom began doing Market Fresh's deliveries each morning. That the business had not been affected by Dom's absence for three hours every morning mattered not one iota to his father—with him, it was always the principle.

"I was five hours down last week," Dom reported. "You'll see I've deducted it from my wages."

He'd been working extra hours at the beginning and end of each day to ensure Bianco Brothers' wasn't adversely affected by his involvement with Market Fresh, but it was impossible to make up all the time. He'd told his father when he'd first started doing the deliveries that he'd deduct any hours he lost, and he'd stuck to his word.

His father squinted at the page briefly, then grunted. Dom hid a smile. Stubborn old bastard. Then he remembered something Lucy had told him while they were on deliveries last week—that it took two to tango and he was just as stubborn as his old man.

Probably it was true. But acknowledging it didn't mean he was going to do anything about it.

At least things had eased between him and Lucy at last. It had been awkward at first, there was no doubt about it. They'd both been on their best behavior, wary of putting a foot wrong. But it was impossible to remain stiff when you were trapped in a small tin can with someone every day. By the end of the first week, they'd relaxed enough to squabble over where they stopped for lunch and whose music they'd listen to during deliveries. By the end of the second week, they'd been swapping childhood stories and family anecdotes.

The fact that there might have been something else between them was almost forgotten. Almost.

Dom was pulled out of his thoughts as his father kicked the box of envelopes he'd stored beneath the table earlier.

"What is this?" his father asked.

"Invitations. The Web site is ready to go, and Lucy and I are having a launch party at my place to showcase it to our clients," he said.

He stooped to pull the front envelope from the box. It was addressed to his parents. He offered it to his father.

"We'd like you to come. It'll be good for people to meet the man who supplies most of their produce."

His father stared at the envelope as though it was contaminated.

"Why would I want to go?" he said with a dismissive wave of his hand. "I not know anyone there. Is nothing to do with me."

Dom kept the invitation hanging in the air between them.

"Then come for me, to see what we've been doing. You never know, you might get something out of it."

It was the wrong thing to say. His father's heavy eyebrows came together and his jaw clenched.

"There is nothing for me to get," he said, then he walked away.

Dom gritted his teeth and slid the invitation back into the box. So much for that great idea.

"Yo! Bianco!"

He glanced up just as a scarf hit him in the face. Lucy grinned at him from behind her trolley.

"You left it in the van yesterday," she said.

"Thank you for returning it so promptly."

"Always my pleasure to be of assistance," she said.

Just as he did every day, he had to fight not to let his gaze drop to her body. She'd grown noticeably rounder in the past few weeks, but she was still beautiful and he still wanted her.

Who was he kidding? He'd passed *wanting* a long time ago. He longed for her, and not just in a physical sense. The smell of her hair. The way she tilted her head when she smiled at him. The way her hands got busy when she was nervous, pleating her clothing or fiddling with paperwork. The sound of her laughter. The thoughtful look in her eyes when she was listening to him. The occasional spark of wickedness in her.

She was…extraordinary.

And he was wholeheartedly, tragically, hopelessly in love with her.

Which just went to show what a masochist he was. She'd warned him off, told him she wasn't prepared to risk exploring the attraction between them. And in response he'd fallen the rest of the way in love with her.

As if he'd had a choice. She was irresistible. Adorable. Sexy. Funny. Warm. And out of his reach thanks to the bump that no longer allowed her to button her coat.

And he was doomed to travel the streets of Melbourne with her until that bump became a baby and she wouldn't need him anymore. He wasn't sure if he was looking forward to that moment or not, sad case that he was.

"Did you get your invitations done?" she asked.

They'd divided their guest list to split the labor, although he'd done his level best to ensure he got the lion's share.

"Sealed and ready to go," he said, stooping to collect his box.

He rounded the table to dump it on the trolley.

"Should have known. Do you ever let anyone down?" she asked lightly.

Briefly his thoughts flashed to Dani, to the bitter disappointment he'd visited on her.

"I've had my moments," he said.

Lucy frowned, but his father arrived to draw her curiosity away. Despite the fact that Dom had been in the doghouse since investing in Market Fresh, his father still doted on Lucy. Go figure. Not that Dom would want her to be subjected to the same moody disapproval. That would only have made a difficult situation more impossible. But still…

"Lucia. You are looking well. So wonderful," Tony said, holding his arms wide. "Every day you look wonderful."

She laughed. "Does Mrs. Bianco know what a ladies' man you are?"

His father's chest swelled. Dom was sure his father had never seriously looked at another woman in his life, but the idea of being a lady-killer clearly appealed to his vanity.

"Mrs. Bianco knows she is on to good thing," he said roguishly.

Lucy laughed, her hand absently going to her belly to smooth a reassuring circle on her bump. The baby had to be kicking—she always did that when the baby was active.

"I have something for you, Mr. Bianco," she said.

She avoided Dom's eye as she reached into her coat pocket. He tensed as he saw what she held—a second invitation to their Web site launch. She'd obviously decided to do her bit to heal the rift between father and son.

Dom crossed his arms over his chest. Good luck to her. He just hoped his father was more polite in his refusal second time around.

"This is for the party Dom and I are having to celebrate our new Web site," she said, offering the envelope to his father. "We'd love you and Mrs. Bianco to come. We're going to have catering, all prepared from your produce, and I would really like my customers to meet the person who handpicks all their supplies."

Dom waited for his father to scowl or wave his hand dismissively, as he had moments ago when Dom issued his invitation.

"I not very good at parties," his father said.

"I refuse to believe that," Lucy said. "I've seen the way you talk to your customers. It will be just like that, with food and vino."

She leaned forward and tucked the invitation into the pocket on his father's apron.

"If you don't come, I'll be very disappointed. I ordered the caterers to make some Sicilian cannoli for you because I know how much you love them."

"Hmmph. I will show Mrs. Bianco, see what she says," Tony said. Then he gave Lucy a wave and moved off to serve another customer.

Immediately Lucy turned to him and pointed a finger at his chest.

"Not a word. I refuse to be the reason you and your father aren't on good terms," she said.

He simply looked at her until her cheeks turned pink.

"What? Did I forget to brush my hair or something?" she asked, reaching up a self-conscious hand.

"I already gave my father an invitation to the launch party."

"Oh." Her color deepened. "I'm sorry. No wonder he looked so surprised. He must think I'm an idiot."

"He refused to accept it. Wouldn't even take the envelope out of my hand."

Lucy frowned, then a small smile appeared on her mouth.

"Huh. Well, I guess you just have to know how to handle Italian men," she said.

"And you do, do you?" he asked.

She breathed on her fingernails and pretended to buff them on her coat collar. "I've got a few tricks up my sleeve."

"Such as?"

He couldn't help it, he'd moved closer to her. She was too beautiful, too funny.

"Well…it helps if you have one of these," she said, pointing to her belly. "The bigger it gets, the more power I have."

"Is that so?"

"Definitely. Any good Italian boy is helpless in my hands. Want me to demonstrate?" she asked, her brown eyes shining with laughter.

"You don't need to," he said.

She glanced up at him, then seemed to suddenly realize how close they were standing. Her mouth parted. He stared at her lips for a long moment, then he took a deep breath and a step backward.

Man, but honoring the deal they'd made got harder every day.

"You got today's shopping list?" he asked.

She handed it over and they both concentrated on filling the order. When the trolley was stacked high, he shifted the boxes into the back of the van. Lucy took over from there, allocating orders with a speed and efficiency that always amazed him. She seemed to have a photographic memory for each customer's requirements and only ever consulted their lists once or twice. She also made sure that at least once a week there was a surprise in their package—maybe some fruit that had just come into season, or an order of herbs they hadn't requested. She understood the importance of making people feel valued.

As she had every day that they'd driven together, she slid into the driver's seat once the orders were allocated. She knew he liked to drive, too, but he'd yet to win that battle.

"Stop giving me that look," she said as he slid into the passenger seat.

"Soon you won't be able to reach the wheel," he said smugly.

"Soon we'll have two vans and you won't have to covet mine," she said.

She smiled, and as he did every day, he wondered how

any man could walk away from her. He couldn't, and he'd never even had her.

On the way back to the city after their deliveries, Lucy kept checking the time on the dash, her gaze darting between it and the congested roads ahead of them. When she started biting her lower lip, he decided it was time to speak up.

"What are we late for?" he asked.

"Not we, me. I've got a checkup with the doctor." She flashed him an uncertain look. "It's been four weeks."

Right. They were going to scan to see if her placenta had moved. As far as he knew, she'd had no more problems since that first bleed. Although they weren't exactly on gynecological terms, he figured she would have told him if something further had happened.

"If you're going to be late, head straight to the hospital. I don't mind waiting," he said.

She shook her head automatically, then checked the time again.

"Don't be a stubborn idiot," he said.

"Lovely," she said, but she turned off and started working her way toward the Royal Women's Hospital.

She found a parking spot and turned off the engine, then simply sat behind the wheel, her fingers drumming repeatedly as she frowned out the front window.

"You okay?" he asked after a few seconds.

"Nervous," she said. "The doctor didn't say this, but I read that if the placenta's moved down instead of up, I'll probably have to be admitted to hospital for the rest of my pregnancy."

He nodded. She would hate being bedridden, and she would worry about the business and feel guilty, but she would do it.

"It's unlikely. Really rare. Probably why he didn't bother mentioning it," she said, her fingers beating out a rapid staccato now. "And I haven't had any more bleeds, so the odds are good everything is fine."

"Want me to come with you?" he asked.

She glanced at him, then quickly looked away.

"Thanks, but I should probably go alone," she said.

Right.

"I don't know how long I'll be," she said. "Sorry."

The next hour crawled by. He couldn't understand what was taking so long. He got out of the car twice, ready to go inside and track her down to make sure she wasn't sitting somewhere, struggling to deal with bad news on her own. Both times he forced himself to stay put. Lucy had defined the parameters of their relationship. He needed to stick to them.

He couldn't stop himself from getting out of the car when he saw her walking across the asphalt after nearly an hour and a half. She was smiling, and there was a new swing to her walk.

Despite his worry, he couldn't help smiling in return.

"Good news?"

"The best. My placenta is midway, just where it should be. I am now officially a normal twenty-five weeks pregnant woman. No special instructions, no restrictions. Woo-hoo!"

She was practically skipping, and he couldn't help laughing.

"We're going to have to tie a string to you so you don't float away," he said.

She stopped in front of him and her expression sobered.

"Sorry it was so long. They were running late."

He shrugged it off, but she reached out to touch his arm.

"I was thinking while I was waiting. I want you to know I really appreciate everything you've done for me over the past few weeks. The extra work, all the support. You're a good man, Dominic Bianco."

He stared down at her, frustrated. He *was* a good man— he was also a man who desperately wanted to kiss her. A man who felt a fierce desire to protect her and belong to her.

"You make it easy," he said.

She stood on her tiptoes and pressed a kiss to his cheek.

"You make it easy, too," she said. "Too easy, sometimes."

It was just a peck, a kiss between friends, but his body roared to life anyway. Before he could stop himself, his arms came up to stop her from stepping away.

They stared at each other. Lucy's eyes dropped to his mouth. Four weeks of careful diplomacy flew out the window. He wanted to kiss her. He was going to kiss her.

She sighed as his lips met hers. His tongue slid inside her mouth, tasting her sweetness and warmth. He slid his hands into her hair, cradling her head as he kissed her deeply.

He'd kept a tight rein on himself for so long, but he could feel his control slipping. He wanted to slide his hands beneath her clothes and touch her. He wanted to see her breasts, feel them in his hands. He wanted to feel her legs wrapped around his waist. He wanted to be inside her, part of her.

He backed her against the van and kissed his way across her cheekbone to her neck. She dropped her head back, her breath coming quickly.

"Dom," she said.

He pressed an openmouthed kiss to the tender skin beneath her jaw, unable to get enough of her. She smelled so good, felt so good….

"Dom. We need to stop," she said. "This can't go anywhere."

She sounded reluctant, and her body was still clinging to his. But she'd said it. He stilled, his face pressed against her skin. He was hard and he wanted her, so much. Not just physically. In every way.

Slowly he lifted his head and looked into her face. Her pupils were dilated, her mouth swollen from his kisses. But her eyes were serious. It was enough for him to release her.

They stared at each other for a long moment. There were so many things he wanted to say to her. He understood her reluctance to complicate her life, but life *was* complicated. The feelings between them were very real. She was prepared to risk so much in her professional life, but in her personal life she had all the hatches battened down tight.

"You know I want more from you than just a few kisses in a parking garage," he said.

She shook her head. "I can't risk it."

"I'm not Marcus, Lucy. I'm not going anywhere."

She simply stared at him. He ran a hand through his hair and stared out at nothing for a moment.

"Okay. I understand. We'd better get back to the market," he said.

He slid into the passenger seat. She got into the car and put the key in the ignition but didn't start the engine.

"I'm attracted to you. It's not that I don't want you," she said quietly.

"Yeah, I got that." He sounded like a sulky kid and he sighed heavily. "Look, we agreed to keep things about work, and I crossed the line. I'm sorry. But like Ma always says, we don't choose the ones we love. It's just the way it is."

She stilled beside him and he closed his eyes.

Way to go, Bianco. Why not write some bad poetry and carve her name in a tree while you're at it?

He waited for her to say something, but after a short, tense pause she turned on the engine.

They were both silent for a few minutes. Then she cleared her throat.

"Sorry for keeping you so long from the market. I hope your dad won't be too upset."

"He'll be fine," he said.

So this was how they were going to handle his inadvertent declaration—ignore it and hope it went away.

A pity he couldn't do the same thing with his feelings for her.

Loving Lucy Basso and not being able to have her was turning out to be the toughest thing he'd ever done.

CHAPTER NINE

THE DAY OF the Web site launch party, Lucy dropped her silver earrings into her makeup bag and zipped it shut. She threw the whole thing into her overnight bag, then checked to make sure she hadn't missed anything. Her dress was on its hanger, suspended from the top of the bedroom door. She had her shoes and makeup and jewelry and perfume. Dom already had all the brochures and other materials at his place.

She was ready to go.

Lucy hung her dress carefully in the van before tossing her bag onto the passenger seat. It was three hours before their guests were due to arrive, but she'd insisted on helping Dom set up. In return, he'd insisted that she shower and dress at his place rather than return home. At the time, it had made sense. Now, it made her nervous. Somehow, the thought of getting naked in Dom's house, even when he was in a far distant room, made her feel distinctly...edgy.

It had been almost two weeks since Dom had told her he loved her. Two weeks of neither of them mentioning it or referring to it in any way. Her fault—she was the one who'd sat in stunned silence when he'd spoken the words. She was the one who had started the car and changed the subject instead of addressing what he'd said.

She'd gone over and over the moment a hundred times, justifying her response to herself, trying to convince herself that what he'd said had been a generic, sweeping kind of statement and not about her, about them.

But she knew it was. Deep in her heart, she'd known for a long time that the way he looked at her, the way he behaved around her was not just about lust or desire. She understood him so much better now, after all the time they'd spent in the van together, after all the working dinners and spirited discussions.

He was loyal to a fault. He was honest, committed. He cared about everything he did. And he was kind—he'd proved that to her time and time again with his generous, selfless actions.

He was also incredibly sexy and clever and witty.

And he loved her.

The knowledge had been working on her like water on rock. Every time she looked at him she thought about what he'd said.

We don't choose the ones we love.

She pushed the memory away as she parked her van in front of his house. She had no idea what to do with it, so she avoided it, the way she'd avoided responding to him at the time.

"Hey. Let me grab that for you," Dom said when he answered the door. He took her dress and bag from her.

"The caterers will be here soon. I've left the flowers for you. I'm still trying to get the patio heaters working."

She followed him up the hallway but stopped awkwardly when he turned through a doorway into a bedroom. One glance was enough to let her know it was his—his suit and shirt were on the bed and his aftershave tinged the air. Briefly she took in the neutral decor, the wooden bed with a mocha linen quilt and the pile of books on his bedside table before she looked away.

He hung her dress on the hook behind the door and left her overnight bag beside the bed.

"There are fresh towels in the bathroom," he said, indicating the door to what was obviously an ensuite.

"Great. Thanks," she said. Her palms were sweating and she wiped them down the sides of her leggings.

She would never have said yes to this if she'd known it would feel so…intimate.

She was relieved to see the armful of cut flowers waiting on the kitchen counter. Work—that was what she needed right now. Lots of work to keep her mind from going places it shouldn't.

"I'll leave you to it," he said.

He picked up a remote control and clicked a CD into play as he exited the house to the covered deck out the back. The smooth tones of Duffy filled the room in his wake. She watched for a minute as he bent to examine the gas bottle on one of the three large outdoor heaters they'd rented to warm the patio. He was wearing a pair of old cargo shorts and a faded T-shirt, and he frowned with concentration as he adjusted something. She was so used to that look now, his I'm-trying-to-work-this-out expression. It made her want to laugh and smooth away the lines at the same time.

She forced herself to look away and concentrate on her own tasks. Within minutes she was immersed in trimming and arranging great bunches of Oriental lilies, saw grass and birds of paradise into what she hoped would pass as professional displays. Duffy's voice rose and fell around her and she hummed along. She placed the first vase just inside the front door on the hall table Dom kept there. The second she placed on the front corner of the kitchen counter. The third went into the center of the dining table. She kicked her shoes off as she surveyed the living area, looking for a home for the last vase.

She saw that Dom already had his laptop linked to his flatscreen TV. They planned to use it as a giant monitor throughout the evening, with their Web site demonstration repeating over and over, showcasing their new services to their customers.

She decided the living space had more than enough color, so she headed outside. She smiled as she caught Dom singing to himself as he manhandled the last heater into position. He flashed her a grin, sheepish at being busted. She placed the vase in the middle of his outdoor table and stepped back to assess the affect.

"Perfect," she said.

"Even if you do say so yourself."

They smiled at each other again and she found herself thinking how natural this felt—being with Dom in his house, sharing with him.

She clamped down on the thought. It had no place in the reality of her life, like a lot of other thoughts she'd had lately.

The caterers arrived on time, and she spent another hour checking over their marketing materials and their Web site display.

She looked up when Dom's bare feet appeared in front of where she sat on the sofa, hunched over the laptop.

"You want first shower?" he asked.

She stared at his feet, not surprised that even they were attractive—brown and strong-looking, his toes even and regular.

"Aren't you cold?" she asked stupidly.

He glanced down at his feet. "Nope. First or second shower?"

"Um, second," she said.

"Okay. I'll yell out when I'm finished."

He left. She finished with the laptop and put it out of

the way. Then she fidgeted, waiting to hear his voice calling her to the shower, trying not to think about him standing under a stream of water, big and naked and wet. It seemed like a long time before she heard a door open.

"All yours," he called.

"Thanks."

She entered the bathroom from the hall, noting with relief that he'd closed the door to his bedroom. Fluffy towels were piled on the shelf at the end of the bath and he'd left her overnight bag beside the vanity. She closed the hall door and started to pull her top over her head. She froze as she heard movement in his bedroom, then rolled her eyes at herself. Of course he was in there—he was getting dressed.

A wave of totally inappropriate heat swept over her as she imagined him getting dressed. Pulling boxers over his strong thighs. Buttoning his shirt over his broad chest. The image was so clear in her mind's eye she had to blink to dislodge it.

She growled at herself and whipped her top over her head. Within seconds she was beneath the shower, washing herself with soap that smelled like Dom. She tried to get a grip by staring hard at her belly, but all she could focus on was what he would think of her pregnant body. Her belly was taut and smooth, but it was undeniably a belly. Her breasts were full, bigger than they'd ever been, and her nipples were darker and very sensitive to the touch. Her legs were still long and slim, her best feature. And she'd only widened marginally in the hips….

Lucy flicked the water off briskly. It didn't matter what Dom might think of her pregnant body. He was never going to see it.

She pulled on her underwear and did her makeup and hair, taking more care than usual. She'd chosen a sleek, modern maternity dress, but she needed the confidence of knowing her hair and face were at their best. She swept her hair up and left several strands down to tickle her neck. She colored her lips with a deep plum lipstick, then made her eyes smoky with kohl. Lastly she slipped her earrings into place, smiling as they brushed her neck as she tilted her head.

Then, her towel wrapped tightly around her, she tapped lightly on the door through to the bedroom. There was no answer and she opened it carefully. The room was empty, but Dom's aftershave hung heavily in the air. The quilt cover was wrinkled from where he'd sat to put on his shoes. His watch lay curled on the tallboy, the leather band curved to the shape of his wrist.

She stood for a moment, looking around. This was where he slept. His clothes were behind those sliding doors. She was in his most private space.

She was doing it again: fixating on a man she couldn't have. Frustrated with herself, she let the towel drop as she reached for her dress. The dark blue fabric slipped down her body and she smoothed her hands over the fine black beading on the bodice and skirt. It was only when she tried to zip the dress that she remembered Rosie had helped her try it on in the store. She bit her lip. Dom would have to zip her up.

Her heels clicked quietly on the floorboards as she walked to the living room. Dom was talking to one of the caterers but he looked up when she entered. It was wrong to feel a rush of pleasure at the way his eyes darkened. Wrong, but impossible to deny. As it was impossible to deny the slow burn in the pit of her stomach as she looked at him, tall and gorgeous in his charcoal suit.

"Can you zip me?" she asked.

He stepped forward. She turned her back, and she felt the slow tug as her zipper closed. When he reached the top, he lingered for a moment, his hand heavy on her back.

"You look very nice," he said. She almost laughed at how much meaning four little words could hold. Except the way she was feeling—at war with herself—wasn't very funny.

"Excuse me, but did you want to start with just the champagne or offer all the wines when people first arrive?" the caterer asked.

Dom turned to answer and she tried to catch her breath. *Don't,* she told herself. *Don't forget what's at stake.*

But for the first time it hit her that maybe she had more to lose than she had to gain by keeping her distance from Dom.

It was a revolutionary thought. And a very disturbing one.

"HURRY UP! We're going to be late," Rosie called as she took one last swipe at her eyelashes with her mascara wand.

"Sweetheart, I've been ready for half an hour," Andrew said dryly.

She turned from the mirror and saw that he was, indeed, fully dressed and reclining on the bed, arms behind his head as he waited patiently.

"Right. Sorry. Won't be long."

"No rush. I like watching you turn yourself into a man-trap." He wiggled his eyebrows suggestively.

She smiled to cover the wave of guilt that swept through her. He was the perfect husband. Her soul mate. Her better half.

She didn't deserve him. Not by a long shot.

Her hand was shaking when she slid the wand back into the tube.

That's what you get for being a liar, she told herself.

Lucy's advice sounded inside her head for the fiftieth time since their heart to heart: *talk to him.*

Simple words but they opened the door to a whole world of doubt and fear.

Rosie and Andrew handled on average sixty divorces a year. She'd sat opposite puffy-eyed men and women more times than she could count, listening to tales of woe and acrimony and disillusionment. She knew better than anyone the kinds of issues that killed marriages. Whether to have children or not was right at the top of the list, rubbing shoulders with money problems and old-fashioned infidelity.

You can't go on like this, a little voice whispered in her ear as she smoothed on lipstick.

She knew it was true, but the alternatives terrified her.

"Want me to call the cab yet?" Andrew asked. They'd decided to catch a taxi to and from Dom's place so they could both drink without worrying about driving.

"Um, sure. I only need another few minutes," she said.

She could hear him confirming their address for the automated taxi service as she checked her hair and slid her earrings into her ears. The pearls Andrew had bought her for their eighth anniversary were cool against her skin as she fixed the clasp around her neck.

"Five minutes," he said as he ended the call. "Just long enough for me to ruin your lipstick."

He crowded into the bathroom behind her, his arms sliding around her waist. He angled his head into her neck and pressed a kiss against her nape.

"You smell so good."

She watched him in the mirror, her love for him so strong inside her it brought tears to her eyes.

I don't want to lose you, I love you so much, she told him in her head.

"Hey, I just remembered. Do you have cash for the cab? I meant to go to the bank earlier but I forgot," he said.

"I'm tapped out, too. We'll have to stop at an ATM on the way to the party," she said.

He grunted his agreement and pressed his face into her neck again.

"Oh, wait. There's a fifty in the zip pocket in my work bag. Lucy's share of the water bill," she said.

"I'll grab it. Your bag in the study?"

"Yep."

He left the room, and she hit her pulse points with one last spray of perfume before moving into the bedroom to collect her coat and evening bag. She wondered how Lucy was doing, aware that a lot was riding on the success of tonight's party. Dom and Lucy had set themselves the target of signing up a quarter of their existing customers to their new Web-based order system by the night's end. Rosie had confidence in their combined skills, but she wished that every hurdle wasn't quite so high and quite so urgent for her sister. Lucy deserved to catch a break.

Then she thought of Dom and corrected herself. Her sister had already scored the biggest break of them all— she just hadn't recognized it yet.

She heard the sound of a car engine out the front and tweaked the curtain aside to check out the window.

"Taxi's here," she called.

There was no response from the study. Which was when she registered how long it had taken Andrew to collect the money.

She'd completely forgotten—

It hadn't occurred to her—

She strode through the house on legs that felt like lead.

His head came up as she stopped in the doorway. She didn't need to see the shiny foil strip in his hand to understand that he knew. It was in his face, in the hurt, shocked disbelief in his eyes.

She felt dizzy. As though she needed to sit down and throw up and scream all at the same time.

"I'm sorry," she whispered.

Andrew fingered the packet of contraceptive pills, his thumb pressing into the little indent where today's pill used to live.

"Did you stop at all? Was there ever a chance?" he asked.

She swallowed, the sound very noisy in the too quiet room.

"The first month. But then I…I filled the rest of my prescription."

A car horn sounded from outside the house.

"That's the taxi," she said lamely.

Andrew stared at her for a long moment, then he stood and walked past her, angling his body very carefully so that they didn't brush against each other in the doorway. As though he couldn't stand touching her.

And why not? She'd betrayed him, made a fool of him. Lied to him every day. Had sex with him and let him hope each time that they were making a child when in fact she'd made very sure they weren't. Commiserated with him when her period came. Talked about what it would be like when it didn't come, the plans they'd make.

She heard the front door click shut and Andrew's footsteps in the hall. She gathered herself and went to join him.

"I'm ready now," she said.

He gave her a disbelieving look.

"I sent the cab away."

Of course he had. They weren't going to Lucy's party, not after what had just happened. Crazy to even think it, but she couldn't seem to think at all right now.

"I can explain," she said.

"Can you?"

She didn't like the way he looked at her, couldn't stand the unfamiliar, angry hardness in his eyes.

"I should have said something earlier."

His eyebrows rose. "*Earlier?* The only reason we're having this conversation at all is because I found the pills in your bag."

She pressed her hand to her throat.

"Just tell me one thing. How far were you willing to go?" he asked.

"Sorry?" Why couldn't she think? All she could see was the anger in his eyes, and all she could hear was the thump of her panicked heart.

"Weeks, months? How long did you figure it would take for me to lose heart and accept it wasn't going to happen for us?"

"It wasn't like that," she stammered. And it was true. She hadn't planned or plotted. There was no method to her madness—she'd been acting on pure, fear-driven instinct.

"You'll forgive me if I find it hard to believe a word you say right now," he said.

She took a step toward him, but he raised a hand to ward her off and she stopped in her tracks. He closed his eyes and took a deep breath.

"Jesus. I can't believe this, Rosie."

He walked past her to their bedroom. Tears burned at the back of her eyes but for some reason they didn't fall. She took a deep breath, then another. Reason told her to give him a moment to calm down, but instinct drove her to chase him, to throw herself at his feet and explain and beg forgiveness.

Andrew was at the wardrobe with an armful of clothes when she entered.

"What are you doing?" she asked.

Then she saw the open suitcase on the bed behind him.

"Please don't. Oh God. Can't we talk about this?" she begged.

Andrew tossed the clothes into the case.

"Now you want to talk?"

"I'm sorry. I know what I did was wrong but I was so scared and I didn't know how to raise it with you. I just needed to buy some time, that's all."

He didn't stop throwing clothes in the case. Far more than he needed for one night, she noted. Bile surged up the back of her throat.

"You don't want kids," he said flatly.

"That's not it," she said.

He nailed her with a look. God, even now she had trouble getting the truth out of her mouth.

"I don't know," she said more honestly. "I have reservations."

"Right."

He crossed to the chest of drawers and began tossing underwear and socks into the open case. He didn't say anything more, and she watched him with growing panic.

"Please, Andrew, say something," she said.

"I don't know what to say to you right now. I feel like I don't even know you."

"I'm not saying I definitely don't want kids. I just need more time to get used to the idea."

"This is not about whether we have kids or not, Rosie!" he said, anger in every line of his body. "You lied to me. You looked me in the eye and lied to me *every freaking day*. What the hell am I supposed to do with that?"

"I'm sorry," she said, because she could think of nothing else to say. There was no excuse or explanation for her actions. Reasons, yes, but nothing that made what she did more palatable or forgivable.

"I thought you were my best friend. I thought we were going to grow old together, that I could trust you with anything," he said.

"You can. I am," she said.

He shook his head. "No."

She gasped at his stark denial. He zipped the case shut.

"Please don't go. We can work this out. We just need to keep talking," she said.

He hefted the case off the bed.

"Not tonight."

"Please. Please don't go."

They'd never spent a night apart because of an argument. They'd never even gone to bed angry. The thought of letting him walk out the door made her dizzy all over again.

"I can't be with you right now," Andrew said.

He stood in front of her, the case in one hand. She looked into his face, tried to summon the words that would make everything all right. Nothing came.

She stepped to one side and he moved past her. She trailed him to the front door.

"Where will you go?" she asked again.

"Does it matter?"

"Can you at least call me and let me know where you're staying?"

"Fine."

He could barely look at her. She reached for him, needing to touch him. He stiffened as her hands found the lapels on his jacket.

"I love you, Andrew. Please believe that I never meant to hurt you," she said.

He just looked at her until she let her arms fall.

She watched him walk down the path to the carport. He threw his case in the backseat and started the car. Then he was reversing down the driveway. And then he was driving off into the night.

She stood on the threshold well after the echo of the engine had died away.

He'd gone. He'd really gone.

Panic and fear and regret and hurt threatened to choke her. She barely made it to the bathroom before she lost her dinner to the toilet bowl. Her anniversary pearls clanked against the porcelain as she rested her elbows on the seat.

What have you done? What have you done?

And how would she ever make it up to him?

Her mouth bitter with bile, she sank to the floor. She opened her mouth on a soundless cry as the tears came.

What have you done?

THE HOUSE WAS FILLED with savory cooking smells by the time the doorbell rang for the first time. Dom answered it and greeted their first guests and soon the house was filled with the sound of laughter and conversation. Like Dom, Lucy worked the room, talking to her clients, introducing people to each other, making sure everyone had a good time.

One of the last arrivals was Dom's father and mother, both looking uncomfortable in their Sunday best. She saw the surprise on Dom's face when he spotted them. He hadn't expected them to come. She made sure they both had drinks—good Italian red wine—and introduced them to one of her favorite customers.

Vaguely she was aware that Rosie and Andrew were late. Around 9:00, her cell phone beeped with a text message from her sister:

Not feeling well. Sorry. Catch up tomorrow. Good luck.

It was unlike her sister to text instead of call. And Rosie had seemed fine when she saw her earlier in the day. Lucy wondered for a moment if she should call home to make sure everything was okay. Then one of her customers approached her to ask some questions about the site and she pushed her sister to the back of her mind. Andrew would take care of Rosie if she was feeling under the weather.

As the night wore on, the feeling of nervous anticipation in Lucy's blood settled. Their clients were having a good time, and by 10:00 almost half of them had signed up for Market Fresh's Internet-based service, well beyond her and Dom's target for the evening. Dom's father had overcome his social nerves and was holding forth on the patio, and a hum of convivial goodwill filled Dom's house.

They'd pulled it off.

At 10:30, she glanced across the room and caught Dom's eye. He smiled and raised his champagne glass. She raised her orange juice, pulling a sad face to let him know she'd rather have bubbles. He laughed and something undeniable caught her in the chest.

He was so beautiful. So wonderful.

And he loved her.

Unexpected tears stung her eyes as the full import of his declaration hit her. This man—this incredible, amazing man—loved her. He'd shown her in a million different ways how much she meant to him. He'd saved her business, helped save her baby's life, stood by her and supported her even when she pushed him away.

She blinked rapidly. Across the room, he frowned. She watched as he put down his drink, preparing to come to her side. Quickly she shook her head, gesturing for him to stay where he was. If he came to her now, she didn't think she would be able to trust herself.

He stopped, the frown still on his face. She forced a smile and turned to the nearest customer. Slowly, the rush of emotion ebbed. She told herself it had simply been the excitement of the evening. Nothing more.

Her feet were aching by the time they ushered the last guests from the house. Dom's father went smiling, full of bonhomie after an evening of playing the expert. Most of their clients went home happy, full of food and wine, clutching brochures for Market Fresh's Web site.

Dom sighed as he shut the door on the last customer and leaned against it.

"Done."

"Like a dog's dinner," she said.

He rubbed his eyes. "I don't think I have kissed so much butt in my entire life."

She laughed. "At least it was for a good cause."

They returned to the living room and surveyed the damage: glasses and plates of half-eaten food everywhere, platters of finger food on every flat surface. The caterers had left over an hour ago and would only return to collect their glassware and serving platters in a few days' time.

"Oh boy," she said.

Dom shook his head.

"Forget about it. You go home and I'll take care of this tomorrow."

She toed her shoes off. "If we at least do some of it now, it won't be so bad," she said.

She crossed to the kitchen and started to empty wineglasses into the sink.

"Lucy, go home," he said with a laugh. "What is it with Italian women? They never know when to stop."

He was behind her, and he reached over her shoulder to pluck a glass from her hand.

"I want to help," she said.

The truth was, she wasn't ready to go home yet. She

didn't want the night to be over. Which was stupid, because she had to go home. The alternative was...well, reckless, to say the least.

"We've got a ton of stuff to go over tomorrow. You can help by getting a good night's sleep," he said.

She half turned toward him, then turned away again. She couldn't say what she wanted to say while looking at him. She reached for the edge of the counter and gripped it tightly.

"What if I don't feel like sleeping?" she asked.

She closed her eyes, immediately wishing the words unsaid.

She had to be crazy. She was pregnant, huge. Dom may have kissed her once and told her that he was interested in something more and maybe even indicated that he might love her but she'd gone from round to bulging since then.

There was a profound silence. She heard Dom take a deep breath.

"Lucy."

She knew she had to face him. She let go of the counter and slowly turned.

He was standing very close and her stomach brushed his hip. Finally she met his eyes.

"Does that mean what I think it means?" he asked.

"Yes. If you think it means I'm asking if you'd like me to stay the night. If you're still interested, that is."

He went very still. She had no idea what was going on behind his eyes. She could feel heat burning its way up her neck and into her cheeks.

"You know how I feel about you," he said. His voice was very low, very deep.

"Yes. I mean, no. I mean, sort of," she said. Her hands fluttered pointlessly in the air between them. As though he needed more clues that she had no idea what she was doing. Even at the best of times she was no femme fatale. Now, tonight…she felt about as sleek and sexy as a Volkswagen.

His mouth quirked into a little smile.

"Maybe I should repeat myself," he said.

His gaze dropped to her mouth and he leaned forward. She closed her eyes as his lips found hers. Warm and firm, his mouth moved over hers. Then his tongue was in her mouth and she was tasting heat and wine and need. Her hands found his shoulders, curling into his collar in case he tried to pull away before she'd had her fill of him. She angled her head to give him more access, but he pulled away from her and broke the kiss.

They were both panting. They stared at each other across the few inches that separated them.

"This isn't just tonight for me, Lucy," he said.

His voice had a tremble in it. It gave her the courage she needed to take the leap of faith he was asking of her. He'd asked her to trust him. She did. He'd told her he wasn't going anywhere. He hadn't. And he'd told her he cared. That he loved her. Tonight, she chose to believe him.

"I know that. This isn't just about tonight for me, either," she said. "I don't know why this has happened in my life right now. The timing couldn't be worse. I'm not exactly at my best. I'm definitely not a great catch. But I can't look at you and not want to touch you. And I can't stop thinking about you. And I'm sick of trying to be sensible when so much of me wants to believe…."

His face softened and his gaze traveled over her features.

"Believe," he said, then he kissed her again.

This time his arms slid around her, pulling her close. Her belly pressed into his, but she forgot all self-consciousness as need long denied swept through her.

It had been a long time since she'd felt sexy or attractive. A long time since she'd allowed herself to be a woman and not a mother-to-be. A long time since she'd been with anyone except Marcus.

But the way Dom kissed… He made her knees weak, stole the air from her lungs. Brought all the forgotten parts of her body roaring back to life.

His mouth slid from her mouth to kiss a trail up her cheekbone to her ear. She shivered as he circled the curve of her ear with his tongue, then sucked lightly on her neck. She let her head drop back and moaned as he pressed open-mouthed kisses to her throat again and again. It felt so good, he felt so good.

She ran her hands over his shoulders, her fingers digging into the big muscles of his back as Dom began to kiss his way down her neck. One of his hands slid up her side to cup her breast, and she shuddered as white-hot desire raced through her.

Had she ever felt so hungry for a man's touch? Had she ever been so desperate to feel skin against skin?

His thumb grazed her nipple once, twice. She grabbed his shoulders, not sure how much longer she could support her own weight.

"You're so beautiful," Dom murmured as he kissed his way down into her cleavage. "So beautiful."

She bit her lip as he nuzzled the neckline of her dress then tugged the fabric to one side to reveal the stretch lace of her black bra. She closed her eyes as his hand closed over her, warm and large, then he was pushing the lace to one side and his hot mouth was on her breast.

"Oh!" she said. "That feels so good."

She felt him smile against her skin. Then he lifted his head and looked into her eyes.

"Come to bed?" he asked. There was still doubt in his eyes. She liked that, liked that not for a second did he take her for granted.

"Yes."

CHAPTER TEN

HIS HAND CLASPED hers and he tugged her after him as he walked to his bedroom. The bedside lamp was on, the light soft and golden across the bed. He pushed the door shut, then pulled her into his arms again.

Perhaps it was being in the bedroom, or perhaps it was simply the growing knowledge that soon they would be naked with each other and her body would be revealed in all its rounded glory, but she was self-conscious this time, more aware of where her stomach pressed against him.

He kissed her long and slow, then slid a hand onto her breasts again. He drove her crazy rubbing his thumb across her nipples through her dress, but not for a moment did she stop worrying and thinking. After a few minutes, Dom kissed his way to her ear, one of his hands sliding to her nape, the other to the small of her back.

"What's wrong?" he murmured, his question more vibration than spoken word.

She considered lying, bluffing. But she trusted him. If this was going to happen, it was going to be honest, right from the start.

"I'm nervous. I haven't done this for a while. And things are kind of…different."

His hand slid around from her back to rest on her belly. "You mean this?"

"Yes. That tiny, insignificant little thing."

"You're worried about the baby?" he asked.

"No. No, the doctor said sex was okay. As long as it's not hanging off the chandelier or something," she said. This was so hard. But she wanted him, wanted this.

"I'm worried you won't want me once you see me without my clothes on," she confessed in a rush.

He stilled for a second, then pulled back so he could look into her eyes.

"Never going to happen," he said.

"But still," she said, shrugging one shoulder. "It might."

He smiled slightly.

"You have no idea how long I've wanted you, do you? Since we were kids. And in the past few years, so much that it made me feel guilty even though my marriage was already history. I've been dreaming about getting you naked for years, Lucy Basso. And this—" he caressed her baby bump "—only makes you more gorgeous."

She nodded. She wanted to believe him. Realistically, there was no way to get past this other than to forge ahead, as it were. If she took off her clothes and he ran a mile, she'd have her answer.

She turned and offered him her back.

"Unzip me," she said.

"Lucy…"

"Please."

Silence for a moment, then she felt the tug as he unzipped her dress. He pressed a kiss onto her shoulder, then her nape as he slipped the dress off her shoulders. She held her breath as he helped the dress slide down her arms. She pulled her arms free and felt the slither of silk against her skin as the dress fell to the floor.

Dom's hands landed on her shoulders as though he

knew this was a big moment for her. She closed her eyes and took a step forward. His hands fell away. From behind, she knew, she looked almost normal, apart from a little extra weight she'd put on around her hips and backside. She held her breath and turned to face him. She knew what he was seeing—her breasts stretching out a black lace bra, the matching panties riding low beneath her bump. And in between, her belly, round and undeniable.

"Lucy. You want to open your eyes?" Dom asked, his voice full of gentle amusement.

"I don't know. Do you still want to do this?" she asked.

"More than ever."

She opened her eyes then and saw the naked desire in his face.

"You need more proof?" he asked.

He stepped closer and took her hand. Holding her eye, he slid her hand to the front of his pants. Her fingers curved instinctively around the hard length she found there. He felt very big and very erect.

No chance he was faking that.

"Good enough?" he asked.

"Hell yeah," she said.

He laughed. "I wasn't fishing for compliments," he said.

"Well, you got one anyway." She pressed her palm against him. Soon, they would be naked and all this hardness would be inside her....

"You're wearing way too much clothing," she said.

She wasn't sure where her sudden boldness came from, but she was too far gone to care. He wanted her. She wanted him. He was a man, and she was a woman. A pregnant woman, yes, but still a woman.

"You want to help me with that?" he asked.

There was something about the way he said it, a catch

in his voice that made her wonder if her undressing him was something he'd thought about before.

The idea made her smile and suddenly she felt infinitely saucy, incredibly sexy. She stepped closer and hooked her finger into the neckline of his shirt. She'd admired his body so many times. The thought that she was about to lay hand and mouth on him made her a little dizzy.

One button slid free, then another, then another. She pushed the sides of his shirt open and pressed her mouth against the wide triangle of chest she'd uncovered. His skin was very warm, his muscles firm. He smelled delicious—spicy and masculine.

She fumbled the rest of his buttons and pushed the shirt off his shoulders and down his arms. He had a beautiful chest, his pectoral muscles well defined with a silky sprinkling of hair that narrowed down into a sexy trail as it headed below his belt.

"Wow," she said as she smoothed her hands over him. "Lifting boxes of fruit really agrees with you."

He laughed and reached out to draw her close. She shook her head.

"I'm not finished yet."

She undid his belt buckle, then tackled the button and fly on his trousers. Her hands were shaking as she pushed his trousers down over his hips. He was wearing black boxer-briefs, the fabric snug over his impressive erection. He shoved his pants down his legs and toed off his shoes. Then he stepped free of his clothing, naked bar his underwear.

She stared at his thighs. Hard and muscled, they made her want to purr with anticipation.

"You have the best legs ever," she said reverently.

He grinned.

"You're good for my ego," he said. "Come here."

This time she didn't stop him when he pulled her close. The first press of his bare skin against hers was breathtaking. She made an impatient sound and reached behind herself for her bra clasp, wanting to feel all of him against all of her. Her bra loosened around her rib cage and she shrugged it off. Dom inhaled sharply as her breasts were bared and his eyes got very dark and very intent.

"If you had any idea…" he said, then things got a little crazy.

Soon they were on the bed with nothing between them but heat. All the weeks of watching and secretly wanting him, all the doubt and uncertainty, and now there was nothing but the slide of his body inside hers, the warmth of his skin on hers, the sound of his breath near her ear.

This was right. This was meant to be. This was perfect.

Her climax came quickly, sweeping her away. She cried out, held him to her. And then he was saying her name and his body was shuddering into hers one last time.

He kept his weight on his forearms afterward, always careful. He lowered his head to kiss her, long and deep. Then he withdrew and disappeared for a few seconds into the bathroom.

She kept her eyes closed, savoring the satisfied warmth spreading through her body. The bed dipped as he returned. His legs tangled with her own as he moved close and slid an arm around her.

"Okay?" he asked quietly.

She opened her eyes and stared into his face.

"More than okay."

They stared at each other, suddenly very serious. Words crowded her mouth, but she hesitated to give voice to them. Not so long ago, Dom had been someone she only saw across the trestle tables at the market. In a few short months, he'd become inextricably entwined in her life, her business and her heart.

"Lucy Basso," he said, smiling. "At last."

He kissed her forehead, her cheek, the end of her nose. Then he gathered her close and rested her head on his chest. She listened to his heart beating, slow and steady. And she swallowed the words. There would be other nights, other moments like this. She had all the time in the world to tell Dom that she'd fallen in love with him.

Closing her eyes, she snuggled closer. For now, she had this. It felt like more than enough to be going on with.

DOM WOKE WITH LUCY'S hair tangled across his chest, her face resting on his shoulder. She was deeply asleep, her chest rising and falling evenly. He smiled as he saw that one of her hands was curved over her belly—even in sleep, she thought of her baby.

Last night had been…well, suffice to say he was a lucky man. A very lucky man. Never in his wildest dreams had he imagined Lucy in his bed. Okay, that was an exaggeration. Many of his wildest dreams featured Lucy in a starring role in just that location. But he hadn't expected her to let him close, not for a long time, anyway. He'd known he'd been paying the price for her ex's faults, that she was cautious and scared and that she had good reason to be.

But last night she'd let him in in a spectacular way. He remembered the way she'd undressed for him, the uncertainty in her eyes, the way her chin had lifted as she stood before him wearing only her underwear.

She had no idea how fine she was, how perfect. She was beautiful, with her big, full breasts, her swollen belly, her long slim legs. She was beautiful and last night had been a gift. Touching her, holding her, being a part of her…

When things had fallen apart with Dani, he'd wondered if maybe he'd had his one shot at happiness and messed it up. Lying here with Lucy in his arms made him believe in an infinite number of tomorrows.

He loved her. Had been half in love with her for years and was now totally besotted with her.

A small frown creased Lucy's brow and she stirred against him. He watched as her eyelids flickered, then opened. He knew the exact moment she remembered what had happened last night, saw the slow smile dawn on her mouth and the warmth in her eyes.

"Morning," he said.

"Morning," she said. Her smile widened and she put her hand on her belly. "Someone else is up, too."

She looked at him uncertainly.

"Do you want to…?"

Hell, yes. It had been weeks since he'd felt the baby's first movements, and he'd been aching for a chance to share the experience with Lucy again. He slid his hand onto her stomach and she guided his hand to where the action was at.

"Of course, she'll decide to go to sleep now," she said dryly.

It took a few minutes of patience, but at last he felt the strange and wonderful surge of movement beneath her skin.

"Wow. That's pretty full on. Much stronger than last time," he said.

He realized Lucy was watching him carefully, just as she had last night when she'd taken off her clothes and stood nearly naked before him.

"This really doesn't make a difference to you, does it?" she asked.

"Not in the way you mean."

"You know that in about another thirteen weeks, I'm

going to be cranky from lack of sleep and I'm going to smell like milk and barely have time to wash my hair, right?"

He pulled a comic face.

"That bad, huh? How soon can you be out of my bed?"

She shoved a hand into his shoulder and he captured it in both of his.

"Lucy, you're going to have a baby. I want to be with you, I want to help you. Caring for you means I already care for your baby. It's not a big deal," he said.

"It would be for some men. It's Marcus's baby, and he practically ran in the opposite direction when he found out."

"Maybe he never wanted children. Maybe he's never wanted to be a father."

He said the words without thinking. Lucy's face softened and she pulled his hand to her face and pressed a kiss into his palm.

"That's one of the nicest things you've ever said to me," she said.

He stared at her, feeling like a fraud. Not because what he'd said wasn't true—being a father had once been one of his most important dreams—but because it was never going to happen for him. And she needed to know that before their relationship went much further.

Tell her. Tell her now. The longer you put it off, the more it's going to mean. And the harder you'll fall if she decides she can't live with it, the way Dani did.

Lucy slid an arm around his waist and rested her head on his shoulder. He loved the feel of her hair on his chest and the warm rush of her breath across his skin. He loved the feel of her slim, strong arm across his body.

He loved her.

I'll tell her tonight. Not now, tonight.

The moment the decision was made, his body grew

tense. He tried to imagine her face when he told her, how she might react. With pity? Disappointment? Anger?

"What time is it?" Lucy asked, lifting her head to look into his face.

"Nearly ten." He was surprised he could speak, his chest felt so tight.

She grimaced ruefully. "I'd better get going. Rosie will be ready to send out a search party. Or she'll be waiting to interrogate me. I'm not sure which is worse, to be honest."

She smiled at him and he pushed thoughts of the future away. Lucy Basso was in his bed, in his arms. That was the important thing. Everything else would follow from that. He had to believe that, or he might as well give up on life and go live in a cave in a hillside somewhere.

Lucy moaned with despair when they walked into the kitchen in search of breakfast.

"Oh my God. I told you we should have put some of this way last night," she said as she stared at the debris from the launch party.

He pulled her into his arms.

"You telling me you'd rather have cleaned?"

She smiled. "No. No way."

"Good."

He made them eggs on toast then washed her in the shower. Saying goodbye took some time, between Lucy's insistence that she help him tidy up and his that she go home to rest and the mandatory bout of kissing that occurred on the doorstep.

Finally he was alone. He put something loud and pumpy on the stereo and started cleaning, but it wasn't enough to distract him from his thoughts.

Lucy had feelings for him. She was attracted to him. She enjoyed his company. He wanted to believe she'd fallen in love with him, the way he'd fallen in love with her.

More than anything, he wanted to believe that loving him would be enough for her. It hadn't been enough for Dani.

She's not Dani. She's a completely different person.

But he couldn't help remembering the fights, the blame, the rejection. He couldn't help remembering the pain of losing the woman he'd vowed to love and honor for the rest of his life.

This is Lucy. This is different.

He looked around at his living room, still scattered with dishes and glasses. He would clean later. Right now, he needed to run.

He pulled on shorts and trainers and was out the door within five minutes. The pavement was wet, and a fine rain misted his cheeks. He didn't care. He ran past the cemetery, through the university and into Royal Park. By the time he returned home he was soaked with sweat and rain and his legs were trembling. He leaned against the tiles in the shower and let hot water wash it all away.

He would tell her. He would sit her down and explain about getting sick in his early twenties, then he'd tell her about his marriage and how he and Dani had tried everything to have the child they so desperately wanted. And then he would tell her to think about what he'd said for a few days, even a week, then come back to him and give him her answer. Was she willing to live with a man who could not give her more children?

It would kill him to have to wait for her answer, but she deserved the time. He wanted her to go into this with her eyes open. He wanted to love her unrestrainedly, unreservedly, without fear of a later rejection.

The man staring back at him from the mirror was grim as he toweled himself dry. There was every chance Lucy would be angry with him, that she'd think his infertility was something she should have known about before she took the huge step of staying with him last night. His only defense was that he hadn't expected her to proposition him. He'd resigned himself to waiting until after the baby was born and she'd found her feet as a mother before he approached her again. Then she'd looked at him last night and asked if he was still interested, if he still wanted her…

He threw the damp towel to the floor. It was useless to speculate. He'd already made his decision. He was telling her. How she responded was not something he had any control over.

He was shrugging on a clean T-shirt when he saw the blinking light on his answering machine. Lucy had called while he was out. He frowned when he heard the emotional quaver in her voice as she asked him to call.

He grabbed the phone and called her back.

"Lucy. What's wrong?" he asked the moment he heard her voice.

"Can you come over?" she asked. She sounded as though she'd been crying.

"I'll be there in ten minutes, but first tell me what's wrong."

"It's Rosie and Andrew. They had a big fight last night. Andrew stayed at a motel. Rosie's a mess—"

"Okay. I'll be there in ten," he said.

He made it in eight thanks to a little bending of the road laws and some luck with green lights. Lucy didn't say a word when she answered the door, she simply walked into his embrace and pressed her cheek to his chest. He soothed circles on her back and rested his cheek against the crown of her head.

"It will be all right," he said, even though he had no idea what he was dealing with. Rosie and Andrew had seemed like a solid, loving couple to him. Definitely not the type to have the kind of fights where one of them had to find somewhere else to sleep the night. But no one ever knew what really went on in other people's marriages.

"I'm sorry," Lucy said as she finally pushed away from his chest. "I just got myself so upset when I started thinking all this through. I wanted to see you."

He smoothed the hair back from her troubled face. She would never understand how honored he felt to be the person she sought comfort from. She trusted him. Better—she felt safe with him.

She led him to the couch and spilled out what she knew of the story.

She'd come home to find Rosie and Andrew's house in darkness, all the curtains drawn, Andrew's car gone, but Rosie's still in the driveway. She'd waited for Rosie to come knocking with an inquisition's worth of questions about why her younger sister hadn't slept in her own bed last night, but it had never happened. After an hour, she'd gone through the connecting door to the house and found her sister curled on the couch in her study, huddled under a blanket, still wearing last night's cocktail dress.

"I'm really worried about her. I've never seen her like this," Lucy said. "She's always been the fiery one, the bolshy one. But she doesn't want to talk, I can't make her eat. And Andrew isn't answering his phone."

She paused then, and he guessed she was trying to work out in her mind what she was free to tell him and what was too private.

"They've been trying get to pregnant," she said. "For maybe a couple of months now. But I found this on the study floor."

She pulled a strip of foil from her pocket. It took him a moment to understand what it was.

"The pill," he said.

She bit her lip and tears filled her eyes.

"Rosie told me a few weeks ago that she was scared of being a mom, scared she wouldn't be up to it and that she wouldn't be able to bond with her baby because she's never been very maternal. When I found the pills, she admitted she's been taking these in secret. Last night, Andrew found them."

Dom sank back against the couch, imagining his own reaction in similar circumstances. He could understand the other man leaving the house. Being very angry with someone you loved was never an easy thing.

Lucy shook her head.

"They have always been so happy, you know? Perfect for each other. They fell in love at first sight at university. I know that sounds crazy, but it's true. I knew the first moment I saw them together that they would get married. And now…"

"Hey, they're not divorced yet. They've hit a pothole. Shit happens in relationships. There's every chance they can get past this."

She looked at him, her eyes clouded with doubt.

"And sometimes shit happening destroys relationships. Look at us. I was with Marcus for eight years, you've just gotten divorced. There are some things that people can't get past. And I'm scared this is one of them."

Something inside him went very still at her words.

"You don't think Rosie and Andrew can work this out?"

Lucy bit her lip. "I think wanting to have a family is one of the most powerful urges in the world. Andrew has always been gung ho, always. I can't see the compromise in this situation. He either gives up on the dream of having children, or my sister has children just to please him. Not exactly a recipe for success, whichever option they go with."

"You don't think that Andrew might decide that Rosie is more important to him than having children?"

She tucked her head into his neck, and he couldn't see her face when she next spoke.

"Maybe. It's possible. I guess I'm just speaking from my own experience. I've always wanted to be a mother. Believe it or not, my first reaction to learning I was pregnant was happiness, even though Marcus had gone and I was all alone. To me, family is what makes the world go round. I'm going to have a little girl, and I want her to have brothers and sisters to lean on and share stories and memories with when she grows up. I want her to have what I have with Rosie, you know? A sense of belonging. Continuity. Love. I don't think I could deny that part of myself and pretend it wasn't there."

She had to have felt him tense, because she lifted her head and pulled back so she could look him in the eye.

"I've totally freaked you out, haven't I?" she said, and he could see she was only half-joking. "I know exactly what you're thinking. One night with a pregnant woman and she's already lining up the cribs in the nursery."

"You haven't freaked me out," he lied. "Family is important to me, too. I understand."

He did, too. He understood exactly what she was saying. He'd heard it all before, after all, in fights across the kitchen table, arguments in the car, tearful discussions in specialists' waiting rooms. He'd been over and over the same ground with his ex-wife, and he knew exactly how undeniable the urge to be a parent was.

He looked down into Lucy's face, into her warm brown eyes, and he acknowledged a truth he'd been hiding from himself for the past months. Lucy was a lover, a giver. A natural caregiver, a nurturer. She was born to be a mother.

And he was sterile.

Sitting in her flat with her head on his shoulder, he could only see one future for their relationship. He could only see pain on both sides. Anger. Resentment. All places he didn't want to go again. Couldn't. It had taken him a year to drag himself out of the depression he'd fallen into at the end of his marriage. He didn't want to even imagine what it would be like to have to get over Lucy.

But he was going to have to. Because he was holding an impossible dream in his arms. ·

He tucked a strand of her hair behind her ear, then traced her cheekbone with his thumb. She looked into his eyes, a small frown creasing her face. He lowered his head and kissed her, closing his eyes so he could consciously savor the moment.

I love you. I think you're wonderful. I want you to be happy.

Lucy's eyes remained closed for a few seconds when he lifted his head. He studied her face, wanting to remember her like this—soft and loving in his arms.

Then he reached for his cell phone.

"What are you doing?" she asked.

"Calling Andrew."

"He won't pick up. I've tried already, three times."

"He might pick up if he doesn't recognize the number," Dom said.

"Oh. Good idea. Sneaky, but good."

He smiled tightly. Lucy gave him Andrew's cell number and he punched it into the phone.

As he'd hoped, Andrew answered almost immediately.

"Andrew, it's Dom. Lucy wants to speak to you," he said.

He handed the phone over and listened as Lucy spoke to her brother-in-law, explaining Rosie's state of withdrawal, asking him to make contact with her, wondering when he planned on coming home. It was a short call, and he could tell by Lucy's face that she wasn't satisfied with the answers she received to any of her questions.

"He's still angry. And hurt," she said.

"He'll get over it. He loves her."

"Sometimes love isn't enough, though, is it?"

He shook his head. "No, sometimes it isn't."

No one knew that more than him.

Lucy stood with an effort and rubbed the small of her back.

"I'm going to go check on Rosie again, let her know I've spoken to Andrew. Even if it wasn't very satisfactory."

"Okay."

He glanced toward the door. He wanted to go. Needed to go, because he wasn't sure how much longer he could keep it together.

"Would you mind waiting?" she asked tentatively.

He wanted to reassure her that he would always be there for her, that she would never have to doubt his support. But she was going to hate him enough in the weeks to come without him digging a deeper hole for them both.

"Sure. Whatever you need," he said instead.

She smiled gratefully before turning away.

"Remind me when I get back how lucky I am," she said.

He remained silent as she opened the connecting door to the house and slipped through.

Lucy *was* lucky. She was about to become a mother. And he was about to spare her the pain of choosing between loving him and her lifelong dream.

For a moment, he was so overwhelmed by anger and frustration that he wanted to throw back his head and howl.

He didn't. He took a deep breath, let it out again, and

waited. There would be time enough for him to withdraw from Lucy's life over the next few days and weeks. Soon enough she would understand that it wasn't going to happen between them. Today, right now, she needed him, and he couldn't deny her what she needed. Not yet, anyway.

There'd be plenty of time for that later, when she hated him.

ROSIE HADN'T MOVED from her curled position on the couch. Even though she was covered with a thick blanket, her hand was cold to the touch when Lucy sat on the edge of the couch and took it in both of hers.

"I just spoke to Andrew. He answered his cell when Dom called."

Rosie opened her eyes and turned her head slightly toward her sister.

"You spoke to him? Is he okay?"

"He sounded angry," Lucy said. There was no point lying.

Rosie's eyes closed again. "Did he say anything?"

"He doesn't know when he'll be home. I told him you were pretty upset. That might make a difference."

Her sister's body tensed beneath the blanket.

"Why did you do that?"

"I thought it might make him come home."

Rosie wriggled around beneath the blanket so that she was facing Lucy and not the back of the couch.

"I don't want him to come home because he feels sorry for me."

"Isn't the important thing that he's here? That you guys start talking again?"

Rosie glared at her, then started pushing the blanket off herself.

"When he comes back I want it to be because he wants

to, because it was his decision. Not out of pity or a misguided sense of responsibility."

Rosie swung her legs to the floor and shoved the blanket all the way off. Lucy stood.

"Sorry. I thought he should be here," she said.

Some of the indignation left her sister's face and her shoulders slumped.

"It's okay, Luce. Thank you."

"It's going to be all right," Lucy said.

"Sure it is. I lied to my husband every day for six weeks and he just found out about it, and everything is going to be dandy."

Lucy winced at her sister's acid sarcasm but she figured that fiery, angry Rosie was better than apathetic, catatonic Rosie. Much better.

"God, my mouth feels disgusting," Rosie said. She walked to her bedroom then into the ensuite bathroom. Lucy stood in the doorway as Rosie began to undress.

"What are you going to do?" Lucy asked.

"I don't know."

"Maybe we could go to the hotel so you guys can talk."

"No," Rosie said firmly. "He's angry with me. He has every right to be angry with me. The least I can do is let him have the space he needs."

"You're a better woman than me, then."

"I didn't say it was going to be easy," Rosie said as she turned on the shower. "You think I don't want to go over there and throw myself at his feet? I tried that last night and it didn't work."

Lucy watched her sister sadly. She had no idea what to say, what advice to offer.

"What about counseling?" she finally suggested.

Rosie's head came up.

"You mean, like a shrink?" Her sister looked appalled.

"Hey, if it's good enough for Tony Soprano…" Lucy joked.

Rosie frowned. "I don't think so."

She stepped beneath the spray, and Lucy went to sit on the bed while her sister showered. She wasn't long and soon she came into the bedroom, the towel wrapped sarong-style around her. She was frowning, her wet hair dripping down her back.

"I mean, I wouldn't even know where to find a counselor," she said. "And what would I say to them?"

"Claire Miller saw someone last year when she was going through her divorce," Lucy said. They'd both known Claire since they were kids, and she knew her sister respected the other woman. "I could get the number from her. And I guess you just tell her what's going on and how you're feeling. She'll take care of the rest."

"It's a woman?" Rosie asked.

"Yep. Claire said she was great. Helped her get her shit together."

"I've got a lot of shit that needs getting together," Rosie said grimly.

Lucy shrugged. "Gotta start somewhere."

Rosie nodded, looking thoughtful.

"I need to do something. I need to show Andrew that I care, that this means everything to me."

"You need to stop giving yourself a hard time for feeling the way you feel, too," Lucy said. "There is no edict from the skies that says every woman must have children. You're allowed to not want them."

Rosie sighed and sat next to Lucy on the bed.

"If only it was as simple as that. It's not like I can't imagine a little baby who looks like Andrew. A little part of him.

When I think of a baby in those terms, it seems crazy not to do it. But then I start thinking about everything else…"

Lucy looked at her sister, hating the worry and sadness and fear creasing her face. Her sister had always been there for her. When they were kids, she'd made sure Lucy never missed out on anything, even if it meant sacrificing herself. She'd protected Lucy in the schoolyard and stepped in to take the brunt of their mother's temper or sadness when things were precarious at home. Even as adults, she'd been the stalwart of Lucy's life, the person she turned to before her mother, before her lover. Lucy understood that was partly because deep down she'd always known Marcus was unreliable, but it was also because she trusted her sister implicitly, with any crisis or problem or secret.

"You know," she said slowly. "You say you're not maternal, but you've been looking after me for years. And I've seen the way you fight for your clients, the way you go beyond what's required to support them. You care, Rosie."

"Then why am I so scared of being a mother? So scared I lied to my husband?"

"I don't know. Maybe because you bore the brunt of all the uncertainty when we were growing up. I always had you to turn to, but you had no one when Ma was out working or was too wound up to be there for us. Maybe in your head, you equate being a mom with all of that."

"If that's true, then why don't you?" Rosie asked.

Lucy kissed her sister's cheek and smoothed her damp hair from her forehead.

"Because I had you to be my mom, stupid. I learned from the best."

Rosie stared at her, her eyes filling with tears.

"It's going to be okay," Lucy said.

This time, she meant it.

Dom was waiting when she returned to her flat. He looked up from reading a magazine when she entered.

"Sorry I was so long. She's up, she's talking, I think she's even going to have some breakfast."

"Good stuff. What can I do to help?" he asked.

"Kiss me?" she asked.

He put down the magazine on the coffee table.

"Like that's a hardship."

His arms were strong and warm as they came around her. She pressed her face into his chest and inhaled his smell. It was like coming home. She couldn't believe she'd been so foolish as to deny herself this happiness and comfort. Dom was not Marcus. Dom was…one in a million.

"I think you're wonderful," she said, her words muffled by his sweater.

He squeezed her a little tighter in response. She closed her eyes. That wasn't what she'd really wanted to say. Not even close. She took a deep breath.

"I also think I'm falling in love with you," she said.

He went very still, then she felt his hand on the back of her neck.

"Lucy," he said.

She waited for him to say something else, anything else, but he didn't. She told herself that he'd already made his declaration to her that day in the car, but she'd be lying if she didn't admit to feeling disappointed. Quickly she pushed the feeling away. They'd had one night together. She trusted him. She knew he felt the same way. It was there every time he touched her or looked at her. She didn't need to hear the words.

That night, Dom collected takeout Indian and she, Rosie and Dom watched an old action movie in the flat. Andrew still hadn't made contact and Rosie couldn't settle in the house, so they made up a bed for her on the sofa when it was clear that exhaustion was kicking in after a day of high anxiety and emotion.

"I appreciate this, Luce. And sorry for cramping your style," Rosie said as she pulled the blankets up to her chin. Her gaze slid over Lucy's shoulder to where Dom waited in the kitchen.

"I'm not sure I know what you're insinuating, young lady," Lucy said primly.

Rosie smiled wearily. "Good night."

Dom turned from rearranging the magnets on her fridge door when Lucy approached.

"Don't worry about deliveries tomorrow if you want to spend the day with Rosie," he said.

"Thanks. Maybe I can start chasing up clients from last night," she said. She had no idea if her sister was planning on going into work, but it was nice to have the option of supporting her if she needed to.

"Let me know if there's anything else I can do," he said. He stepped forward and kissed her gently on the lips.

As always, his touch heated her blood, and she pressed closer and opened her mouth beneath his. He didn't pick up on her cue to deepen the kiss, however. Instead, he pulled back, but not before pressing a kiss to her forehead.

"You know, you don't have to go home if you don't want to. Just because Rosie's on the couch doesn't mean you can't stay," she said.

"Not that it's not very tempting, but I'll be up early and you might as well grab sleep while you can," he said.

She wanted to tell him she didn't mind being woken in the morning, but then she remembered the way he hadn't responded to her declaration earlier. For the second time that day, doubt gnawed at her as he pulled away from her.

She reminded herself of the certainty she'd felt last night, the rightness of being with him. She trusted him.

"I'll see you tomorrow, then," she said as she followed him to the door.

"I'll call," he said.

He kissed her once more, then he was gone.

It wasn't until she'd shut the door and turned out the outdoor light that she realized he'd avoided answering her directly.

CHAPTER ELEVEN

ROSIE WOKE from a restless sleep to the sound of a door opening. She squinted at the glowing digital clock on her sister's DVD player. Three in the morning. She guessed Lucy was going to the bathroom and rolled onto her side, hoping she'd be able to kill a few more of the long, dark hours till dawn with sleep rather than staring at the ceiling the way she had last night.

"Rosie?"

Her heart slammed against her chest as she recognized Andrew's voice, lowered to a whisper.

"Rosie, are you in here?"

She sat up. She could see his tall body silhouetted in the doorway to the house.

"I'm here," she whispered back.

"Thank God. The bed was empty and I was worried…"

She stared into the darkness.

"You were worried?"

Hope flared inside her. Andrew had come home in the middle of the night and he'd been worried when he hadn't found her in their bed.

Maybe he wasn't angry with her anymore. Maybe he was ready to talk.

She started to get off the couch but he was already moving toward her. She settled for pulling her knees in tight to her chest as he sat beside her.

"I was worried," he confirmed.

She could see his face now her eyes were adjusting to the dark. He looked tired and concerned, just like he'd said.

"Don't worry about me," she said, shaking her head. She didn't deserve his consideration.

His eyes searched her face.

"I'm sorry. I shouldn't have left last night. I should have stayed and let you explain—"

She leaned forward and pressed her fingers to his lips.

"No! Don't apologize to me. I *lied* to you, Andrew. I was a chickenshit and I lied to you and I hurt you. Don't you dare let me off the hook."

"Rosie," he said, but again she pressed her fingers to his lips.

"No. No," she said.

His hand came up to pull her fingers away from his mouth.

"You always were stubborn. And tough on yourself."

She swallowed a lump of emotion as he wove his fingers with hers. His hand felt so big and strong and precious. So familiar.

"Do you mind if I finish what I was saying?" he asked.

She just stared at him.

"I'll take that as a yes." His thumb swept across the back of her hand. "I was sitting in my hotel room, feeling hard done by, going over and over it all again. How pissed I was at you for lying to me. How stupid I felt. How I couldn't believe you'd do this to me. I mean, you never lie, Rosie. You're one of the most honest, forthright people I know. You can't even fib on a survey. I've seen it eat you up. And then it hit me. I realized how absolutely terrified you must have been to take those pills and not tell me. What it would have taken for you to get to that point."

She started to cry as he lifted their joined hands and pressed a kiss to her knuckles.

"I've been pushing for us to have a family for so long, and you've been doing everything you can to push back. And I ignored it, because I didn't want to think about it, because I figured it was just cold feet or worry about money or worry about the practice. I didn't give you many options, did I?"

She sniffed inelegantly and wiped her face on the sleeve of her pyjamas. "I could have talked to you. Like any sane, normal person would have. I could have told my husband how I was feeling."

"I know. And the fact that you didn't is what kills me the most, Rosie. Because it means you were so scared you couldn't, and I hate that more than anything. I hate the idea of you being so messed up about something that you couldn't even share it with me."

He shifted his head and she saw shiny streaks on his face. He was crying. It was the final straw. Even though she didn't deserve his comfort or his understanding, she threw herself into his arms.

"I'm so sorry," she whispered as his arms came around her.

"So am I."

They held each other so tight it hurt. She didn't ever want to let go. Andrew kissed her temple, her cheek, her nose, her mouth. She kissed the tears on his face, rubbed her cheek against the stubble of his beard.

"I love you so much," she said.

"I love you, too. Let's never do this again," he said.

She hiccupped out a laugh and he pulled her into his lap. She sniffed back fresh tears and made an effort to pull herself together. Andrew had come to the party, and it was time for her to step up, too.

"I'm going to go see someone," she said. "Lucy knows a counselor. I think maybe I have some things to work out."

She could almost hear him thinking, processing what she was saying.

"Is this something you want to do alone or together?" he asked.

She squeezed him tighter and pressed her face into the angle of his neck.

"Together and alone, maybe. Depending on how screwed up I am."

"You're one of the most together people I know," he said.

"At the moment, that's not saying much."

He tilted her chin up with his finger and kissed her fiercely.

"Whatever it takes," he said.

She stared into his face, so beloved and precious to her.

"Yes. Whatever it takes," she said.

They both blinked as the overhead light flicked on. Lucy stood in the doorway to her bedroom, squinting against the brightness of the light.

"Andrew. Thank God. I thought it was either thieves or Rosie was talking in her sleep," she said.

The concerned look left her face as she took in the way they were sitting.

"Anyway. I didn't mean to interrupt. Sorry. As you were."

"Thanks, Luce," Rosie said. She hoped her sister understood the world of gratitude the single word represented.

Lucy waved a dismissive hand, then flicked off the light and retreated to her bedroom.

"Is there room on this couch for two," Andrew asked, "or should we go back to the house?"

It was a no-brainer. "The house."

She wanted to be in her own bed, with her husband beside her.

She felt his thighs flex beneath her, then he stood with her in his arms. She grabbed at his shoulders.

"Andrew! God, you'll kill yourself," she said.

"Do you mind? I'm having a moment here," he said.

He was smiling foolishly, and she couldn't help laughing. Somehow he managed to get the door to the house open without dropping her, although he did knock her feet against the door frame a few times.

"Sorry," he said.

She rested her head on his shoulder as he made his way through the darkened house. He set her down gently on the mattress and she fell silent as he knelt in front of her.

They stared at each other. Rosie's chest ached with gratitude and love.

"Whatever it takes," he said again.

"Always."

SINCE SHE DIDN'T HAVE to babysit her sister for the day, Lucy got up at her usual time and drove into the market. Dom had left her his car and taken the van, and she parked the Mercedes carefully before hunting him down at his father's stand.

He was sorting through a crate of apples when she found him, his head lowered as he selected produce for an order. She smiled to herself as she took in his jeans and steel-toed work boots. She loved him in his suit, all shiny and polished, but this was how she thought of him—a hands-on man, physical and ready for anything.

"Dom," she called as she approached.

His head came up, and his gaze searched for her in the crowded market. He frowned as he caught sight of her, but by the time she was by his side his expression was unreadable.

"Rosie's okay?" he asked.

"Andrew came home last night. Or this morning. It was dark, that's all I know. They're talking and sleeping in the same bed, so I figure they're well on their way."

"You didn't need to come in, though. You must be tired," he said.

"No more than usual. Besides, I wanted to see you."

She stepped closer to greet him properly, but he tensed and all her doubts from last night crashed down on her.

"Is everything okay?" she asked.

She expected him to give a quick and easy affirmative, maybe tell her that he'd just had an argument with his father or a problem with a customer. Anything to explain away his reaction.

But he didn't. Instead, his gaze shifted over her shoulder for a few seconds, then he shrugged.

"This probably isn't the best place to talk," he said.

He took her by the elbow and started to lead her toward the coffee shop. She jerked her arm free.

"What's going on, Dom?" she asked, fear squeezing her diaphragm.

"Come on." He gestured for her to keep walking, but she dug her heels in.

"Tell me what's going on."

He sighed heavily. Then he slid his hands into the front pockets of his jeans and hunched his shoulders.

"I'm not sure this is going to work out," he said.

For a moment she thought she had to have heard wrong. She blinked.

"You don't think this is going to work out," she repeated. "What exactly does that mean?"

"The other night was great, but I think you're looking for something that I can't give you."

Again she shook her head. This was the man who had touched her so reverently, so passionately the other night that he'd made her feel beautiful and shiny and new all over again. This was the man who had moved heaven and earth to help her save her business. This was the man who had held her hand when she'd been afraid her baby was going to die.

This was the man she'd trusted enough to love.

And he was telling her…what?

"What exactly is it that you think I want that you can't give me?" she asked carefully.

Maybe this was all a misunderstanding. Maybe she was reading this all wrong.

"I think you want a husband. A father for your baby. More children. And I can't give you any of that."

His voice was flat. Distant. She stared at his face, trying to understand what was going on. How did a person go from so much intensity, so much connection, to this… emptiness? In the space of twenty-four hours?

"I don't believe you," she said.

For the first time he met her eyes.

"It's true. Believe me," he said.

"What about the other night? The things that you said. That you wanted more than one night. That you cared for me."

His eyes traveled over her face.

"I meant them at the time."

She gasped. He might as well have slapped her.

"Look, Lucy, I'm sorry. But I didn't realize how intense things were going to get so quickly. I'm fresh out of a divorce. I don't know if I'm up for so much so soon."

She shook her head.

"No. You're the one who wanted this," she said. "You're the one who told me your feelings wouldn't change. You told me I could trust you. You pursued me." She stared at him, at his distant eyes and his tight, unreadable face. "You made me fall in love with you."

He had the good grace to look away then.

"I'm sorry."

He was sorry.

It didn't even come close. Didn't even touch the sides of the pain and hurt opening inside her.

She looked around, trying to find the words or the actions or something, some way of responding to the colossal hurt he'd just inflicted on her. She felt hoodwinked, swindled, cheated. For weeks he'd wooed her, and she'd held him at arm's length because she was afraid, because Marcus had taught her not to trust. And finally she'd taken the leap of faith—and Dom had pulled the rug out from beneath her.

"Listen. I never meant to hurt you. Believe me, that's the last thing I wanted," he said.

"Too late," she said.

She turned on her heel and started walking. After a few feet she stopped and retraced her steps.

"Give me the keys to the van," she said.

He frowned. "I'll do the deliveries today."

"Give me the keys to the van."

"You can't do the deliveries on your own, Lucy."

"Give me the freaking keys!" she yelled.

People stopped to stare. Out of the corner of her eye she saw Mr. Bianco start to move toward them.

"What about the baby?" Dom asked.

She wanted to punch him in the face. Mash his nose, split his lips, pummel him until the rage bubbling up inside her was gone.

"I'll worry about my baby. Give me the keys," she demanded.

"What is going on? Is there problem?" Mr. Bianco asked as he came up beside them.

Lucy didn't take her eyes off Dom. After a long moment he pulled the keys from his pocket and handed them over. Her hand closed around them. They were warm from his body and her hand curled into a fist, squeezing the keys tightly.

"You're an asshole," she said to Dom. She threw the keys to the Mercedes at his feet.

More than anything she wanted to walk away and never see him or hear from him again. But she didn't have that luxury. She had a business to run, and his father was her key supplier. Worse, Dom was her business partner.

She turned to Mr. Bianco. There would be time to work out how to disentangle her life from Dom's later.

"Can you help me fill my order for the day, Mr. Bianco?" she asked.

Tony darted a glance at his son before nodding.

"Of course, of course, Lucia. No problem."

She didn't look at Dom as she turned away. She didn't so much as glance his way as Mr. Bianco helped her load her trolley over the next fifteen minutes. And she kept her head down as she pushed her load back to the van.

Only when she was alone in the privacy of her van did she sit down on a stack of empty crates and let herself howl. Hands clutched to her belly, she rocked back and forth as all her shock and disappointment and hurt streamed down her face. She cried till she was gasping for air and her chest ached.

It had been so hard for her to trust him. But she had. And he'd thrown her trust back in her face, along with her love.

I can't give you what you want.

"Oh God," she said.

How could something so new hurt so much?

Soon, she knew, she would be angry, and that would be a good thing. But right now, she was devastated and she didn't know where to put herself.

A rapid fluttering inside her belly drew her mind back into her body. Her baby was kicking in agitation, clearly distressed by her distress.

She took a deep breath and let it out on a shudder. She needed to get a grip. She had orders to deliver. More importantly, she had her daughter to consider.

There would be plenty of time to brood over her stupidity and gullibility later. All the time in the world.

She wiped her eyes on a wrinkled tissue she found in her pocket, then pushed herself to her feet.

She didn't have the luxury of falling down and staying down. For the rest of her life, she would have to get up and keep fighting on her own. Because there was another life completely reliant on her ability to continually get up and keep fighting.

She set her jaw grimly. She might as well get used to it now, because she would never make the mistake of trusting someone else to fight alongside her again.

DOM COULDN'T CONCENTRATE. Three times he added up the same order incorrectly. Every fiber of his being wanted to chase after Lucy and pull her into his arms and comfort her. But he couldn't offer her comfort when he was the one causing the pain.

He swore under his breath as he fumbled the keys on the calculator for the fourth time. His hands were shaking so much the glowing display shimmered before his eyes, blurring the digits together.

Or maybe that was because he was on the verge of tears. Damn.

Michael was walking past and Dom shoved the calculator at him.

"Could you take care of this order? I've got to do something," he said.

He didn't wait for other man to reply, just took off.

He barely made it into the darkness of the cold storage before his emotions overtook him. He swore out loud in English and Italian, then kicked an empty orange crate so hard it skidded along the ground and shattered against the far wall.

It wasn't fair.

But life wasn't fair, and he'd done the right thing.

Now he simply had to live with the consequences.

Lucy hating him. The mess of their business partnership. His own guilt and pain. The knowledge that he'd hurt her.

"Goddamn," he said, his voice deadened in the metal-lined space.

He sat on a crate and dropped his head into his hands. He pressed his fingers into his eyes and tried to get a grip. Long moments passed where there was nothing but the sound of his own harsh breathing. Then light streamed in as the door opened.

He shied away and tried to wipe his eyes on the tail of his shirt.

"Dom, you here?" his father called.

"I won't be a moment, Pa. Tell me what you need and I'll bring it back to the stand," he said.

He kept his back turned, praying his father would take the hint and leave him alone.

Dom heard the heavy tread of his father's footsteps before his warm hand landed on Dom's shoulder.

"Dominic. Talk to me," his father said quietly. "What

has you so upset? And why is Lucia so upset? What is happening?"

"It's not important. We'll sort it out," Dom said.

He kept his back turned.

"My son," his father said heavily, "when did you stop trusting your papa?"

Dom sighed. After a long pause he half turned toward his father.

"It's not that I don't trust you, Pa. There's just nothing you can do about it. Nothing anyone can do."

His father dug into the pocket on his apron and pulled out a handkerchief.

"Here."

Dom took it and blew his nose, feeling about nine years old. He was pretty sure that was the last time his father had caught him crying. At least that time Dom had had a broken leg as an excuse.

Wood creaked as his father sat on one of the crates.

"You love Lucia?" he asked. He made it sound so commonplace, so matter of fact, Dom almost laughed.

"Yeah, I do."

"I thought so. Your mama not so sure, but me, I see."

Great. His whole family probably knew about it by now—sisters, cousins, relatives back in Italy.

"Lucia does not love you, this is the problem?" his father continued.

"She loves me," he said heavily.

"Ah. You worry about bambino? That you not the father?"

"I don't care. It's Lucy's baby. That's all that matters to me."

He could practically hear his father considering and discarding other options. Dom ran his hand through his hair.

He'd been meaning to tell his father about his infertility

for a long time. And it wasn't as though this day could possibly suck any harder.

"I can't have children, Pa," he said. To his everlasting shame, his voice cracked on the final word and he had to blink back fresh tears. "That's why Dani and I broke up. Remember I had mumps when I was twenty? It doesn't happen very often, but sometimes it can make men infertile. I got lucky."

His father was silent for a long moment.

"No bambinos?"

"No. Never. Dani and I tried everything. But it was no good."

"This is why you divorce?"

"Yes."

"Your mother will be very sad for you. This is hard thing."

"Tell me about it."

He wasn't sure what he'd expected from this moment—Recriminations? Guilt? Shame?—but his father's quiet sympathy in the dark was unexpected.

They were both silent for a while.

"And this is why Lucia and you fight?" his father asked eventually.

"Lucy doesn't know."

"So why for you fight?" his father asked, bafflement rich in his tone.

"She wants brothers and sisters for her baby, a family. I can't give her any of that. So I ended things between us."

"I see. You ended things so Lucia could have what she wants?"

"Yeah."

His father exhaled heavily, then pushed himself to his feet.

"I am very sorry for you, my son."

For the first time in years, Dom found himself drawn

into the all-encompassing embrace of his father. Tony Bianco's big arms squeezed him tight, his hands patting Dom's back comfortingly. Dom breathed in his father's hair pomade and the smell of his mother's laundry detergent.

"This is big sadness for you to carry. I am very sorry," his father said again.

Dom hugged his father back.

"I am very sorry for you, but I think you make big mistake," his father continued.

Here we go.

Dom let his arms drop to his sides. "Pa—"

"Lucia is not Dani," his father said over him. "Lucia is Lucia. You not give her the chance to make her own decision."

Dom shook his head. "She shouldn't have to make a decision. She should have what she wants—brothers and sisters for her daughter."

"You sound like one of your mother's saints, making the big sacrifice." His father mimed someone hanging on a cross.

Dom shrugged uncomfortably. He hadn't meant to come off as a martyr. "I just want her to be happy."

His father nodded as though he was agreeing with Dom. "And you are scared," Tony said.

"I'm not scared. What have I got to be scared of?"

His father tucked his hands into the waistband of his apron. "What if you tell Lucia no bambinos and she says no matter? What if she says she loves you and one bambino is enough? Then she changes her mind and what happened with Dani happens with Lucia, all over again?"

"What am I supposed to say to that?" Dom said.

"That it is true. That it might happen. That you are afraid." His father held Dom's eye, waiting.

"I can't give her what she wants," Dom said. "What's the

point in starting something that will only hurt her more in the end?"

"This is Lucia's decision to make, not yours."

Dom looked away from his father's knowing eyes.

"You know I right, Dominic."

Dom shook his head. What his father was asking was too much. He refused to set himself up for disaster again. He'd done the right thing. For both of them.

To his surprise, his father stepped forward and patted his cheek, just as he used to when Dom was a very small boy.

"You will work out. You smart boy," his father said. "I want you to know, I very proud Saturday night. The party, the people, all the fancy pictures on the television." Tony nodded his head sagely. "Very impressive. Very smart."

Dom smiled ruefully. "You don't have to throw me a bone just because you caught me sooking, Pa."

His father frowned. "No bone. I go home, I look at the thing, the order thing you buy…?"

"The handheld unit."

"Hmmm. Is not so hard."

Dom stared at his father. "You used the handheld unit?"

His father shrugged, but Dom could see he was proud of himself. Dom snorted his amusement and surprise. Talk about leading a horse to water… Except this particular old donkey had taken his own sweet time in lowering his head for a drink.

His father dusted his hands down the front of his apron.

"You coming back to stand now?" he asked.

"In a minute."

"Take your time," his father said magnanimously.

Dom stood in the dark for a few minutes after his father had left. After months of conflict, his father had finally come around. Unbelievable. Maybe now they could start streamlining the business, making things more efficient and cost-effective.

Any satisfaction Dom felt faded as he remembered the look on Lucy's face when she'd thrown his car keys at his feet.

He'd hurt her. The last thing he'd ever wanted to do.

He leaned against the cool metal wall, forcing himself to remember the passion in Lucy's voice when she spoke of the importance of children in her life. It was all very well for his father to pat him on the cheek and say wise words, but he hadn't been there when Lucy talked about wanting siblings for her daughter. And he hadn't watched the wife he loved turn into a bitter stranger because a harmless virus had taken away his ability to be a father.

Lucy would thank him in the long run.

LUCY SPENT THAT NIGHT with her sister going through her accounts with a fine-tooth comb, trying to find a way to buy Dom out of their partnership. Between bouts of pacing and ranting and sitting and sobbing, she ate chocolate-chip ice cream and far too many Tim Tam cookies.

"I'm sorry," Rosie said for the tenth time. "I feel so responsible. I practically pimped you out to him. I was so sure that you guys had this spark. The look he used to get in his eye when he was with you… But I guess I was wrong."

"You didn't make me kiss him or sleep with him or fall in love with him. I did that all on my own—with a lot of help from Mr. I'm-Not-Going-Anywhere," Lucy said bitterly. "I'm so stupid. I told myself over and over that I couldn't afford to get involved with someone, let alone my *business partner*. I honestly don't think there is a dumber woman alive. What was I thinking?"

"Falling in love isn't exactly a right-brain function," Rosie said sympathetically.

Lucy looked up from the spreadsheet she'd been studying.

"Do you think if I show the bank the Web site and all the customers who have signed over to the new program and our new marketing plan they might reconsider the loan? It might be different now that I've got the Web site running."

"You can try. But there are clauses in the contract about you and Dom buying each other out. You need to get the business assessed by a small-business broker. He owns half of it now. Any improvement you've made means that his half is worth more, too."

Lucy sank back in her chair and reached for her spoon again.

"Why did I do this to myself?"

"Stop giving yourself a hard time. You fell in love. It's not a crime. He made it incredibly easy for you to fall in love, too. And you had every reason to believe what he said to you. Up until now, he's been the perfect man. Kind. Thoughtful. Always honest and reliable. Passionate. Committed."

Lucy felt tears welling again, and she held up a hand to stem the flow of her sister's words.

"Stop. Please."

Rosie pushed the ice-cream tub closer.

"Have some ice cream."

Lucy sniffed and dug her spoon into the tub, but couldn't summon the effort to pry it out again. She wasn't hungry, she was heartbroken.

"Did you get on to the counselor today?" she asked as she reached for another tissue.

"Got my first appointment next week."

Rosie sounded nervous. Lucy blew her nose.

"You'll be fine. If you don't like her, if it doesn't make

sense or feel like something that will work for you, you just don't go again. Simple."

"I know. Just like changing hairdressers."

"Exactly."

"Except we're talking about the inside of my head and not the outside."

Lucy couldn't help smiling.

"I'm so glad you and Andrew are talking again."

Rosie twisted her wedding ring around her finger, studying the single diamond for a moment.

"I'm very lucky."

"He's lucky, too, you know."

Rosie smiled. She looked very wistful.

"There's a stupid part of me that hopes I'll walk in the door of this counselor's office next week and she'll wave a magic wand and everything will be okay. I won't be scared anymore, no more doubts. I know it won't work like that, that it'll be hard. But still…"

Lucy slid the spoon free from the tub and reached for the lid.

"No more doubts. I'd buy a ticket for that," she said.

"Who wouldn't?"

They smiled at each other. Rosie took the ice cream from her and crossed the room to return it to the freezer.

"What are you going to do?" she asked when she came back to the dining table.

Lucy stared at her spreadsheet.

"I'm going to endure," she said finally. "I'm going to suck it up and keep running my business and seeing him every day, even though it will be one of the hardest things I have ever done."

Rosie watched her sadly.

"I can do this," Lucy said. "I'm tough."

"Like an old boot."

"Or one of those black box things that survive plane crashes."

"Or Mr. T, back when he was with the *A-Team*."

They both laughed.

The smile faded from Lucy's lips.

"If only I could stop loving him," she said quietly.

Rosie didn't say a word, simply reached out and rubbed her arm. What more was there to say, after all?

THE NEXT DAY, Lucy sat in the van in the parking lot behind the market for a full ten minutes before she could summon the courage to get out and fill her order. She didn't want to look at Dom, hear his voice, even say his name. But she'd already gone over all of that with her sister. She didn't have a choice. Even if he wasn't her business partner, his father was the best and cheapest fresh produce wholesaler in the city. Their lives were inextricably entwined.

Hands tight around the push bar of her trolley, she walked slowly to the Bianco Brothers' stall. Dom had his back to her as she approached, his head lowered as he talked intently to a tall, gangly young man. She didn't need to see his high cheekbones and strong jaw to know he was a relative.

Her stupid body hadn't quite caught up with the events of the previous day, and her heart gave a ridiculous kick as she stared at Dom's broad shoulders and beautiful backside. For one night, he'd been hers, and it had been wonderful.

Yeah, and you paid a bloody high price for the privilege, her cynical self chastised.

The thought helped her square her shoulders as Dom turned around, almost as though he had sensed her approach.

For a second he simply stared at her. She made a point

of holding his gaze. He'd hurt her. She wasn't about to pretend it was any different and she wasn't ashamed of caring for him. He was the one who should be ashamed of the way he'd treated her—like the latest toy, to be played with until the next amusing thing came along.

After a long silence, Dom gestured over his shoulder toward the young man.

"This is my sister's boy, Michael. He's going to help you out with the deliveries until the baby's due," he said. "If things work out, he's interested in the job driving the second van."

Her gaze flicked to Dom's nephew. Michael gave her a little half smile and a wave, then shifted his feet awkwardly. Poor kid. She figured he had no idea what kind of a mess his uncle had dropped him in the middle of.

"You don't think this was something we should have discussed first?" she said, returning her attention to Dom.

"Of course. But I figured you probably didn't want to talk to me last night and that you wouldn't want me doing deliveries with you today."

"Bingo." She crossed her arms over her chest.

"You can't do deliveries on your own, Lucy."

"What I do or don't do is none of your business."

Dom's jaw tensed again.

"Actually, it is. If you hurt yourself on the job, Market Fresh is liable," he said coolly.

She took a breath to argue some more, but she could feel pressure building behind her eyes. She refused to cry in front of him. Owning her feelings was one thing, but blubbering in front of him was a whole other ball game.

"Fine. Whatever. Michael, pleased to meet you," she said, thrusting her hand at Dom's nephew.

"Oh, um, you, too," he said, shaking hands awkwardly.

"Let's go."

She pushed the trolley past Dom and didn't stop walking until she was as far from him as she could get and still be standing in front of Bianco Brothers'. Michael watched her anxiously as she breathed deeply and sniffed a few times.

"It's okay. I'm okay," she said.

"Do you want a handkerchief?" he asked.

He offered her a neatly pressed white square. The sight of it made her laugh.

"I bet your ma made you put that in your pocket this morning," she said as she took it.

"Won't let me leave the house without one," he grumbled.

She blew her nose, then looked him in the eye.

"Don't tell your uncle I was crying," she said.

He shook his head.

"No way."

Dom kept his distance for the rest of her time at the market, and she didn't look his way once. Still, she felt a little nauseous by the time Michael pushed the trolley back to the van.

This was going to be hard—much harder than she'd thought. Seeing Dom every day. Driving around with his look-alike cousin in the van beside her.

But that was what enduring was all about, right? Doing what you had to do, no matter what.

"Okay, Michael," she said. "Let's get this show on the road."

CHAPTER TWELVE

EIGHT WEEKS LATER, Dom checked his watch for the fifth time in as many minutes.

Lucy was late. He wondered if she'd changed her mind about coming. She hadn't been exactly thrilled when he called to suggest a face-to-face meeting. Not that he blamed her.

It was raining outside, pelting down. Briefly he wondered if he should call her, make sure everything was okay. He quelled the impulse. Probably the weather was slowing traffic.

He pushed his coffee away. He was as nervous as a kid on a first date. Except this was no date. This was almost the exact opposite of a date, in fact—a meeting to dissolve his partnership with Lucy.

He'd cut her free from their relationship, and now it was time to cut her free from their business contract.

She was unhappy. He could see it in her eyes, the dullness of her skin, the downward slope of her shoulders. Being tied to him was difficult. Painful. Once their partnership was dissolved, she wouldn't have to deal with him anymore. Someone else could serve her when she came to the stand. Hell, he'd even make sure he was absent during the times she usually came to collect her supplies. That way, they'd never have to see each other at all. That should make things easier for her.

He rubbed his eyes. He hadn't had a good night's sleep in weeks. He hadn't counted, but he was pretty sure that if he cared to do the math, he'd work out that he hadn't slept a full eight hours since the Sunday he'd realized that he was going to have to give Lucy up.

So his motives weren't entirely selfless in regard to dissolving the partnership. It was killing him having to deal with her all the time, too. He'd tried to make it as easy as possible—hiring Michael to help with deliveries so he could ensure she was looking after herself without physically being there himself, staying away from her when she came to the stand, keeping any business discussions brief and to the point and conducting as many of them as possible via e-mail.

It didn't make any difference. He still wanted her. He still dreamed of her. He still turned automatically toward the sound of her voice. His chest still ached when she laughed. Not that she'd been laughing much lately.

He'd hurt her. But he hadn't had a choice. He'd have only made her even more unhappy in the long run. This was the lesser evil, the kinder cut.

It was the same thing he'd been telling himself over and over, and he was sick of hearing it. He shoved his cup even farther away and coffee lapped at the rim, almost spilling over.

He knew the feeling. Maybe it was the lack of sleep, or the guilt, or the pain of being a part of Lucy's world but not a part of it, but he'd felt damned close to spilling over a number of times lately. He'd been short with his father. He'd even snapped at his mother. He was pretty sure most of the staff members at Bianco Brothers' were going out of their way to avoid him.

He sat back in his chair and stared blindly out the window.

How long did it take to stop loving someone? To stop dreaming of the smell of their skin, the feel of their hands on your body?

How long did it take to kill a dream?

Longer than eight weeks. But maybe dissolving the partnership would help. He bloody hoped so.

The bell over the coffee-shop door rang and he looked up. Lucy met his eyes as she shook out her umbrella. She looked tired, drained. He'd arranged to meet at the end of her delivery run so they'd have more time to discuss things, but now he wondered if he should have made it a morning meeting.

"You look tired," he said as she joined him at the table.

She didn't respond. She dumped her umbrella under the table and lowered herself carefully into the chair. She'd grown in the past few weeks, her belly burgeoning into a classic pregnancy silhouette.

"What did you want to see me about?" she asked.

Her gaze was clear, her eyes distant.

Right. Straight into business.

"I want to dissolve the partnership," he said.

"I see."

He shoved a sheaf of papers across the table toward her.

"I had my lawyer draw this up. This gives you full title to the company. Once we sign, Market Fresh will be all yours again."

She scanned the front page, then quickly flipped through the next few pages.

"It doesn't say how much you want. We need to get the company valued," she said.

"I don't want you to buy me out. I'm signing my half over to you," he said.

She stared at him.

"You're *giving* it to me?"

"That's right."

She let her breath out in a rush, then she looked down at the papers in her hand for a long moment. She stood, her chair scraping across the café floor.

"Where are you going?" he asked as she stooped awkwardly to collect her umbrella.

"Home. Where I won't be insulted."

He stood.

"Wait a minute." He grabbed her arm.

"Don't touch me."

"Lucy. Don't be stupid," he said. "Stay and talk it through."

She shook him off. Her eyes were wide with anger. "I don't know what's wrong with you, but I am not accepting thirty thousand dollars of investment in my business because we slept with each other. I don't believe I've sunk to the level of whoring just yet."

"For Pete's sake—"

"What else is it for then, Dom? It's guilt money, pure and simple. And I am not your freaking charity case," she said. Her voice quavered then broke on the final few words, but she kept staring him down.

"That's not the way I think of you," he said.

"What am I, then? A mistake you need to pay off?"

"No."

She threw her hands in the air.

"What, then? You tell me why you want to give me thirty thousand dollars for nothing."

"I want you to be happy. I want to make sure you're all right."

"Neither of those things are your responsibility," she said.

She turned to go. He grabbed her arm again.

"Lucy—"

She swung around on him. "No! You gave up the right to care about me when you cut me loose like some girl you'd picked up in a bar."

"I did you a favor, Lucy," he said.

She laughed, the sound hard and bitter. "Is that how you sell it to yourself? Wow, what a guy. You should go get yourself measured for a suit of armor. Make sure it's nice and shiny."

She headed for the door. This time he let her go.

She stopped on the threshold to fumble with the umbrella. He was about to head to the counter to pay his bill when she dropped the umbrella and clutched at her belly.

He was at her side in two strides.

"What's wrong?"

"I think I'm bleeding again," she said. "I felt a rush, like last time. Oh God."

She lifted the hem of the stretchy black tunic she wore over a pair of pale gray leggings. They both stared at the damp spreading down her thighs.

"That's not blood," he said.

Her face was pale as she met his eyes.

"My water must have broken."

There was bone-deep panic in her eyes. She was only thirty-four weeks.

His phone was in his hand before he'd even formulated the thought.

"Ambulance," he told the emergency services operator. Immediately he was patched through to the ambulance service. It took only a moment to give their location.

"Two minutes. We're lucky we're so close to the hospital," he said as he ended the call.

"It's too early," she said as he led her back inside the café. "The baby's too small still."

"Lots of babies are born early and survive," he said.

She grimaced and her hand shot out to grasp his arm. Her fingers convulsed around his wrist.

"Oh boy. I think I'm in labor."

She leaned forward, groaning.

"Is she all right?" a voice asked behind them.

It was the shop owner, looking concerned. A crowd of customers was forming.

"The baby's coming," he said. "The ambulance is on its way."

"Oh!"

"It hurts!" Lucy groaned.

The wail of sirens sounded in the distance. One of the customers went out into the street to flag it down.

"We'll be at the hospital in five minutes," he said.

"Rosie! I need Rosie."

"I'll call her."

The ambulance shuddered to a stop out the front of the café, lights circling, its siren piercing until it was silenced abruptly.

Rosie's phone went through to voice mail when he dialed. He left a quick message.

"I'll try Andrew," he said before Lucy could ask.

She nodded her thanks as the ambulance crew entered. While they settled her into the gurney, he called Andrew's cell. Again he got voice mail. He left another message.

"They had a court hearing this afternoon. A divorce," Lucy said as the paramedics began to wheel her out the door.

He grabbed her bag and coat and umbrella.

"I'll meet you at the hospital," he said.

She nodded, but he could see how afraid she was. He hesitated only a second before following her to the ambulance and climbing in after her.

"I'm coming with you," he said.

She bit her lip, then nodded.

"Thank you."

He reached for her hand as the ambulance started up.

"You're going to be okay," he said.

She was about to answer when her eyes rounded and she gasped.

"Oh God!" she groaned, curling forward.

"When was your last contraction?" the paramedic asked.

Lucy was too busy panting to respond.

"Just before you arrived," Dom said.

The paramedic's eyebrows rose. "That's pretty close."

"I guess. Is that bad?" Dom asked quietly.

"It's fast. Her water just broke? There's been no other signs of labor? No backache or any other cramping?" the paramedic asked.

Lucy shook her head and collapsed down onto the gurney.

"Are the pains supposed to be this bad?" she asked, her voice faint.

"When the labor is fast like this, they hit hard."

The ambulance slowed as it turned a long curving corner. Dom guessed they'd arrived at the emergency bay.

Within seconds the doors were open and Lucy was being raced to a cubicle. They transferred her to a bed, and a nurse helped her remove her leggings and underwear. Dom moved to the head of the bed and laid his hand on Lucy's shoulder. He felt utterly useless, but he refused to leave her side.

An older woman with faded blond hair entered the room.

"Hello, Lucy, I'm Julie. I'll be your midwife this afternoon," she said with a warm smile. "How are we feeling?"

Lucy groaned as another pain hit. Dom watched as her belly hardened and her body stiffened. Julie frowned.

"Okay, Lucy, I'm just going to take a quick look and see how far along you are."

Very aware that he had no right to be a part of this experience, Dom glanced away as the midwife checked Lucy's cervix. The midwife was very matter of fact when she straightened.

"Lucy, you're almost fully dilated. This baby wants out, fast. I'm afraid we're not going to be able to give you any pain relief."

Lucy shook her head. "Is my baby going to be all right? It's so early…"

"We have the neonatal team on standby, but thirty-four weeks is very viable," Julie said. "I've called your obstetrician, Dr. Mason, and he's coming in. But I should warn you that you may have delivered before he gets here."

"I don't care. As long as my baby is okay."

She growled low in her throat as another contraction hit. This time she slapped a hand onto Dom's arm and clung on so tightly his skin turned white.

"Hang in there, Lucy. This is going to be fast and furious. The important thing is that I want you to wait until I tell you to push, okay? Pretty soon you're going to want to do that more than anything, but I need you to wait until I give you the go ahead. Okay?" Julie asked.

Lucy nodded. Dom reached out to push the damp hair off her forehead.

"You're tough. You can do this," he encouraged her.

"It's not like I have a choice. I never have a choice," she panted.

Her mouth opened on a silent cry and her fingers tightened around his. He watched her body quiver for what felt like forever, then she collapsed back onto the bed.

"I want my sister," she said, staring forlornly at the ceiling.

"I know. I'm sorry," he said.

She turned her head to look at him.

"You don't have to stay. I know you feel guilty, but you don't have to stay."

"If you want me to go, I'll go," he said.

Lucy's face screwed up with pain and she clutched at his hand as another contraction hit. Over the next fifteen minutes, her contractions came faster and lasted longer. Sweat rolled down her face. Dom offered water, his hand and words of encouragement. He'd never felt more helpless in his life.

"Oh! It's burning," she gasped. She grunted, her chin buried into her chest, tears rolling down her red face.

Julie checked between her legs.

"You're crowning, Lucy. Don't push right now. Give your vagina a chance to stretch. I know you probably want to push like hell, but give your body a chance to adjust."

Lucy tucked her chin down more and panted.

"Right. Go for it, Lucy. Whatever feels good. Give me all you've got," Julie said.

Lucy strained upward, letting go of Dom's hand to clutch at the mattress, both hands fisting into the sheets. Dom moved close, his arm sliding around her shoulders to support her, wanting to take some of the pain for her or help her in some way.

"Good girl. You're doing great, Lucy. I can see the baby's head," Julie said.

"Oh!" Lucy said, her eyes widening suddenly.

And then a thin, high wail sounded and Julie was holding a small, red-and-white bundle in her arms.

"Is she okay? Is she all right?" Lucy asked.

"She's breathing well. Our neonate specialist, Dr. Wilson, is just going to check her over," Julie said.

Dom took Lucy's weight as she relaxed. Not for a second did her gaze waver from the small shape in the doctor's arms. Dom stared down at Lucy's face, damp with sweat, tendrils of hair clinging to her temples. She was amazing. Absolutely amazing.

"Lucy, I need you to stay with me for a bit," Julie said.

Lucy tensed and groaned, a look of utter surprise crossing her face.

"More pain. Isn't it supposed to stop now?" she gasped.

"That's the placenta. Just push when you need to."

The next few minutes passed in a blur as Lucy grimaced and panted and bore down.

"Okay, I've got it. Well done, Lucy," Julie said.

"How is my baby?" Lucy asked for the fifth time.

"She's six pounds three, a good weight for thirty-four weeks," Dr. Wilson said. "Good color. Good movement."

"Can I hold her?" Lucy asked.

"I don't see why not. We'll want to get her into an incubator and check her out more fully, but she's a good, strong, healthy baby for thirty-four weeks," Dr. Wilson said.

He brought the baby to the bed. Lucy held out her arms and the doctor placed her on Lucy's chest. She looked impossibly tiny to Dom, her body curled in on itself, her skin still speckled with blood and a white, waxy substance. Her dark hair was matted to her skull, her tiny face screwed up in outrage as she mewled her objection to the rude awakening she'd just experienced.

"She's beautiful," he said, his voice rough. "She looks like you."

Lucy laughed. Tears rolled down her cheeks. She reached out and ran a finger gently down her daughter's cheek.

"Hello, little one. I've been waiting so long to meet you."

"Congratulations, Lucy. Do you have a name picked out?" Julie asked, a warm smile on her face.

Lucy nodded, never taking her gaze from her child.

"Mariella. It was my grandmother's name," she said.

"That's lovely. Does it mean anything?" Julia asked.

"Beloved," Dom said quietly. "It means beloved."

Lucy looked up at him. There was nothing he could do about the tears on his face, so he just held her eye.

"Lucy, how about we see if she will take the breast?" Dr Wilson suggested. "She may not, but she's so strong I'd like to at least give it a try."

Dom let her rest back against the pillows while Julie helped adjust her hospital gown. Lucy cradled her daughter close to her breast while Julie offered a few quick instructions.

At first Mariella screwed up her face and turned her face away as Lucy brushed her nipple across the baby's mouth. Lucy tried again, and finally the baby's mouth opened. She nuzzled the nipple curiously, then instinct took over and she drew it into her mouth.

"That's fantastic. Wonderful," Dr. Wilson said.

A slow smile spread across Lucy's face as Mariella suckled. She glanced up at Dom, her eyes big and soft.

"Isn't she incredible?"

"Yes."

Emotion choked his throat. More than anything today, the sight of her breastfeeding her child hit him in the gut and the chest.

"I'll go try Rosie again," he said, backing away from the bed.

Lucy nodded, not taking her eyes from Mariella.

"Tell her to hurry. She's missing out."

"I will."

He stepped out into the corridor and strode down the corridor quickly until he could see daylight outside the emergency entrance doors. Then he was sucking in the damp cool air of a wet afternoon.

He had just witnessed a miracle. It was the only way he could describe it. The birth of a tiny new person. Lucy's child. Mariella. Beloved.

He took a deep breath, fighting for control. He would never forget the past hour, ever. It was burned into his memory, the most privileged and precious moments of his life.

For a man in his position, it had been the ultimate gift. A priceless blessing.

And he was well aware that he was the last person Lucy would have chosen to share the experience with if she'd been given a choice.

He pulled his phone from his pocket.

Now that the emergency was over, Lucy would want her family by her side.

LUCY FRETTED as the nurses cleaned her up and helped her into a hospital gown and transferred her to a ward. They'd taken Mariella away for a more thorough examination but promised to return her to Lucy for another feed.

A tired smile curved her mouth as she thought of her daughter. So small and pink and angry. She was perfect and fragile and terrifyingly small. The love that had risen up inside Lucy the moment she'd looked into the daughter's face had been so overwhelming, so undeniable it had taken her breath away.

A footfall sounded in the corridor and she tensed. Maybe they were bringing Mariella back to her.

Or maybe it was Dom.

He hadn't come back. Not since the birth. She'd waited for him to come back after calling Rosie and Andrew again, but he hadn't.

She frowned down at the blanket she was pleating between her fingers. She knew better than to expect anything from him. After all, he was the man who "couldn't give her what she wanted." Seeing her give birth wasn't going to change anything. If anything, it would probably make him run in the opposite direction.

Even if he had cried when she held her daughter for the first time.

"Lucy!"

Rosie rushed into the room, Andrew following.

"I'm so sorry. We were in court, it went on and on. We broke the sound barrier trying to get here," her sister said. "Are you okay? Is the baby okay?"

"I'm fine. The baby is good. The doctors wanted to check her out again, but she's really healthy. Big for thirty-four weeks."

"I'm so sorry I wasn't here for you," Rosie said.

"Dom was here," Lucy said.

"So I gathered." Rosie gave her a careful look and Lucy shrugged.

"That'll show him for dumping me."

"Yeah, way to punish him. Make him witness childbirth," Rosie said.

Andrew leaned forward and kissed Lucy's cheek.

"Congratulations. Do we have a name?"

"Mariella."

Rosie's eyes filled with tears. "Oh. That's beautiful."

Andrew smiled and put his arm around his wife.

"When can we see her?" Rosie asked.

"She's in the preemie nursery on the second floor."

Andrew and Rosie looked at each other.

"Off you go," Lucy said with a rueful smile. "I can see I'm no longer the star of the show."

"We won't be long," Rosie said. "I love you."

"I love you, too."

Rosie and Andrew headed for the door.

"Oh, and your mother's on her way in," Andrew said.

She settled back down onto her pillows as they left and closed her eyes. Her body ached. She had two stitches and some bruising from the rapid labor. She was exhausted. She wanted her daughter.

And she also wanted Dom to come back.

ROSIE STOOD at the window to the nursery, staring at the rows of tiny babies in front of her. They were all so small, most of them with tubes in their noses and mouths, and drips in their arms.

"They're so tiny," she said.

"Not ours," Andrew said. He gave her a nudge and she saw that the crib closest to the door was labeled Mariella Basso and was playing host to the biggest baby in the nursery.

"Good lord, she's a giant," Rosie said.

Andrew laughed. "Only by comparison."

They moved closer, pressing their hands against the glass. A few dark strands of hair poked out from beneath the baby's bonnet.

"She's got dark hair, like Lucy."

"And she's got Lucy's nose and mouth."

"Thank God. Can you imagine Marcus's nose on a girl?"

A nurse came forward to check on Mariella. Rosie frowned and moved to the doorway.

"Excuse me, sorry. I'm her aunt. Is everything okay?" she said.

The nurse smiled.

"Absolutely. She's a firecracker, this one."

She gestured for Rosie and Andrew to come in.

"Come closer. She won't bite."

"If you're sure…?" Rosie said.

"Of course. Aunts need to meet their nieces straight-away. Makes it easier to ask for babysitting duties later on," the nurse said with a wink.

Rosie moved closer to the clear-sided crib. She glanced at Andrew and he smiled, his eyes soft.

Mariella lay curled on her side, her hands pressed to her mouth. Her eyes worked behind her eyelids, and her mouth opened and closed rhythmically.

"Mariella. It's very nice to meet you," she said quietly, leaning close. "You certainly came in a big hurry, didn't you?"

The baby shifted her head fretfully.

"Hello, little lady," Andrew said. He reached out a finger and ran it over her cheek. "She's so soft."

He smiled at Rosie, and she reached out a tentative hand.

This was her sister's child, her blood. The next generation of her family. A part of Lucy, and a part of Rosie, too.

She stroked Mariella's cheek, then traced a tiny pink ear.

"She's perfect," she said.

Love welled up in her, and she let the tears slide down her cheeks. That was something she'd learned in her once a week therapy sessions—that it was okay to cry, to feel compassion for herself. She'd learned a lot of other things, too, about herself, and her relationships with her mother and her sister and her husband.

Nobody had waved a magic wand. She still had her moments of doubt and uncertainty. But she was starting to understand herself better, and how the patterns of her childhood had impacted on her adult life.

She traced one of Mariella's tightly fisted hands. To her surprise, the baby uncurled her fingers and opened her hand. Rosie hesitated a moment, then pressed her finger into the tiny palm. Immediately little fingers closed around her finger in a tight, instinctive grip. Rosie swallowed noisily and sniffed. Then she looked at her husband.

"I want this," she said fiercely.

He leaned across and kissed her.

"We'll get there."

Looking into his blue eyes, she could only believe that they would.

"Whatever it takes," she said.

It had become their mantra.

"Whatever it takes."

LUCY WOKE TO THE RUSTLE of plastic bags. She'd dozed off while she waited for her sister to return. She opened her eyes as Dom moved quietly toward the door.

"I thought you must have gone home," she said.

He looked caught out.

"Sorry. I didn't mean to wake you. The nurse said you might not have small enough clothes for Mariella since she was so tiny, so I went and grabbed a few things for her."

She pulled herself higher in the bed and saw her overnight bag was sitting on the guest chair, alongside two shopping bags.

He'd gone to her flat to collect her baby bag. She frowned, and he shifted uncomfortably.

"I hope you don't mind. Your keys were in your purse, and I figured Rosie and Andrew wouldn't have a chance to stop by home on the way in…" he said.

"It's fine. It's lovely, actually. I hate hospital gowns. Thank you. That was…thoughtful."

He was always thoughtful. She'd been so hurt and angry over the past few weeks it had been easy to ignore the many little kindnesses he showed her every day. But the truth was, even though he was no longer interested in her, he still looked out for her. To the extent that he'd actually offered to give her business back to her today.

"Is there anything else I can get for you? Anyone else you need me to contact?" he asked.

She shook her head.

"No. Thank you for looking after me today. You always seem to be there when I need you."

He shrugged again and looked away. She didn't think she'd ever seen him looking so uneasy.

Was it because he felt guilty? Was that why he was so generous and considerate and compassionate toward her, and why he was so uneasy now? He couldn't give her what she wanted—him—so he tried to give her everything else?

The thought made her feel very sad. For both of them.

"I suppose this has put you off babies for life," she said. "All the moaning and groaning."

"No."

He glanced toward the door.

"If you need to go, it's okay," she said.

"It's just I know you'll have all your relatives here any minute."

"It's okay. I understand. This is probably the last place you want to be."

He frowned, started to say something, then shook his head.

"I'll, um, check in with Rosie tomorrow, see how you're doing," he said.

"Sure."

He turned for the door. She struggled to contain the words rising up inside her, but she couldn't help herself.

"For what it's worth, I'm glad it was you," she said before he could go. "I'm glad you were the one who was with me. I know that probably makes you uncomfortable, but it's true. It's crazy, but I can't think of anyone who could have made me feel as safe as you did today."

His step faltered. She could feel heat rushing into her face.

"Lucy," he said. His expression was pained as he turned to look at her.

She held up a hand. "It's okay, you don't have to say it. I don't need to hear how you did me a favor again. You're not the only guy who'd run a mile at the thought of an instant family. The miracle is probably that you even looked twice at me in the first place."

She knew she sounded angry and self-pitying and bitter, but she wasn't a woman who loved easily. And for better or for worse she'd fallen in love with Dom and it was going to take more than eight weeks for her heart to mend. Maybe that made her soft or stupid, but it was just the way it was.

"It's not you, Lucy," he said. "Or the baby. Believe that. No guy in his right mind would walk away from you."

She didn't look up from the blanket. She didn't want to see the pity in his eyes, or the guilt.

"It's not you, Lucy," he said again.

She could feel him watching her. She was very afraid she was about to cry.

"You should go," she said.

She rolled over onto her side so her back was to the door. She waited for the sound of footsteps, but it never came. She sighed.

"Look, I shouldn't have said anything. Pretend I didn't. Just go."

"I can't have children."

His voice was so quiet, his words so totally unexpected, she almost didn't hear him.

She stared blankly at the wall. Then she looked over her shoulder, certain she had to have misunderstood. He stood stiffly in the doorway, his dark eyes steady on her.

"I'm sterile, Lucy," he said simply. "That's why my marriage broke up, and it's why I ended things with you, okay? Not because of anything you did or didn't do, or because of Mariella. You are the most…" He paused and lifted a hand to rub the bridge of his nose. His shoulders lifted as he took a deep breath.

"One day soon, some lucky bastard is going to find you and give you everything you need and want, and all of this won't mean a thing."

She stared at him. She thought about the way he'd gone quiet the day they discussed Andrew and Rosie's baby problems in her flat, and she thought about the way he'd been so distant the next day. And she remembered what he'd said to her, over and over: *I did you a favor.*

For eight weeks she'd lain awake, sifting through every second of her time with him. The way he'd looked at her, the way he'd talked to her, the way he'd touched her, the way he'd made her feel. For the life of her, she hadn't been able to understand how she'd gotten it so wrong, misread all the signals, been suckered so completely.

And all along...

"You walked away from me because you're sterile?"

"Because I can't give you what you want."

Her hands clenched the edge of the blanket as she understood what he'd done: sacrificed himself—*them*—for her. For what he believed she wanted.

"How do you know what I want?" she asked quietly.

"You want more children. You think family is the purpose of life. You want brothers and sisters for your daughter. That's more than enough to rule me out."

He said it like it was carved in stone, immutable, unchangeable, unarguable.

"How do you know what I want?" she repeated, her voice louder. "Did you ask me? Did you give me the choice? Did you sit down and have a conversation with *me* so that *I* could decide what my future was going to look like?"

He shifted his weight.

"I didn't want you to have to give up your life's dream for me, Lucy. I've played that game before, I know how it ends. I did what I thought was best."

"Then you're an idiot, Dominic Bianco!" she said. "You think guys like you grow on trees? You think people fall in love the way we fell in love every day? I did everything I could not to love you, but it was impossible and you dared to make a decision on my behalf without even consulting me?"

She thumped the bed with her fists, her body vibrating with fury.

"Lucy, calm down," he said.

"I have been miserable for two months, crying myself

to sleep, dragging myself through each day, eating my heart out over you! Don't you dare tell me to calm down!"

He took a step forward, but she grabbed the plastic water jug from her tray table and threw it at him. It glanced off his arm and hit the ground with a clatter, water splashing everywhere.

"You should have asked me!" she said. "You should have bloody well asked me and bloody well let me choose. You stupid, stupid idiot."

She was crying, her face crumpled with distress.

"Lucy," he said.

He crossed to the bed and tried to take her in his arms.

"Sweetheart, don't cry," he said. "Please."

She hit him on the chest, the shoulder, the arm but he caught her fists easily and held them to his chest with one hand as his other pulled her close. Then her head was on his shoulder and she was breathing in the warm, woody smell of him.

"You idiot. Don't you know how much I love you? I took my clothes off for you when I was the size of a whale. Surely that must have told you something?" she sobbed into his chest.

She felt him press a kiss onto the top of her head.

"I want you to be happy," he said quietly. "Can't you see that? I want you to have everything."

She pulled back to look him in the face.

"Life doesn't work like that, Dom. No one has everything. And if I get to choose whether I have you in my life to love and laugh with and grow old with and lose my marbles with, I'm going to choose you every time. Every. Time."

He searched her face as though he couldn't quite let himself believe what she was saying.

"You want children," he said.

"Yes. Don't you?"

He sighed heavily, and she could see years of grief and resignation in his eyes.

"More than anything, Lucy. But it's not going to happen."

"Ever heard of adoption? Sperm donation? Fostering? How many ways do you need to have children in your life, Dom?"

He stared at her. "Dani didn't want to adopt. She wouldn't even consider sperm donation."

Lucy reached up and grasped his chin in her hands.

"I'm not Dani, in case you hadn't noticed. I'm Lucia Carmella Basso, and I love *you,* Dominic Bianco. I want *you.* Anything else is a bonus."

For a moment Dom just stared at her. Then he closed his eyes and pulled her close, burying his face in her neck. His shoulders shook and Lucy's arms tightened around him.

He'd been so hurt by his ex-wife's rejection. So wounded. Lucy held him as close as she could, trying to convey with her body how much she needed and wanted and loved him.

"I love you, Dom. You're more than enough for me."

He held her tighter, his arms like steel around her.

"Lucy. God. I love you so much," he said over and over.

"I know," she said, pressing her hand to the back of his head. "You love me so much you were prepared to give me up. I should probably warn you, I'm not that noble. I plan on hanging on to you for the rest of my life. So if you have a problem with that, speak now or forever hold your peace."

He laughed. He pulled back to look into her face and she reached up to wipe the tears from his cheeks.

"My sweet idiot," she said softly, lovingly.

Then she pulled him close and kissed him. It was like coming home after too long away. It was perfect, as good as she remembered.

Better—because this time she understood exactly who she held in her arms and how lucky she was and how lucky he was.

"Hey, Luce, guess who we found in the elevator? Oops!"

"Lucia!"

Dom broke their kiss but didn't immediately turn to acknowledge her sister and mother. He smiled and caressed her cheek. She smiled back.

Later, they would talk some more. He would hold her, and she would tell him over and over how much she loved him—whatever it took to remove the shadows of the doubt he'd lived with for so long.

"Does someone want to tell me what is going on? Why are you kissing Dominic, Lucia? I thought there had been a falling out? Why does nobody tell me anything?" Sophia asked.

Lucy's smile broadened as she looked over Dom's shoulder at her family. Rosie had a smug smile on her face while Andrew was doing his best to look as though he found his sister-in-law in a lip-lock with her estranged business partner after giving childbirth every day of the week. Her mother was flushed and expectant-looking, far more curious than she was outraged.

Lucy took Dom's hand in hers and tangled her fingers with his.

"Relax, Ma. Everything's going to be all right."

And for the first time in a long time, she knew it was true. She knew the weeks and months and years ahead would bring with them their fair share of problems and heartbreak and troubles. But she also knew she could take on anything with Dom at her side.

She glanced at him, and he raised their joined hands and pressed a kiss to her wrist.

She smiled. This was going to be good.

* * * * *

Celebrate 60 years of pure reading pleasure with Harlequin®!
Silhouette® Romantic Suspense is celebrating with the glamour-filled, adrenaline-charged series
LOVE IN 60 SECONDS *starting in April 2009.*
Six stories that promise to bring the glitz of Las Vegas, the danger of revenge, the mystery of a missing diamond, family scandals and ripped-from-the-headlines intrigue. Get your heart racing as love happens in sixty seconds!

Enjoy a sneak peek of
USA TODAY *bestselling author Marie Ferrarella's*
THE HEIRESS'S 2-WEEK AFFAIR
Available April 2009 from Silhouette® Romantic Suspense.

Eight years ago Matt Shaffer had vanished out of Natalie Rothchild's life, leaving behind a one-line note tucked under a pillow that had grown cold: *I'm sorry, but this just isn't going to work.*

That was it. No explanation, no real indication of remorse. The note had been as clinical and compassionless as an eviction notice, which, in effect, it had been, Natalie thought as she navigated through the morning traffic. Matt had written the note to evict her from his life.

She'd spent the next two weeks crying, breaking down without warning as she walked down the street, or as she sat staring at a meal she couldn't bring herself to eat.

Candace, she remembered with a bittersweet pang, had tried to get her to go clubbing in order to get her to forget about Matt.

She'd turned her twin down, but she did get her act together. If Matt didn't think enough of their relationship to try to contact her, to try to make her understand why he'd changed so radically from lover to stranger, then to hell with him. He was dead to her, she resolved. And he'd remained that way.

Until twenty minutes ago.

The adrenaline in her veins kept mounting.

Natalie focused on her driving. Vegas in the daylight wasn't nearly as alluring, as magical and glitzy as it was after dark. Like an aging woman best seen in soft lighting, Vegas's imperfections were all visible in the daylight. Natalie supposed that was why people like her sister didn't like to get up until noon. They lived for the night.

Except that Candace could no longer do that.

The thought brought a fresh, sharp ache with it.

"Damn it, Candy, what a waste," Natalie murmured under her breath.

She pulled up before the Janus casino. One of the three valets currently on duty came to life and made a beeline for her vehicle.

"Welcome to the Janus," the young attendant said cheerfully as he opened her door with a flourish.

"We'll see," she replied solemnly.

As he pulled away with her car, Natalie looked up at the casino's logo. Janus was the Roman god with two faces, one pointed toward the past, the other facing the future. It struck her as rather ironic, given what she was doing here, seeking out someone from her past in order to get answers so that the future could be settled.

The moment she entered the casino, the Vegas phenomenon took hold. It was like stepping into a world where time did not matter or even make an appearance. There was only a sense of "now."

Because in Natalie's experience she'd discovered that bartenders knew the inner workings of any establishment they worked for better than anyone else, she made her way to the first bar she saw within the casino.

The bartender in attendance was a gregarious man in his early forties. He had a quick, sexy smile, which was probably one of the main reasons he'd been hired. His name tag identified him as Kevin.

Moving to her end of the bar, Kevin asked, "What'll it be, pretty lady?"

"Information." She saw a dubious look cross his brow. To counter that, she took out her badge. Granted she wasn't here in an official capacity, but Kevin didn't need to know that. "Were you on duty last night?"

Kevin began to wipe the gleaming black surface of the bar. "You mean during the gala?"

"Yes."

The smile gracing his lips was a satisfied one. Last night had obviously been profitable for him, she judged. "I caught an extra shift."

She took out Candace's photograph and carefully placed it on the bar. "Did you happen to see this woman there?"

The bartender glanced at the picture. Mild interest turned to recognition. "You mean Candace Rothchild? Yeah, she was here, loud and brassy as always. But not for long," he added, looking rather disappointed. There was always a circus when Candace was around, Natalie thought. "She and the boss had at it and then he had our head of security escort her out."

She latched onto the first part of his statement. "They argued? About what?"

He shook his head. "Couldn't tell you. Too far away for anything but body language," he confessed.

"And the head of security?" she asked.

"He got her to leave."

She leaned in over the bar. "Tell me about him."

"Don't know much," the bartender admitted. "Just that

his name's Matt Shaffer. Boss flew him in from L.A., where he was head of security for Montgomery Enterprises."

There was no avoiding it, she thought darkly. She was going to have to talk to Matt. The thought left her cold. "Do you know where I can find him right now?"

Kevin glanced at his watch. "He should be in his office. On the second floor, toward the rear." He gave her the numbers of the rooms where the monitors that kept watch over the casino guests as they tried their luck against the house were located.

Taking out a twenty, she placed it on the bar. "Thanks for your help."

Kevin slipped the bill into his vest pocket. "Any time, lovely lady," he called after her. "Any time."

She debated going up the stairs, then decided on the elevator. The car that took her up to the second floor was empty. Natalie stepped out of the elevator, looked around to get her bearings and then walked toward the rear of the floor.

"Into the Valley of Death rode the six hundred," she silently recited, digging deep for a line from a poem by Tennyson. Wrapping her hand around a brass handle, she opened one of the glass doors and walked in.

The woman whose desk was closest to the door looked up. "You can't come in here. This is a restricted area."

Natalie already had her ID in her hand and held it up. "I'm looking for Matt Shaffer," she told the woman.

God, even saying his name made her mouth go dry. She was supposed to be over him, to have moved on with her life. What happened?

The woman began to answer her. "He's—"

"Right here."

The deep voice came from behind her. Natalie felt every

single nerve ending go on tactical alert at the same moment that all the hairs at the back of her neck stood up. Eight years had passed, but she would have recognized his voice anywhere.

* * * * *

Why did Matt Shaffer leave heiress-turned-cop Natalie Rothchild?
What does he know about the death of Natalie's twin sister?
Come and meet these two reunited lovers and learn the secrets of the Rothchild family in
THE HEIRESS'S 2-WEEK AFFAIR
by USA TODAY *bestselling author*
Marie Ferrarella.
The first book in Silhouette® Romantic Suspense's wildly romantic new continuity,
LOVE IN 60 SECONDS!
Available April 2009.

CELEBRATE
60 YEARS
OF PURE READING PLEASURE
WITH **HARLEQUIN**®!

Look for Silhouette®
Romantic Suspense in April!

Love In 60 Seconds

Bright lights. Big city. Hearts in overdrive.

Silhouette® Romantic Suspense is celebrating
Harlequin's 60th Anniversary with six stories that
promise to bring readers the glitz of Las Vegas,
the danger of revenge, the mystery of a missing
diamond, and family scandals.

**Look for the first title, *The Heiress's 2-Week Affair*
by *USA TODAY* bestselling author
Marie Ferrarella, on sale in April!**

His 7-Day Fiancée by **Gail Barrett**	May
The 9-Month Bodyguard by **Cindy Dees**	June
Prince Charming for 1 Night by **Nina Bruhns**	July
Her 24-Hour Protector by **Loreth Anne White**	August
5 minutes to Marriage by **Carla Cassidy**	September

You're invited to join our Tell Harlequin Reader Panel!

By joining our new reader panel you will:

- Receive Harlequin® books—they are FREE and yours to keep with no obligation to purchase anything!
- Participate in fun online surveys
- Exchange opinions and ideas with women just like you
- Have a say in our new book ideas and help us publish the best in women's fiction

In addition, you will have a chance to win great prizes and receive special gifts!
See Web site for details. Some conditions apply.
Space is limited.

To join, visit us at
www.TellHarlequin.com.

Harlequin® Historical
Historical Romantic Adventure!

Undone!

THE RAKE'S INHERITED COURTESAN
Ann Lethbridge

Christopher Evernden has been
assigned the unfortunate task of minding
Parisian courtesan Sylvia Boisette.
When Syliva sets off to find her father,
Christopher has no choice but to follow
and finds her kidnapped by an Irishman.
Once rescued, they finally succumb to
the temptation that has been brewing
between them. But can they see past the
limitations such a love can bring?

Available April 2009
wherever books are sold.

www.eHarlequin.com HH29541

HARLEQUIN®
Super Romance®

COMING NEXT MONTH

Available April 14, 2009

#1554 HOME AT LAST • Margaret Watson
The McInnes Triplets
Fiona McInnes finally has the life in the Big Apple she'd always wanted. But when her father dies, she's forced to return home to help settle his estate. Now nothing's going as planned—including falling back in love with the man whose heart she shattered.

#1555 A LETTER FOR ANNIE • Laura Abbot
Going Back
Kyle Becker is over any feelings he had for Annie Greer. Then she returns to town, and suddenly he's experiencing those emotions again. But before he and Annie can share a future, Kyle must keep a promise to deliver a letter that could make her leave.

#1556 A NOT-SO-PERFECT PAST • Beth Andrews
Ex-con Dillon Ward has no illusions about who he is. Neither does his alluring landlord. But Nina Carlson needs him to repair her wrecked bakery—like, *yesterday*. And if there's one thing this struggling single mom knows, it's that nobody's perfect…

#1557 THE MISTAKE SHE MADE • Linda Style
Tori Amhearst can't keep her identity secret much longer. Ever since she brought Lincoln Crusoe home after an accident took away his memory, she's loved him on borrowed time. Because once Linc knows who she really is, she'll lose him forever.

#1558 SOMEONE LIKE HER • Janice Kay Johnson
Adrian Rutledge comes to Middleton expecting to find his estranged mother. He doesn't expect to find Lucy Peterson or a community that feels like home. Yet he gets this and more. Could it be that Lucy—and this town—is the family he's dreamed of?

#1559 THE HOUSE OF SECRETS • Elizabeth Blackwell
Everlasting Love
As soon as Alissa Franklin sees the old house, she knows it will be hers. With the help of handyman Danny—who has secrets of his own—she uncovers the truth about the original owners. But can a hundred-year-old romance inspire her to take a chance on love today?